FAMILIAR SCENTS

SCENTS

T.S. KAY

FAMILIAR SCENTS
T.S. KAY

Science Fiction and Fantasy Publications

https://scififantasypublications.com

An imprint of DAOwen Publications

Familiar Scents / T.S. Kay

Edited by Douglas Owen and MJ Moores

ISBN 978-1-928094-26-5

EISBN 978-1-928094-27-2

Jacket art: MMT Productions

10 9 8 7 6 5 4 3 2 1

To Ann, for putting up with me all these years.

1

My phone rang, startling me awake. The clock proclaimed it Monday morning, 2:00 AM. I sat up and grabbed the receiver before it could ring again.

"Hello?"

"Detective Steckler? Precinct dispatch. You're needed at Park Avenue and East 21st. Multiple units responding to a break-in and robbery. One injured, one witness on the scene."

I rubbed sleep from my eyes and jotted the address on the pad beside the phone.

"On my way."

With a groan, I shoved myself out of bed and stumbled to the bathroom. Running the cold tap, I grimaced through bloodshot eyes at the face in the mirror. *God, it must be a madhouse out there tonight*, I was third in line for on-call. I hated this job – always being called after the crime, always too late. The only thing I hated worse was having nothing to do.

On autopilot, I dressed, tightened my underarm holster and scooped up my keys, badge, and phone. I paused at the faded photo by the door.

"Miss you, Sis. I'm still looking."

I touched the edge of the photo with a sigh, then hurried to the garage.

Parking my black, unmarked sedan in front of a hydrant, I made for the flashing crimson and blue lights. Patrol cars, ambulances, and the squawk of communicators led me to a strange four-story building: glass and stainless on the ground floor, and some kind of weird-ass baroque façade with fancy swirling plaster above. After the patrolwoman at the door glanced at my badge, I pushed into the front room, filled with uniformed police. The name on the door read, "e-Scents." *E-Scents? What the hell was that supposed to mean?*

The smells assaulted me: sweet citrus, vanilla, bile, blood, and excrement. *Jesus*, I covered my nose and choked back a gag reflex. How was I supposed to breathe much less solve a crime? With a shudder, I turned around, taking in the room and pictured it without the cops, as it might have appeared before the break-in.

An upscale retail space – elegant, minimalist with polished hardwood floors; museum-smooth, eggshell-white walls and ceiling. At the back, two uniforms looked over the remains of a party table covered with shambles of hors d'oeuvres and pricey champagne. White podiums dotted throughout the floor, each displaying a spotlighted object with a metal plaque. I crouched to examine a bottle of perfume. Rescue Me. *The break-in was about perfume?* I hoped the witness could tell me.

Before I could ask about where he or she was, EMTs pushed through a door in the back, rolling a stretcher. Another straddled a female victim. I flattened against the wall to give them room. The technician looked up from her patient and shook her head; the victim dead.

As soon as they wheeled the stretcher out the door, a Patrol Officer approached me.

"You Steckler?"

I nodded and flipped open my notepad; keeping track of a crime was a nightmare without notes.

"Bently," he introduced himself.

"What happened here?" I looked around the store.

He glanced at his own notepad before answering. "I spoke to the other victim; sounds like a robbery gone bad, but something doesn't make sense. The owner, Anthony Patronio, is in the back room." He nodded at the door behind me. "They had a party here tonight with the local rich and famous. It ended an hour and a half ago, about 11:30. Patronio and Lisa Taylor – that's the dead victim – were in the back room. Two men broke through the back door wearing ski masks and carrying handguns. Patronio and Taylor wound up on the ground, and Taylor was shot." Bently flipped his notebook to the next page. "Here's where it gets weird. Patronio says the perps also brought bleach and ammonia and either spilled or sprayed it on the floor and shelves. Everyone started choking. Patronio escaped and called us."

"Ammonia and bleach, that's poison, right? Are the bottles back there?" I wrote in my notepad to be sure they were checked for prints.

"They aren't there now," he answered.

"Patronio is in the back room?" I glanced at the door.

"I don't think he's got anything to do with it, Detective."

I looked at Bently, curious.

"You'll see, he's not the type." Bently pointed over my shoulder.

A man stepped out of the doorway. A familiar feeling came over me. Intuition? Instinct? I'd felt like this many times over the years. Whoever he was, I would keep a close eye on him.

"Mr. Patronio, I'm sorry about what happened here tonight." I reminded myself about the value of keeping an open mind and not making snap judgments.

A small, thin man; approximately five foot, six inches tall, stood wearily before me. I loomed over him by eight inches and a hundred pounds. Clad completely in white: white suit, white shirt, white shoes, even a white ascot, under normal circumstances he would stand out brightly. Now they were smudged with dirt and blood. The diamond studs he wore in each ear sparkled against his dark tan, and thick, black hair. His deep-set, brown eyes ringed with even darker circles.

"Thank you." He took a deep breath, tilted his head, and looked at me more closely. "Detective Steckler? Have we met? Perhaps at a salon or a soiree? There's something familiar about you."

Bently snorted.

Patronio's body stilled and he looked over my shoulder.

I smelled something burning and looked around, but not seeing anything, shrugged.

"Did you say something, Officer Bently?" Patronio's eyes didn't waver. Police radio chatter interrupted the silence, but Patronio waited patiently.

"No. Nothing," Bently replied.

Patronio held his gaze a moment longer then nodded.

"Bently, find out when the forensic team will get here," I said.

"Thank you," Patronio said after Bently left.

"No, I don't know you," I said.

He paused and then shrugged.

"Mr. Patronio. I'm afraid I'm going to have to ask you to go over everything in detail. You seem very focused for someone who's been through hell."

4

He frowned. "I'm trying to think of a way to find these people. In my workroom, I might be able to provide you with definitive clues as to who the murderers are."

"Why? Did something happen there?"

"I never saw their faces, but there was something distinctive about the way one of them smelled."

That took me by surprise. "Great, but that will have to wait. You need to come to the station to give your statement."

"It would be more useful to get to my workroom now to identify what the smell was." He narrowed his eyes. This man was used to getting his way.

"No, Mr. Patronio, we'll go and let the crime scene team get started."

Patronio's eyes narrowed to squints. His nostrils flared as he took a deep breath and peered at me. Then his eyes widened. "Fine, we'll do it your way."

The three of us sat around the plain, square table in the precinct's interview room. No matter what we used to clean it, the smell of fear and sweat lingered in the air.

"Detective Steckler, I have nothing more to add; we've gone over it three times. I'm exhausted. Lisa Taylor was killed next to me in my gallery. My clothes are covered in dirt, blood, and God knows what. Let me go home, or somewhere, to get warm and clean. Please, can't I just go now?" Patronio's voice faded to a whisper.

We'd taken his coat, shirt, and ascot as evidence, leaving him wearing his t-shirt and pants. His earlier determination at the gallery faded into weariness. Even the tremors during his recounts had stopped.

"Once more." This would be the last time. He was not faking it. If he was involved with Lisa Taylor's murder, if he hadn't slipped yet, he wouldn't anytime soon.

"Fine," he sighed.

"You don't want a lawyer?" Dwayne, the other detective working the case with me, checked each time we began. Reamed once by the District Attorney's office for not asking about a lawyer before an interview, he's overcompensated for it ever since.

"I don't need a lawyer. I had nothing to do with Lisa's death."

"Good. Just checking. Let's start from the beginning. You had a party at your store," Dwayne said.

"Detective Washington, that store you so quaintly refer to, is a perfume gallery. It is the premier location worldwide to acquire it – each unique fragrance crafted by me." His words were clipped and clearly articulated. He sounded that way every time during the interview when he grew annoyed.

"Why'd you have the party?" I ignored the sarcasm.

"I launched a new line of perfume and invited all of my customers."

"Was Lisa Taylor a customer?" I wanted to understand the nature of their relationship.

"Not really. She is – was – a close friend. I've *given* her perfume. She didn't have the money to buy it."

"She's a lawyer," Dwayne countered.

"She hasn't worked for eight years. Her partner is a programmer. They have two kids. They didn't have extra money."

"Do you have a list of everyone who was there?" Dwayne and I would need that to have them verify different facts.

"Yes, it's on my computer at work. I have names, home and email addresses, even pictures. Security webcams and the internet have made it easy."

"Why use pictures?" I wouldn't like my image in any company's data base.

"My customers are the type of people who wouldn't come back if I didn't recognize them after they bought something."

"Do you have cameras in the gallery?"

"Yes, but they weren't on during the party."

"Why not?" Dwayne had gotten tired of watching *me* ask the questions.

"Liquor and cameras don't go well with my clients."

"What time did it end?" I checked my watch out of habit. The hours had flown by.

"Just before midnight," he answered.

"The break-in didn't happen until one. What were you doing until then?" Dwayne's tone implied he thought there were more to their relationship and chumming around.

"Drinking, talking, drinking some more." A faint smile appeared then faded.

"If Lisa wasn't a customer, why was she at your party?" Dwayne tried one more time.

"She was going stir crazy. Her partner, Angie, stayed with the kids. Lisa came over toward the end of the evening. We planned to go to a bar"–tears slid down his cheeks–"but I still had two bottles of Dom Pérignon left. We decided to finish them. God, I wish we just went out."

"So, you were drunk when it happened?" Dwayne accused him.

"Not really, but I wasn't sober either."

"Then what happened?" I pushed.

"As I've already stated, two men entered the gallery from the backroom. They had masks and gloves on. One was thin and my height. The other one was closer to your size." Patronio looked at Dwayne.

"How do you know they were men?" Dwayne's question must not have made sense to Patronio who shook his head.

"Only one of them spoke. He made us lay face-down on the ground and covered our heads. I never saw them but I got a good whiff of them."

"Grrreat, but what good does that do?" I was being sarcastic but Patronio answered me.

"I have an incredible sense of smell; I've become a wealthy man because of it. Each person has his or her own unique olfactory signature. Using my nose and the implements in my lab above the gallery, I can recreate their scents and, perhaps, find a clue to their identities." He ignored our skeptical looks. "I think I have already found a useful one."

Dwayne and I exchanged a glance. This was the first information Patronio volunteered.

"What is it?" For the first time since meeting Patronio, that intuition stirred in my mind, and I felt that thrill of excitement when I found a clue.

"I don't know yet." Patronio shook his head.

"Grrreat." I fell back on my favorite catchall sentiment.

"One of them had a distinct scent. One I have not come across before."

"What good does that do?" I tried not to let my annoyance show.

"Detective Steckler, above my gallery there are thousands of distinct bottled scents. Each distilled and cataloged by me. If I haven't smelled something before, it's uncommon. I have years of experience tracking and labeling scents. This one could lead to the killers."

"That's great, Mr. Patronio, but don't get any ideas about taking action on your own. Let's go through what happened tonight. What did they cover your heads with?"

"Black ski masks."

"Did they use their own masks?" I knew his answer but wanted to get through this run-through.

"I think so. I heard one of them being taken off and the smell of hair gel became stronger."

"Just one?" Dwayne jumped in, checking Patronio's story against what he wrote in his notes.

"Yes. I think they were surprised when they saw Lisa with me. They paused a second when they noticed her. One of them had a ski mask in his hands when they entered."

Another new piece of information. Dwayne scribbled something in his notebook even though we recorded our interviews.

"You were on the floor, and they were about to cover your head with the ski mask. I'm sorry, but please walk us through what happened next," I said.

Patronio closed his eyes and sighed.

"I was on the floor, my hands behind my back. Lisa was in the same position on my left. We were looking at each other. I knew she was thinking about Angie and her children. She was so scared; she cried. I hoped they'd just rob us, take the perfumes and whatever else they wanted, and leave. One of them crouched down next to me – it must have been the one with the extra ski mask – and covered my head. For a second, I thought there were three men then."

"Why?" Another new tidbit of information. That small thrill of excitement went through me as I made another note.

"I smelled a different scent but then it faded," Patronio answered.

"Then what?"

"The one who covered my head said something, but he had a strong accent. It sounded East Asian, but I can't be sure. The other one answered him. He had a deep, gravelly voice. He said, 'She hasn't seen our faces. Just use my mask and we'll tell them to keep their eyes closed.' Then I heard one of them take off his mask and put it on Lisa. The one with the accident said, 'Just shoot them both.' The deep-voice man growled something. Lisa screamed and a gun went off. I felt something splatter me. I called out Lisa's name, but she didn't answer. I started crying. I knew she was dead, I just knew."

He trembled again. I felt bad but he had to go through the next part, it still didn't make sense to me or Dwayne. We waited.

"The men were silent like they hadn't expected that to happen. I can't be sure but one of them whined like he was about to cry. Then they yelled at each other and I smelled ammonia, then bleach. They must have mixed them. The chlorine gas was overpowering, and they coughed. It was hard to breathe. We all coughed, except Lisa, and I heard the men stumbling. I think they had trouble standing."

"Did you have bleach or ammonia in the gallery?" This was the part of the story that made the least amount of sense. I knew the answer but I hoped my question would get him to say something new.

"No. I couldn't. It doesn't mix with the perfume and would damage my sense of smell."

"Did you hear them take out containers or open or spray them?" Dwayne tried a new question to see if we could dig new information out from him.

"No, I didn't hear anything like that."

"Where do you think it came from?" Dwayne asked the question as if he were talking to child. That approach could annoy Patronio enough to make him think of something new.

"It's possible they had it in their pockets," he answered as he shrugged his shoulders. "I realized that I might be able to escape while they coughed. I took off my mask and ran out through the front of the gallery. Then I called the police on my cell phone. I hid in a doorway and waited until they arrived. That's it."

Despite myself, I had to admit that Patronio was no push-over. Not many people go through such an ordeal and are coherent hours later. There was something different about him, maybe self-confidence. But unless Angie Taylor provided a motive or something showed in his background, I doubted Patronio had anything to do with the break-in and murder. Lisa's death was violent and messy. That was definitely not Patronio's style; poison maybe, but not guns. It bugged me, I couldn't figure out how he got out alive. The bleach and ammonia made no sense.

"I know you're tired, Mr. Patronio. Each time we go through it, I think of different questions that lead to new information that gets us one step closer to catching them."

He wasn't the only one who was tired. Dwayne rubbed his eyes and motioned me toward the office door.

"Excuse us, Mr. Patronio. We'll be right back." He nodded his head. I expected him to complain again about being kept longer; maybe shock was setting in.

Dwayne held the door for me as we left the interview room, then shut it behind us. We checked the squad room for civilians who might overhear us. It was safe on Tuesday morning at 03:30 hrs. Bently and another patrol officer from the scene sat completing paperwork. *Even in the city that never sleeps, this is a pretty quiet time.*

Well over six foot tall, Dwayne looked down at me and most other people. He was a former third-stringer for the Jets who still carried a lot of weight and muscle. At times like this he tried to use it to his advantage.

"Carl, this is a robbery gone bad, clean and simple. The bad guys thought they'd get money or perfume to sell. Instead, they opened the door to find pansy-the-perfumer and his BFF–"

"Dwayne, the last thing we need is Patronio claiming bias."

He ignored me.

"They panicked and shot Lisa when she didn't shut up. They decided to kill him and cleaned any traces of themselves with the ammonia and bleach they brought with them. Idiots didn't know not to mix the stuff and choked. While they stumbled around, Tinkerbelle took flight. Then so did they."

The door behind us opened. Patronio walked to us. "I also have very good hearing," he said to me, then headed toward the office exit.

"Mr. Patronio, we aren't done yet. I want to go over it one more time," Dwayne said.

I looked down to hide my frown. This was how Dwayne reacted when he wanted to dominate someone he didn't like.

"Detective Steckler, am I under arrest?" Patronio's tone had gone flat. He didn't look at Dwayne.

"No, but I still have questions I'd like to ask you. I think they'll help us identify and catch these people."

"Detective Steckler, am I a suspect or a person of interest?" he used that same tone.

"If we say you're staying, you're staying," Dwayne answered for me.

Yeah, that's gonna help; Dwayne, you idiot.

"Detective Steckler, talk to my lawyer."

"You could wait for your lawyer in the cells instead of our offices. That'll only take a few hours … or days. A guy like you ought to make a lot of friends down there." Dwayne took a step toward him.

Patronio didn't blink or move. The guy had balls. Not many men could ignore Dwayne. I put myself between the two of them and caught a whiff of burnt food. The place was still empty but I looked around for evidence of a pizza delivery anyway.

"Okay, Mr. Patronio, we can call it a night. I'll phone you later today. If you think of anything, get ahold of me."

I reached into my shirt pocket for my cards, but they weren't there. Thankfully, Dwayne kept his mouth closed, grunted at me, and walked away. "My cards are in my jacket."

Patronio turned to leave.

"Wait." I touched his arm. "There's more in my desk." I pointed near the exit. "It's on your way out." Patronio shrugged and followed me.

My desk wasn't exactly orderly. I opened several drawers to search for my cards and looked apologetically at Patronio. He stared at the picture on my desk – the same as the one at home. I hesitated to do it, but maybe I could gain ground back with him.

"That's my sister, Denise," I told him. "We're twins." I avoided using the past tense.

"It's an old picture." He picked it up to look more closely.

I squashed the impulse to snatch it back.

"Yes," I agreed. "Twenty-two years ago. The last picture I have. She went missing a few months later. We never found her."

"That must be very hard for you."

I stopped searching for my cards. Something changed; he was still exhausted but now stood straight and looked at me with hostility rather than sympathy.

"Please sit." Maybe he recalled something new.

"Here's one." He interrupted me and grabbed a card that had been hidden behind the picture.

"I'm leaving now. We'll talk soon, Detective," he called as he walked out.

The squad room was quiet. Most of the other detectives were either out pursuing cases or in meetings. The phone rang as I went through my case notes and tried to come up with a new angle.

"Steckler," I answered with resentment. Phones and I didn't get along. Since Denise disappeared, I hated to depend on them for news.

"Good morning, Detective Steckler."

I heard Patronio's distinctive voice. It was little over a day since the interview. I'd left messages for him, but Captain Perez insisted I back off until we had something specific on Patronio. Perez received a call from the Mayor whose wife was Patronio's customer and friend.

Dwayne was off the case as well. He threw a fit, but if the sphincter fits … I told him. His big mouth got him into trouble, and I paid for it with leg work, calls from the press, and a sharp word from Perez.

"Thanks so much for returning my calls, Mr. Patronio."

"Spare me, Detective. I have enough to deal with at the moment. I've spent the day with Lisa's family." My frustration drained. No one deserved that.

An hour earlier, I'd spoken with Lisa's partner, Angie, about what happened. She didn't know who would want to kill Lisa or Patronio and was incredulous when asked if Patronio could have been behind it.

"He's richer than God! He owns the freaking building the gallery is in and gave us the down-payment on our co-op as a wedding present! I wish you moronic homophobes would start working on finding these murderers!" She had shown me to the door without another word. Thanks again, Dwayne.

"You're right. I was outta line," I said.

"No apology necessary, neither of us is having a good time of it. Angie said you hadn't made any progress. Is that still true?"

"That depends."

"On?"

"If I can trust you not to rat me out to the Mayor again."

He laughed. "Detective, if this is your idea of a peace offering, you need to go back to negotiation class."

"Probably."

"Treat me with the same respect you'd accord anyone else and we'll be fine."

"That won't be a problem," I answered. "No one gets my respect."

He laughed again.

"What about your lawyer?" I wanted to get that cleared up as soon as possible.

"If I'm still a suspect for the break-in or Lisa's murder, I'll bring him in."

"No, don't do that … yet."

"That's a good enough answer for now, Detective," he said, surprising me. "I left you with almost as many questions as you started with. I'm prepared to answer them now."

"Good, come to the precinct. I'll meet you in the lobby." I was ready to leave my desk right then.

"No. No, not your office."

"Why not?" I liked meeting in my office. I had more control.

"I'm afraid."

"If you're not guilty, there's nothing to be afraid of, Mr. Patronio."

"Relax, Detective Steckler. The Mayor wouldn't let me be arrested. I think I'm being watched."

"By who?" I didn't believe him, but knew I had to humor him.

"The same people who killed Lisa."

"How do you know?"

"By the way they smell."

My hand tightened on the receiver.

"I know you don't believe me yet, Detective. Meet me this afternoon, I'll answer your questions and by the end of our conversation you'll understand why someone is watching me."

"Talk to me in my office," I tried again.

"To make new friends in the jail cells?"

"I'm sorry for what my partner said the other night, Mr. Patronio. It was late and we were all tired. That's no excuse, but it was Dwayne, not me. Come into the precinct, please?"

"Not unless you're arresting me."

"Fine. Where and when?"

He started to speak and I stopped him.

"I'll head toward Gramercy Park then call your cell. Tell me where to meet you then. If your phone is bugged, they won't have time to do anything." It was the prudent thing to do. He would think I was on his side. Before he could protest, I dropped the phone into its cradle.

I drove by Patronio's gallery. Private limousines were double parked in front. The crime scene team cleared it yesterday, rushed by the Captain's pressure to avoid another run-in with the Mayor. *Business looked brisk.* White-clad employees talked with customers. I shook my head – the rich and indolent had their fair share of carnage junkies. The same sort of people surrounded us when Denise first disappeared.

"Hello, Detective Steckler. Where are you?"

"In front of the gallery. Lots of people in there," I mentioned, not pleased with what I saw.

"Yes, our phones haven't stopped ringing these past few days."

"People love the misery of others, right?"

"Actually, most have brought donations. We've started a college fund for Lisa's children."

Moments like that made me think I've been a cop too long.

"I can write a check for twenty, Mr. Patronio."

"Every little bit helps. I'm at the Rose Bar in the Gramercy Park Hotel," he said, changing the topic.

"Got it." I disconnected.

Luckily there was space next to a fire hydrant. I parked and threw my "Official Police Business" plaque card on the dashboard. Patronio could pick up the tab; a drink here cost the same as a meal anywhere else.

The doorman held the entrance open for me. A quick look around the lobby showed me the entrance to the bar.

Walls and furniture colored a dusty rose, made masculine by wooden accents and deep blue floor-to-ceiling curtains, explained why it was named The Rose Bar. Empty now, the place was packed with the rich, famous, and assorted wannabes on the weekends.

Patronio sat at a table.

I completed and handed him the check for my donation as promised. He nodded his thanks.

"You're in a good mood, Detective. Has there been a break in the case?"

"No, not unless you've got something useful."

"It's good, trust me. But have a drink first. You may need it." He signaled to the barman.

"What can I get for you, Mr. Patronio?" The waiter asked with a slight smile and a glint of speculation in his eyes as he looked back and forth between us.

"A vodka martini, up, very dry, and dirty," Patronio answered. "Use your best vodka and make it a double."

Great, he's getting sloshed.

"I'll have coffee with cream and sugar."

"Bring an extra martini, just in case," Patronio called after him.

"Tell me what you're going to tell me so I can get back to work."

"Just a moment, Detective." Patronio pointedly looked at the barman. A few moments later, the bartender placed a martini glass and a large shaker in front of Patronio. With a smile, he put an empty glass down next to my coffee.

"William, are you expecting a crowd in the next hour or so?" Patronio checked the room for other people. I glanced at my watch; it was just past 10 AM.

"No, Mr. Patronio. There's nothing scheduled today. It won't get busy until after 11:30."

"Excellent. Please close the bar until then. I don't want us interrupted." William looked at him expectantly. "Yes, I know. It'll cost me. Put it on my tab and give yourself a generous tip."

"Thank you, Mr. Patronio. I'll see to it."

We watched as William rummaged under the bar and emerged with a laminated piece of paper stating 'Closed for private party.' He taped it to the entrance and left.

"Detective, I have a lead for you which you won't believe until I share information about myself. Something I've told very few people. Perhaps it will lead you to trust me with your secrets as well?" Patronio smiled but his eyes remained cold.

I shrugged, not sure what he intended.

"Seriously, you can't share it with anyone else. Can I trust you?" His smile faded.

"I can't make any promises, Mr. Patronio, especially about anything with a bearing on the case."

"Wait and see. Maybe we can make a deal."

"I don't make deals, Mr. Patronio. I do what's necessary to find people like Lisa's killers and build the case against them. If I have to make anything public to do that, I will."

Patronio thought a moment then sighed. "Fine. I'll trust you to make the right decision." He sat back, trying unsuccessfully to make himself comfortable; his hands shook. "I'll get to the point then. You have questions about how I escaped that night, correct?"

2

Mr. Patronio and I were the only people in the Gramercy Park Hotel's Rose Bar. He knew I still had questions about how he escaped the men who killed his friend, Lisa.

"Yes," I told him.

An intense smell of bleach assaulted my nose. I jerked away from the table and shook my head.

"What the hell!" I spat at him. Strong onion replaced the bleach. My eyes began to water.

"What are you doing? Stop it!" I rubbed at my eyes, glared first at Patronio, then around and under the table. Whatever I found, I'd use it to smack him upside the head. Then the onion smell was replaced with lemon, which then faded to nothing.

Patronio hadn't moved while I was under siege. He watched as I wiped my runny nose.

"What the hell are you doing?" I yelled.

Patronio, folded hands in plain sight on the table, waiting for me to calm down.

I checked again for some sort of nozzle or spray bottle but there wasn't a place to hide it.

"That's how I got away, Detective, but much more intense and painful for them. I ran out while they were choking."

"You sprayed their faces with something, is that it? Why didn't you just tell me?"

"Detective, you know I never moved."

"You set it up before I got here. Your gallery is rigged the same way. Why the stupid games?"

"Did your crime scene team find any devices in my gallery or the backroom?" He waited as I moved the cups, glasses, and utensils, and searched under the other tables.

His white clothes, this time, a jacket, t-shirt, and jeans, didn't have wires or unusual bulges. I examined his jacket, searching for a device.

"You're not making a difficult task any easier for me, Detective. May I take off my jacket?"

"Just don't spray me again, okay?" I wanted to reach for my gun.

He nodded, stood up slowly, and took off his coat. The short-sleeve t-shirt clung to him. His painted-on pants couldn't hide anything, and I mean anything.

I held out my hand and searched his jacket, no longer angry, just curious how he did it. "You win. It's a great trick. I have no idea how you did it or how you got it past the crime scene techs. Tell me. Now." We both sat down.

"It's not a trick, Detective. It's my gift." His facial expression implied it was my turn to share.

"What are you talking about?" I felt my patience slip away, tired of

20

riddles.

"There are no tools or tricks. I think it and it happens." An edge sounded in his reply.

I rolled my eyes.

"Name a scent, anything," he said.

"No."

"Do you have another explanation?"

"No, but I'll find one."

"Any smell you want," he returned.

"No."

"Anything."

"No."

"Chicken?" I was surrounded by the aroma of roasting chicken. My mouth started to water.

"Cucumber," I threw out, following up with "Road tar, vanilla, vomit, baked beans, tuna fish, body odor ..."

One after the other, I smelled them. Each strong and unmistakable.

"Oranges," I added just to get the last one out of my nose. "Hypnotism?" I tried to sound definitive.

"Do you consider yourself susceptible to suggestion?"

"Nope." I frowned, desperate to figure why he would go to such lengths to spin such a strange story. "Drugs in my coffee or smeared on the table?"

"What would be the point?"

"I haven't figured that out yet. But when I do, if you're playing some kind of a game on me to get away with Lisa's murder, you'd better start running. Fast."

"Lisa was my best friend, Detective Steckler," Patronio said. His eyes welled.

Crap, I so don't want him to cry. "Okay. Let's pretend you have this gift. How does it work?"

His tears stopped and the anger disappeared. He seemed relieved and sniffed loudly. "I think of a scent I want you to smell, dialing the intensity up and down as necessary. At the low end, a person simply smells what I want them to. At the high end, the air becomes saturated with the scent which leaves a residue."

"Is that how you make your perfumes? Recreating them?"

"No." He honestly sounded offended. "My gift helps me remember and craft them, but I work very hard to create them."

"You remember smells?"

He shrugged. "Other people have eidetic memories for what they read. I have an eidetic memory for scents. Once I smell a particular scent or a new combination of scents, my mind catalogs them, and then can recreate it."

"Grrreat." Whatever delusions of power or *gifts* he had, I needed to get back to my sane world of murders. "You said you had a lead for me."

"And I'm being watched."

"Right."

"You still believe I tricked you?"

"I don't know what I believe."

"Well, to paraphrase Sherlock Holmes, when you have eliminated the impossible, whatever remains, however improbable, must be the truth."

"I've not eliminated the impossible yet."

"It's hard to accept, but it's the truth. I have no need to lie and every reason to try to persuade you."

"What reason?" I felt wary again.

"I'm in over my head. I've caught the scent of one of the two men who killed Lisa three times today. They are either going to kidnap or kill me."

"Can you go away for a while? Until we catch them?"

"No."

"Why not?"

"Two days ago I used my gift to protect myself. I'm not running from a fight anymore. Never again. Ever. Besides, suspects can't leave town, right?"

"You're not really a viable suspect," I confessed. "The forensics don't point to you. We found the heaviest gunpowder residue on the side of your coat, not your sleeves or hands. The investigation hasn't turned up any reason for you to have killed Lisa. I know you didn't do it."

"But I did nothing to stop it either! I was so worried about hiding my gift, Lisa died!"

"You didn't think they'd kill her, right?" I wasn't sure about the smell-o-rama story, but he shouldn't feel guilty for Lisa's death; he didn't pull the trigger.

"No, I thought they were there to rob me."

"You wouldn't have used your gift to stop them from robbing you?"

"No. Absolutely not," he answered, firmly. "I didn't want anyone to know about it."

"Why not?"

His hands shook but he forced them to stop by tightly gripping the martini glass. "Detective, my parents emigrated from Italy and are old-school Catholic. Mother was a stay-at-home mom. Dad worked with stone, brick, and tile; my two brothers are in business with him. As you may have guessed, I wasn't very much like them. They never understood how to deal with me. I was tolerated, supported as best they could, but never really accepted."

"That must have been rough," I said, with some empathy. This wasn't the first time I'd heard about the tough lives of gay men and women growing up. For a few, it was merely difficult; others, almost torture. I was too busy as a teenager being the man of the house for my family, there was no time for dating and all the drama.

"I was luckier than most living so close to New York City. At fifteen I knew there were people like me just over the bridge from Jersey. It was only a weekend subway to meet people like me."

"I'm not really sure I want to hear anything about your Saturday night escapades."

Patronio rolled his eyes. "Detective, I found a community that not only accepted me but was encouraging and supportive." He paused, becoming serious again. "Then my gift manifested."

"And the problem with that was?"

"Gay people are still human, Detective. They'd be afraid of my gift, or think it a hoax like you do. I'd found an alternative family and wouldn't risk losing them. My gift stayed hidden from almost everyone until today."

"Almost? A friend? Lover?"

"Neither," he replied. "I told an interesting Vietnamese person named Tú." He nodded as if he made a decision.

I got a hunch to keep my mouth shut. The times I've had that feeling and followed it, a major break in a case came of it.

"In for a penny, in for a pound, right Detective?"

"Absolutely." The feeling got stronger.

"Tú is one of two other people I've met that were gifted. Like I am."

"Gifted in terms of being able to create scents?"

"No, their gifts are different from mine. I don't know exactly what Tú's gifts are or how strong. Tú uses smell as well as the other senses, and from what I've observed, it involves bewitching people, in the old-fashioned sense of the word."

"Sounds scary," I said, ready to ask about the second person when he continued.

"Just as mine can be, if used the wrong way."

"What do you mean?"

"Scents are made up of minute amounts of specific chemicals in the air. Poison gasses are made up of chemicals as well. I discovered the other night I can make dangerous scents as well as poisonous gasses. Tú can vary the intensity as well."

"You've told me a lot about Tú. Why?"

"Yes, time to get to the point, but breaking more than twenty years' worth of self-imposed silence is difficult. I hope it's not a mistake." He

24

looked at me expectantly.

"Sure, it's difficult. Thank you for trusting me. I'll do my best to make sure it doesn't come back to bite you in the ass." Still refusing to make promises I couldn't keep. Whatever kept him talking.

Patronio smiled. "Remember I smelled something unique about one of the attackers? He was Asian, based on his accent. There were scents on him associated with Asian communities, but no specific one. Then I caught a whiff of something different than I've smelled before."

"You figured out what the smell was?"

"Yes. When not with Lisa's family, I was at Asian food markets searching. It was the essence of a giant water bug." He had a satisfied look on his face.

"Water bug?"

"It's used in Thai and Vietnamese cooking," he said. "Hence the discussion about Tú. The only Vietnamese person with whom I've spent any time."

"You think Tú had something to do with Lisa's death?"

"I don't know. We were friends of sorts. But Tú's gift doesn't work on me as far as I can tell."

"How do you know?"

"We experimented a month ago. Tú would try to … influence me; I created strong scents around me and countered it. We agreed to try it again using bottled scents I prepared. We hadn't set a date as yet."

"What's Tú's full name?"

"I'm sorry. No idea."

"Then maybe we should go see Tú?" I suggested. "Now."

"I can't. I have to get back for Lisa's services this afternoon and tonight. Besides, Tú wouldn't see us until after midnight. After the show is over.

"What show?"

"Tú runs a nightclub in Chelsea," Patronio told me.

I frowned. Chelsea was the heart of New York City's gay community.

Patronio's widened smile confirmed my suspicions.

"A gay nightclub? A drag show?" I felt a growing sense of discomfort. It was rare for me to think about sex. What people do behind closed doors was their own business and I tried to keep them firmly shut.

"Yes. But it's more of a cabaret than a drag show. I went there for the first time a few weeks ago, after an invitation from a friend."

"Grrreat." I had no idea what a cabaret show was. After Denise disappeared, who cared? "So Tú is a drag queen?" Drag queens freaked me out, even after all my years on the job. I could understand the gay thing; your body and mind were hardwired to like what they like. But a man who may or may not be gay wearing women's clothes was too ambiguous for me.

"I don't know what Tú is."

"What?" That sense of discomfort became a burning pit in my stomach.

"I'm not sure if Tú is a man or a woman."

"How do you not know that? If you've spoken with someone, after a while can't you just tell? Is Tú transgendered?"

"Detective, I'd hoped you weren't so homophobic."

"It's not that. I don't care what a person does but that kind of ambiguity is hard for me to take."

"Imagine how they feel every day." Patronio frowned. "Usually, I can make a reasonable guess by the way they smell. But Tú is very gender neutral and doesn't encourage questions any more than I do."

"Grrreat," I said, ignoring Patronio's smirk. My intuition prompted me again. "But I do appreciate you telling me about Tú. When do you want to go see hi … Tú?"

"I'll call after I've spoken to Tú and set something up for late tonight or early tomorrow."

"That works!" I was excited at the possibility of a break in the case.

Patronio became serious. "Detective, don't underestimate Tú being bewitching. I can counter it. You cannot.”

I moved my jacket aside to show him my Glock 17.

“Okay,” he said with obvious doubt.

“Mr. Patronio, I know how to conduct myself and my investigations.”

“Maybe around average criminals and victims, Detective. But I’m not normal, and Tú is even less so.” The smell of oranges surrounded me again, strong and sweet. “That could just as easily have been mustard gas, Detective.”

“Call me when you’ve set something up.” I strode away before he could do anything else. Halfway to my car I still felt the sense of anticipation that saying the right thing or opening the right door would make something important happen. I spent the rest of the ride trying to figure out what, as well as a way to counter Patronio’s gift.

I ran down a dark alley, chasing after my sister. “Wait! Denise!” I was about to catch her when the phone woke me. Damn thing. The clock read 10:30 PM, after an hour’s sleep. I was tempted to ignore it but it was my father’s number. A spike of adrenaline shot through me – he was old and went to bed early.

“Hi, Dad. Are you okay?” My voice rasped.

“Hello, Carl. Sorry to call, but I didn’t know what else to do.” He sounded okay.

“No problem, Dad. What’s the matter?”

“There’s water in the basement and the sump pump is broken.”

I’d have to go check that. “Okay, be over soon.”

“Thanks, Carl. I’ll buy you a drink.”

“Great, Dad. See you in a while.” I hung the phone up.

“Crap.” First the dream and now Dad. I hadn’t had that dream in years. Denise would be in the distance, get within reach and suddenly far away down another road, hallway, or room. Each time, her face would hold more fear. The sequence repeated until I woke bathed in sweat. I should thank Dad for breaking the cycle.

After putting on a t-shirt, jeans, and waterproof boots, I remembered to bring a dress shirt and slacks for the meeting with Patronio. Captain Pérez, the lead Detective in our precinct, had an unwritten policy that required us to wear professional clothes while on the job.

I went into the extra bedroom that served as a home office. My gun sat stored in a safe box along with notes on the case. The neoprene scuba suit and gear I'd bought while investigating a serial killer who disposed of his victims in the Hudson River, was piled on top of the lock box; I'd cleaned out the closet earlier in the week.

Patronio called, giving me the club's name and address. There was very little about it in any of our databases. It was owned by the Chung Corporation and had changed names several times during the past four decades. There were no citations, infractions, or even a police call. Customer reviews described it as clean, campy, and geared for the geriatric crowd.

My fingers itched to go through the pile of folders containing unsolved cases on my desk. When bored or anxious, which was often, I'd pick at them, hoping something would break. Most of the time it went nowhere. Once in a while, though, a hunch led to a connection to a fact or news item that had me calling in old witnesses or double-checking facts and a case would be broken.

Unlike television cops, I use research and continuous questioning of facts and assumptions to wear away at crimes. After a short stint on a beat, my career kicked into gear when I transferred to the records group. I reviewed case files and made suggestions to detectives. When I helped close a number of cold cases, I moved into an analyst position, then made Detective.

On the other side of my desk a single, thin, tattered and taped folder with everything about Denise's disappearance waited for me. Again, my pulse surged with anger and frustration. After all my closed, ice-cold cases, I made no progress on finding her or learning what happened.

I stopped thinking about it, grabbed my gun and badge and headed to my father's place.

"Hey, Dad," I called, stripped off my dripping coat and hanging it on the hook by the back door. He was probably in the living room waiting for me.

"Hi, Carl. Thanks for coming." Dad startled me once again.

He stood in the back hallway and smiled at me with perfect teeth, a head full of thick, white hair, and a white, neatly trimmed beard. I hadn't heard shuffling feet, and his eyes were clear.

A stroke nearly killed him when Denise and I were ten. Strokes and high blood pressure ran in the family. His sister died when she was only twenty-two, long before we were born. Dad's stroke left him partially paralyzed on his left side and with difficulty speaking. Years of speech and physical therapy got him back to normal but he still had difficulty, especially when stressed. It had been tough on him when Denise disappeared and Mom died. Before then I planned to attend medical school to find a way to prevent and reverse strokes.

"No problem. How's the basement?" I changed the subject to avoid his thanking me again. The appreciation had lost its appeal.

"The water is still coming in. If the sump-pump were working, it wouldn't be a problem."

He backed into the kitchen and stopped.

"Do you want a beer before we get started?" He expected another lecture about him moving to a place that didn't require so much maintenance.

Seeing him fidget, I decided to skip it tonight. "No thanks. I have to work later."

"Coffee then?"

"Great." I moved to the coffee maker on the kitchen counter.

"No, you sit. I'll do it," he said. I sat with a silent sigh.

"Don't sigh at me. Or roll your eyes."

My eyes twitched violently and he laughed.

"I still know you even after two months without a visit."

I sighed, loudly this time, and he chuckled.

"Sorry, couldn't resist. I know you're busy."

Something was bugging him, but, as usual, I ignored it.

"You're right, I should have come sooner." Seeing Dad always involved doing some work around his house, fixing the car, or running errands.

To derail that chain of thought, I scanned the room for something else to talk about. Dad bought this house a few years ago using money from Mom's life insurance policy. It was a beautiful brownstone with a huge original-sized kitchen. Thankfully, the previous owner had done a great job remodeling it – all new appliances, lots of cabinet space, and beautiful wooden floors. The kitchen table seated eight and still left lots of room all around it.

Dad stood doing something with the coffee maker. I didn't interrupt him, not wanting to drink coffee sludge due to a miscount. Pill bottles were centered on the table. Vitamins, blood pressure medicine, aspirin, and tadalafil. My eyes bugged out. Dad was taking erection pills.

"Surprised?" he asked with a nervous smile on his face when I glanced up at him.

"Umm ... you got a girlfriend?" I blinked, nonplussed.

"No, Carl, I wanted to spice up my jerk-off sessions."

"Ugh!"

My face reddened, he laughed and relented.

"Yes, if that's the right term. We met a few months ago."

I thought about it and felt a smile grow on my face. "Great, Dad. Good for you." It was his first girlfriend since Mom died.

He let out his breath.

"What's her name?"

"Barbara DiNofrio."

"She retired too?"

"No, she's a Producer at one of the theaters here in Brooklyn."

"Oh, that explains the little blue pills." I laughed. "A younger woman."

He laughed as well but didn't deny it.

"Well, I'm glad for you Dad."

"Thank you, I hoped you'd say that."

"I'm fine with it. You deserve to be happy." I meant it. He'd had so much crap in his life.

"You can have a few of the boner pills if you want."

Wow. How to kill the moment.

"It gives you a hard-on like you're nineteen again."

"Grrreat." I stood up from the table. The coffee dripped into the carafe. I grabbed a mug from a shelf and poured some into it.

"Carl, find yourself a nice girl … or boy … and have a family."

Here we go again.

"We've been through this before. I don't want to settle down with a girl, boy, or anyone. I don't care about either. Trust me, I'd tell you. Anything to get you to let up!" I threw my spoon in the sink and stomped down the stairs to the basement.

It was an unfinished space with cement walls, beams crossed the ceiling, and utility shelving units leaned against the walls. The water wasn't more than an inch deep.

The sump-pump squatted in the furthest corner of the basement. I sloshed over to it and used the flashlight from the car to look around at the damage. It wouldn't be smart to turn the lights on until I knew the circuits wouldn't blow and electrocute me.

Thankfully only one box stood on the floor and the bottom shelves of the units held mostly dust except for a few old vases and bottles. The water had damaged nothing important.

The sump-pump looked like a humped-back shrimp hiding in the corner. Based on a casual perusal, the pipes and such were in place and intact. I'd learned to check after Dad fell on a heating pipe. It took weeks to discover the crack after the heat stopped working. As a novice handyman, I'd spent hours trying to figure out how to fix the problem.

I knelt down and felt the water seep into my pants and found the problem as soon as my hand went to the bottom of the pump: a bunch of papers and other crap were wedged around the base. The reset button was switched off. The papers clogged it and caused the short. I swore, cleared the area around the base, and hit the reset switch. Within seconds, the pump hummed.

With a groan, I stood and shone the flashlight on the box marked "photos" written in Mom's handwriting. A few months ago I brought it down from the extra bedroom and put it on a top shelf. Dad must have moved it as the flaps were open. The bottom of the box darkened by water, I hoped the contents weren't ruined.

"Sounds like you got it working," Dad said with a grin.

I jumped and swore. He'd always been good at sneaking up on people. Claimed it was his gift. I brandished the soggy remnants from below the sump pump. "It was plugged up with papers."

"Thanks, Carl," he said.

I could tell he had more to say, whether I wanted to hear it or not. "No problem. Easy enough, but we'll have to empty the box." I walked back to the steps and turned on the overhead lights. They revealed Dad looking at me with furrowed brows and thinned lips. Here we go again.

"What? Ask or tell me so we can get it over with and clean up down here." He sighed.

"Carl, I'm worried about you. That's all."

Here we go again.

I bit my lip so I didn't yell.

"Neither Barbara nor I believe that."

I bit my lip so not to yell at him.

"Your girlfriend?"

"Yes."

"How did you meet her?"

"Don't change the subject. I don't understand you, Carl."

"What don't you understand?" I leaned toward him and my tone went flat.

"You can't intimidate me, Carl. I'm your father."

He wasn't going to let this go.

3

My father and I glared at one another as the sump pump slurped and drained water.

"Ask or tell me whatever you want but make it quick, I have to get to work."

He swallowed. "I don't want to wait anymore."

"For what?"

"For you. I wanted you to find someone first, but time is running short. You grew up so fast after I had my stroke. Then when ... Denise ... died, you just stopped. You gave up on everything good in life and waited for her. I can't do it anymore." Tears welled in his eyes.

I put my hand on his shoulder and shook him gently.

"Jeez, you should have said something years ago! Don't hold off on my account. I'm glad you've found someone." I ignored his comment about Denise, not wanting to argue again.

"Thanks. Barbara and I have a lot in common. We don't know where it's going but it's fun and the sex is great." Now there was a smile on his face.

"Yeah, I guessed that from the boner pills." We laughed but his face grew serious again.

"Why don't you have a girlfriend?"

"I just don't."

"If you like men, it's not a big deal. I knew about Denise. It would make sense since you're her twin." I blinked at him.

"You knew what about Denise?" I was intrigued; he always avoided talking about Denise or Mom.

"You don't have to protect her memory. I wasn't happy about it at the time, but times have changed."

"I have no idea what you're talking about."

He squinted at me. "You didn't know about Denise? Really?"

"Nope. Just tell me what's getting you all worked up."

"Denise was gay."

I laughed. "No, she wasn't."

"Yes. She was seeing that girl, Kim."

The kids in high school gossiped about it, but were jealous because Denise was so good at softball and liked the limelight. I was the quiet one, which only made her seem loud and boisterous. They'd said worse about Kim when the two of them took the team to the state championships.

"You've watched too many talk shows. Not everyone is gay."

"I saw them kissing – really kissing."

I felt a twinge of doubt. Denise and I shared about everything but sex. Mom had been a bit of a prude and discouraged that sort of talk. Then I remembered something I hadn't thought of in years.

"Kim gave me a blowjob. I doubt she was gay." It was his turn to look surprised. We'd been at one of Denise's friend's house for a party and somehow I wound up alone with Kim. I didn't find her attractive but a when you're a teenage boy with a good buzz, a blowjob is a blowjob, right?

"So, you're not gay?"

"I'm not anything. Just me."

He blinked and went back to what he really wanted to talk about.

"I don't understand. You're a good looking man. You should have a wife, or someone, to care for you."

"I just don't care about it, okay?"

"Barbara thought it might be something …" He didn't finish his sentence when I glared at him.

"I'm glad you and Barbara can talk about me. What did Barbara think? She must have a lot of insight to share, especially since we haven't met."

"Don't run your mouth! Who else am I supposed to ask? It's not like you and I are close."

"Nice job. Accuse me of a bunch of things and blame me for not talking to you at the same time. I'm impressed." My gaze drifted to the box with Mom's handwriting. He turned to see what caught my attention.

"I'm not accusing you of anything! We thought you were into kinky stuff and didn't want to share it with us."

I didn't stop my eye roll this time. "No. God-as-my-witness, I'm not into *anything* at all. Please stop watching cable TV."

"It's not kids, is it?" he mumbled.

"No!"

"S&M?"

"No."

"Dead people?"

"Ugh. No. Anything else?" I laughed, it was so ridiculous.

"Do you even …" He made a gesture near his crotch.

"No. Since Denise disappeared, I don't have any sex drive."

"See a psychologist about it. You deserve to be happy. What happened to Denise wasn't your fault."

"I'm not going to a shrink. End of discussion. Now change the subject or I'm out of here."

"I had to ask. I'm your father."

"Great. Now you know. That's the last time. Otherwise, I'm not coming back." My voice had gone flat and deadly serious.

"Don't threaten me."

"It's a promise, not a threat."

"Fine, I won't mention it again."

"Good." He would keep his word – at least for a while. "Now let's get the box back up off the floor. Let me get another cup of coffee first." I ran up the stairs to cool off and to stop thinking about what he said about Denise.

The box wouldn't move without the bottom falling out, so I opened the top and found a framed photograph. It was of me, Denise, Mom, and Dad sitting at a restaurant table in Cancun, Mexico.

Everything had been perfect when the picture was taken. Dad had recovered from his stroke and surprised us with the trip. We found the restaurant the first night we arrived and returned each day for a meal. It was the first time Dad let Denise and me have a beer.

We were seniors in high school, both accepted to the same college in upstate New York. Denise received a partial softball scholarship, me going for pre-med. Mom and Dad couldn't have been happier to see us on the road to success. Dad regaled us with tales of his father. He'd been an up and coming orchestra maestro, known for being able to synthesize strangers into a unified whole in minutes to play phenomenal music. He died very young, of a stroke, before he could make a greater name for himself. Dad swore Denise showed the same gift.

"Wow, I haven't seen that picture in a long time," Dad said, looking over my shoulder, a sad smile on his face. "We were so happy then."

"I'll hang it up for you if you want." His smile faded and he just looked sad.

"No. Let's just find another box for it."

"Because Barbara will see it?" I couldn't keep the hurt out my voice.

"No, Barbara wants to see pictures of your Mom and Denise. She wants to meet you too. I told you I just want to …"

"What do you want? Forget about Denise and Mom?" I was angry and could feel the veins in my forehead pounding and throat constricting. To my horror, tears prickled my eyes.

He took a deep breath then sighed. "I don't want to forget them, but do want to move on." He took the picture from my hands and smiled that sad smile again. Tears brimmed his eyes. "I lost everything when Denise disappeared. We all lost Denise, but you and your mother left me too. Your mother drank herself to death. You obsessed over Denise and shut everything and everyone out. Including me."

"Oh." I couldn't think of anything to say. He had a point. Denise and I went beyond being twins. People described us as inseparable. After any time apart, we sought each other to talk, be together, and to understand the world. Until today, I thought we had no secrets from one another— although I never told her about my adventure with Kim. When Denise disappeared I stopped caring about anything but tracking her. I dropped out of high school with only months to finish. Why bother to finish anything without Denise?

The first two years after she vanished, one day I was manic and reviewed every detail of her disappearance, then consumed with depression, stealing Mom's vodka and pills to numb the pain. Not from the pain of loss but from my inability to help her. I knew she'd lived – I had no doubt. Every day I'd felt her need for help; my nightmares told me what happened to her.

"Remind me not to clean your basement anymore. It's no fun."

He chuckled. "At least, you still make me laugh."

I came back to his point. "I'm sorry, I never thought of it that way before."

"Water under the bridge. I never stopped or turned it around. I'm just as much to blame."

"None of us were prepared for Denise's disappearance. We did our best." He nodded, put the photo on the steps and came back. I pushed the box lid open again and we saw what had been under the photo. It was Mom's scrapbook documenting Denise's disappearance. My hand hovered over it.

"You don't have to open it."

"I have to."

He sighed. "Fine. Take it out of the box and get out of my way. I'll move the rest of the stuff in the box to the steps and you can bring it up to the kitchen when you're done."

"You're not going to look at it with me?"

"No. I can't. I won't."

I looked at him, astonished. It was all we had left of Denise. Of Mom. "I don't want to think about it anymore. Denise and your mother are gone. I'm old. It's time to move on and try to be happy during my remaining time. You need to do the same or you'll die old, alone, and friendless. Move out of the way, please."

A part of me was shocked at how blunt he was about how he saw my future. Another part knew he was right, but still didn't care. Without Denise, I was just marking time. I moved to a better lit spot and put the scrapbook on the shelf.

Dad harrumphed and grabbed something out of the box.

I didn't turn to see what he held. The scrapbook captured my attention. Centered on the first page by yellowing tape, Denise's high school senior picture caught my breath in my throat. It still felt like she disappeared yesterday. I quickly turned the page; feeling guilty I hadn't been there to protect her. There were several articles from the local newspaper about Denise and the softball team making it to the state championships. She had been the captain of the team.

Mom even had a clipping from the hospital newspaper. She worked there first as a nurse and then, after Denise disappeared, as an administrator until she died. It described Mom's years of service in the cardiac, intensive care unit where she earned the unofficial nickname, "The Defibrillator", due to the number of patients who she revived after their hearts stopped. The hospital employees and many former patients contributed to a fund to find Denise. The irony of her dying of a heart attack struck me yet again.

I scanned the rest of the article, but didn't need it to repeat the essence of what happened. I repeated to others a million times over the years.

On Sunday afternoon, February 18, thirty-three years ago, Denise and her friend, Kim Pham, went to a professional women's softball game in New York City. Kim had recently transferred to our school and joined the team that fall. It was a big adventure for Denise, a girl from eastern Long Island, to go to Manhattan without an adult. When they didn't get off their scheduled return train, we assumed they missed it and would be on the next one. We tried not to panic when we got home and Dad told us the phone never rang.

Everything unraveled after that. We knew nothing about Kim, Denise's friend. Denise had played on a variety of sports teams over the years. She was popular and friends with a lot of girls; too many to count.

40

While we spent time together, we also tried to have our own friends.

Mom and I called Denise's friends. We prayed they'd heard from her or they knew Kim's telephone number. After two hours and no information about Kim, Mom called the police. Dad took extra drugs to stay calm and avoid another stroke.

Kim's address turned out to be a vacant lot, the phone number disconnected. The police were unable to find her family. Our high school administration took heat for failing to verify any of her information.

The police told us Denise and Kim made it to the softball game and stayed afterward to congratulate a friend on their win. They were invited to a party that night, but declined as they needed to get back to Long Island. That was the last place Kim or Denise were seen.

At first, we put a good face on—both for Dad and ourselves. We cooperated with the police and spoke to television and newspaper reporters. Our church held prayer services and candlelight vigils to call attention to Kim and Denise's disappearance.

Each event was described by increasingly smaller articles in Mom's scrapbook. There were letters and cards from strangers expressing sympathy and support.

Kim Pham was either a victim or a kidnapping conspirator. The police were never able to determine her role. On our better days we included Kim in our prayers, prayed she was safe and, despite not locating her family, she would return along with Denise. On our worst days, we assumed she played an active role in Denise's disappearance and hoped she was rotting alone and unidentified on the side of some road.

Carnage junkies, vultures, and psychos circled us like flies around a feebly-twitching, dying animal. At Mom's urging, Dad cashed in our college funds and spent the money on shady private investigators. Mom met with psychics and emissaries from God. People from all over the world called or wrote, claiming to have seen Denise or Kim; they just needed five hundred, a thousand, or five thousand dollars to help their mother, daughter, or husband before they would share what they knew.

I flipped past the last article and realized the scrapbook was only half full. The notes, cards, articles petered out after a few months. Denise and Kim became anonymous numbers in runaway or missing-persons statistics.

My story didn't stop even though there were days I wished it had. Agonizing months turned into years. I earned a GED., went to a local college for criminal justice, and joined the NYPD. Solving crimes of any sort, from misdemeanors to multiple homicides, became an obsession. Off-time I attended classes to learn anything to help me find Denise or crack another case.

"That didn't take long," Dad commented, coming down the stairs as I shut the scrapbook.

"Not much new in it for me. It's like visiting a grave. I pay my respects, and then I can leave."

"Take it with you if you want," he suggested.

"You don't want it?"

"No. Take it."

I shrugged and walked to the stairs, full of assorted items including two alarm clocks, sodden paperbacks, and a few sweatshirts needing to be washed. Moving the scrapbook to a higher step, I returned to the now empty waterlogged box and crumpled it.

Dad went up to the kitchen and I ran the stuff to the table, the garbage can, or the washing machine. By the time we finished, the pump had sucked the water from the basement. Dad could mop the floor in the morning.

He made me another cup of coffee while I showered and changed into my work clothes. When I returned to the kitchen, only the scrapbook and the family photo were on the table.

"Do you want me to take them with me?" I put on my coat.

"Take the scrapbook. Leave the picture. I want to think about the best place to hang it."

I smiled at him. "Great. I gotta go."

"Call me. I want you to meet Barbara."

"I will." I left feeling good, despite Dad's questions, supposed revelations, and the memories the scrapbook stirred up.

4

"Welcome to 'Rice Queens,' Detective Steckler," a warm contralto voice said as a figure emerged from the shadows and opened the door to the bar. The New York accent surprised me; I assumed they would be Vietnamese immigrants.

At 2:00 AM – the night club had closed thirty minutes before. We huddled outside the entrance, pretending scrunched eyes and ducked heads would keep the rain off us. The collar of my decrepit trench coat wouldn't stay up. Patronio, nattily dressed in a rain coat belted at his waist, a wide brimmed fedora, jeans, and boots, all bright white, appeared dry.

"Anthony." This greeting was far cooler. I held the door for Patronio to take and reached to shake hands but let the gesture die as the person backed into the dim lighting of the bar's entranceway, and leaned against the wall to make way for us. I took in the floor-length black cloak and face-concealing hood before rolling my eyes at the theatrics.

Patronio caught the expression on my face and frowned to warn me to behave.

"Please, sit at the bar."

A thin white hand emerged from the black folds of the cloak and pointed beyond us, deeper into the gloom of the darkened hallway of the closed nightclub.

"Great, we can have a drink with the Ghost of Christmas Future." I followed Patronio down a short flight of steps. At the bottom, muted spotlights allowed us to thread our way through tables and chairs facing a stage with closed curtains. Each light revealed a painting or poster. I could name a few of them: Jamie Lee Curtis, David Bowie, Grace Jones, Boy George, Annie Lenox, and Lady Gaga. All famous for their androgyny.

The place appeared nicely decorated. I expected a drag bar to be cheesy and tacky. The high ceiling, dark fans, and simple, small silver-domed lights above each cocktail table made the room feel cozy, despite easily seating two hundred people. Black fabric billowed out from the walls like bed sheets, except where pictures hung over them. The darkness made it difficult for me to get a good sense of the room.

The bar, situated along the back wall, was big enough for thirty people to sit comfortably in the low-backed stools. At the far end, a dimly lit door quietly proclaimed "employees only". The small stage, hidden by black curtains, took up another wall. In the center of the stage, a set of steps led to the audience-level.

We took seats at the closest end of the bar and our host joined the thin, short-haired Asian man behind it cleaning after the night's show. I noticed he kept his back to us, which caught my attention. *Most people look at newcomers.*

Patronio took off his hat, leaned toward Tú and laughed. "I love the

Lady Gaga portrait, Tú! That wasn't up last time."

"I am not Tú, I am Tú's sibling, Cha^a. But thank you, Anthony. Lady Gaga liked the picture too." Patronio sat back, eyes wide in alarm. He inhaled deeply through his nose. That Tú had a sibling was clearly news to him. He shifted closer to me and my hand snaked toward my Glock in response to his obvious fear.

"It's a pleasure to meet you, Cha^a. Are there more–siblings–like you?" Patronio seemed nervous about the question.

"There are six of us," Cha^a answered.

I heard the bartender whisper, "Always six." The hair on the back of my neck stood up.

Patronio's eyes bulged and I unclipped my holster.

Cha^a saw my movement and pulled the hood back, I lost track of everything.

Cha^a's skin transfixed me. Before the hand looked corpse-like but now it glowed like snow in the moonlight. Lips as red as July cherries, unsullied by lipstick, turned upward with a faint smile. Above them sat a delicate and perfect snub-nose, slightly turned up. Almond-shaped eyes with irises so dark I couldn't be sure if they were black or brown, stared back at me, their corners crinkled in amusement, or perhaps contempt. Thick, lustrous hair surrounded the face and blended with the cloak.

I inhaled deeply, reveling in the smell of jasmine and leaned forward to touch that beautiful skin.

"Cha^a, that's enough!" Patronio yelled and slapped his hand on the bar.

My eyes watered and I coughed as the stench of cut onions assaulted me. Fear swept through me, clearing my head.

The bartender and Cha^a coughed and pulled away. Cha^a lifted the cowl back up, the material thick, almost like canvas. I knocked over a bar stool and pointed my gun squarely at Cha^a's head. The barman's eyes never wavered from Cha^a, filled with lust and envy.

"Detective, I can counter Cha^a's scent, but if you look at the face, you're bewitched," Patronio told me.

I forced myself to look no higher than the neckline of the robe.

Patronio peered around the room. "Tú, I know you're here. I can smell the difference now. You have one more chance, but if either of you attack us, I'll fill the place with toxic gas. Unless Detective Steckler shoots Cha^a first." His eyes flickered to me.

"If anything happens, the police will be all over this place and your secrets will become public," I added.

The barman stared at Patronio, his expression surprised and fearful. Even in the midst of this freakazoidal spook show, I knew he needed to be watched as well. Patronio's eyes kept glancing over at the bartender as well.

A new voice, another contralto, said from the stage, "I apologize for Cha^a's behavior. The urge to assert control is instinctual for us when we are nervous."

A figure emerged from behind the stage curtains and glided down the stage-side steps, garbed in a black canvas robe, head covered by a cowl. Jasmine scented the air as it drew near. My gun swiveled to point at the newcomer and I backed up farther. The click of the safety being switched off shattered the silence.

"Screw this! I'll come back with a S.W.A.T. team. You people and your 'gifts' scare the shit out of me." I backed Patronio toward the exit and sniffed at him, hinted to use his gift to get out safely.

Cha^a gasped and my trigger finger tensed as a hand moved toward the hood.

"Wait!" Patronio blocked my shot at Cha^a and patted the air to calm everyone down. "Let's not do anything rash. I've told Detective Steckler about your gifts. You've made us nervous." A master of understatement.

My gun still pointed at Cha^a as the barman moved toward the door.

"Keep your faces covered." I flicked the gun muzzle at Tú and back at Cha^a.

"Again, I must beg your forgiveness," Tú replied. "We will keep our hoods up but can do nothing about our scent. When we feel threatened our bodies react. I will back away and Cha^a will leave if you will permit it. Then we will talk. My siblings and I are upset you suspect us in the death of Anthony's friend."

Cha^a hissed and made rapid-fire statements in what I assumed to be Vietnamese. While they exchanged curses, I turned to Patronio, touched my ear and pointed at the siblings. Patronio shook his head minutely, speared the barman with his eyes and nodded. By the hatred smoldering on his face, I, as well as the siblings, could tell Patronio recognized the barman's voice and scent from the other night.

Apparently Tú won the argument. As Cha^a stomped from behind the bar toward the exit, the barman whispered, "Tú betrays our family. Tú should die for it." Both Cha^a and Tú turned toward him.

Tú made a chopping motion at Cha^a and said, "Go! I will deal with our little brother, Va^n."

With movement almost too quick to follow, Tú leaned over the bar, facing Va^n, back to us. Va^n's face remained defiant. His rebelliousness melted into a vacuous, lustful expression as Tú's face emerged from the hood. The smell of jasmine became stronger.

Patronio stepped close and orange scent surrounded me.

Tú hissed at Va^n then spoke in a hushed, rapid whisper. I wished I knew what was being said. Va^n nodded several times. Then without another word, he turned and followed Cha^a out. Tú pulled the cowl up.

"He's not going anywhere." I made to go after him.

Tú intercepted me, hand near the cowl, a threat.

"He isn't leaving; he is straightening out the storage area. What do you want with him?"

"He killed Lisa," Patronio said, his tone cold.

The smell of burnt popcorn filled the air and I could tell Tú was looking from Patronio and back to me again from beneath the cowl. Our faces showed no doubt.

Tú's hand dropped as if in defeat "There must be some reason you suspect him. My families' incompetence shames me," Tú said and turned to Patronio. "Cha^a will send him back to us."

We waited for Tú to move to a phone or intercom.

Patronio's narrowed eyes never shifted off Tú. The burnt smell worsened, a sure sign Patronio was pissed.

"I wasn't there, Anthony." Tú knew the meaning of the smell as well.

"You have five other siblings, Tú, not to mention the unhappy little bartender, and didn't vouch for them," I pointed out. "Now get Va^n back here."

"I already asked Cha^a to send him back," Tú answered.

"How?" I pressed my lips together and frowned.

"We siblings can share our thoughts with one another."

I groaned and looked at Patronio for his opinion.

He shrugged an "it's possible" but didn't take his eyes off Tú.

"I don't believe you." I made another move toward the door but Tú blocked me again.

"Why would we kill Anthony's friend, Detective?"

"Mr. Patronio was the real target of the attack."

"Detective, you've had a taste of my gifts," Tú said and a pale hand touched the cowl, then drifted down. "We don't resort to violence to get our way."

"Does that include Va^n? He's not like you and your siblings and was very pissed about something," I said.

"I recognized his voice and scent from the night Lisa was killed, and he was here the night we discovered my ability to negate your gifts," Patronio added.

"Va^n is new to this country, ambitious, and wants to assume a leadership role in our family and businesses. His impatience can be tiresome, but he is still just a boy. You are mistaken about him. We can control him." Again the hand drifted up to touch the cowl. I tried not to think about just how much control they had over him and anyone else close.

"Why isn't Va^n here yet? You don't have as much control as you think," I said and pushed past Tú.

A gunshot sounded. Tú screamed, stumbled into me. I closed my eyes and prayed nothing weird would happen from a touch.

Patronio filled my nose with the smell of oranges and I thought absurdly to tell him I didn't like them that much.

Tú swayed, hand clenched at chest height. Patronio pulled Tú's cowl down further. I nodded gratefully. Neither of us wanted to risk it falling no matter what Tú experienced.

"What's the matter, Tú?" I asked.

"It's Cha^a. Cha^a is hurt." Tú stumbled toward the door. It banged open when Tú fell on it, but he remained upright.

A combination hallway and storage area hid on the other side of the door; a rectangle fourteen feet long by five feet wide. At the opposite end, an open door with an "Exit" sign, led outside. I caught a glimpse of Va^n, with a bundle of black cloth under one arm as he ran down a dark alley before the door swung almost closed.

A pale form, nude except for slippers on the feet, propped the door open. One arm, flung out, acted as the doorstopper. The body laid on its side, a hole gaping in the back. The other arm draped over the chest. Something bothered me about the two arms but I couldn't determine what. A pool of blood widened around the body. Behind me, I heard Patronio gag. Given the long black hair, I assumed it was Cha^a.

To chase Va^n, I moved Cha^a's hand away from the door. I heard a warning yell as I grasped it and, moments later, found myself kneeling next to Cha^a, unaware of the blood soaking into my pants.

Fascinated, I stared at the motionless form, its glowing white skin and the deep red flecks of blood sprinkled over it. My gaze focused on the beating pulse on the side of the neck. I felt warm and safe as the thrum slowed then stopped. The trance-like state lifted and I dropped Cha^a's hand and threw myself up and against the door as far as possible from the body. Va^n was long gone.

My gun pointed at a cluster of people. I didn't remember taking it out of its holster but wouldn't think twice about shooting if anyone touched me now.

The wall on the left held shelves stacked with liquor boxes and bar supplies. A small vial rolled on the floor beneath them. An open door on the right side of the hallway revealed a stairwell with four more figures dressed in robes identical to Cha^a's and Tú's. I made sure not to look at them. Jasmine, intense and cloying, saturated the air.

Patronio stood on the other side of the hallway and stared at the body on the floor.

Tú, next to him, hissed, and the figures in the stairwell covered their faces with cowls.

"I tried to tell you not to touch Cha^a's body, Detective. Cha^a must be dead. Otherwise, you would still be stunned just by seeing him like that."

My eyes grew wide. Tú and the hooded figures spoke in sync with one another.

"Cha^a is dead," they chanted.

"What happened?" I stared at the four figures clustered in the doorway. Each was the same height as Tú. One of them stepped forward.

"We do not know. We were upstairs," they answered. "We came down when we felt Cha^a's pain. We sought to help."

"Who else is in the building?" I rose from the floor.

"Va^n was the only other one here. He told the other staff to leave. He volunteered to clean and close up after the show," they answered.

"Why are you talking in unison? It's freaking me out."

"When we feel threatened, our minds join and act as one."

"Va^n is gone. He won't be back with you waiting for him," I assured them.

Their forms became still and Tú said, "No one asked my permission to send the staff home."

"Va^n said he asked you. We did not think to verify this with you, Tú," the robed figure in the front of the foursome spoke and all four bowed. "Cha^a and Va^n had an intense conversation right after Cha^a told us your friend, Anthony, and the detective, were coming."

"Where do you think Va^n went?" I asked.

"We do not know. It is doubtful he will go to his family's home. They will not welcome him after they learn of his actions. He spent much of his waking hours as our General Manager and handled the bar's day-to-day business with outsiders."

"Why would Va^n murder Cha^a?" I tried to determine a motive.

"There are many possibilities," Tú answered.

"He was one of Lisa's murderers. Your scents confused me and I was distracted by Cha^a at first, but after I heard him speak, I knew his voice." Patronio confirmed what I suspected. He looked wary as he came closer and let the barroom door swing shut behind him.

Tú, Patronio, and I were clustered around Cha^a's body while the other siblings hovered by the stairwell.

"Was Cha^a the other person?" I knew Patronio would know I referred to the night of Lisa's murder.

"No," both Tú and Patronio answered simultaneously. I looked from one to the other.

"I would have recognized the scent right away. It's almost identical to Tú," Patronio added.

"Cha^a was here that night. We are here or at one of our other homes every night. It is difficult for us to be out in public," Tú explained.

The answer made me curious, but I decided to follow up later. "That means he has an accomplice. One that isn't here. Va^n's probably on his way to him, but can't have gotten far yet. I'll call an ambulance for Cha^a and get more patrolmen to track Va^n down." I reached into my pocket for my cell phone.

The four figures by the doorway hissed and reached for their hoods.

"Detective Steckler, we cannot allow you to do that," Tú said.

"You don't have any say in the matter." I flipped my cell phone open. The smell of jasmine became more intense, overwhelming me.

I found myself staring at Tú's hand, thinking how delicate it was, how beautifully white, even in harsh fluorescent light.

Pain washed over me when I bit my lip to clear my head. I leveled my gun at Tú. My mind glazed over when the faint smell of oranges was overwhelmed by jasmine.

"Detective, there are too many of them," Patronio said. "Tú, stop bullying Detective Steckler! We need his help." He stepped between me and the siblings.

I felt a flash of appreciation before my gaze drifted back toward Tú's exposed flesh. Patronio was no push over. I bit my lip again, tasting blood. "I'm a cop, no one else will help you with this." I told them.

"Detective, we will do our best to control our reactions. We mean you no harm. Put your gun away and give us time to explain. The officials cannot be brought into this matter." The air became cleaner and less perfumed. My head cleared, gut telling me something important was about to happen.

The gun dropped down; it wasn't going to help me in this situation. Without a demonstration of their "gifts," I couldn't explain to anyone if I fired it. That didn't change the fact they scared me and a double-murderer was on the loose. I had little choice but to listen, at least for now.

"I'm not making any promises."

I put my hand on Patronio's shoulder, brought him to my side and out of the line of fire.

"Detective, look closely at my sibling." Tú knelt and, before I could stop it, pulled Cha^a's body over flat on its back. An arm flopped onto the floor with a slap and the outside door shut with a clunk. I growled at the damage done to the crime scene.

Then I noticed the chest. On the left was a perfectly formed, small, female breast while the right side was flat like a man's with no scars except the bullet hole. The arms and hands were similarly different. The left one was thinner, more delicate, with child-sized fingers. The arm and hand on the right were masculine and muscled with larger fingers and knuckles. The legs and feet followed the same pattern. No hair adorned the body.

Just like a carnage junky, I felt a shudder of fear and anticipation as I focused on Cha^a's genitalia: a vagina with a small penis rather than a clitoris. Seeing something so strange and in-person made me uncomfortable, but once "cataloged" I moved to the face.

Unlike the rest of the body, the combination of masculine and feminine was seamless. Beautiful even in death; it needed no bewitching power with thick, deep black hair around it. The white skin without blemishes or veins reminded me of porcelain.

"You're a family of intersexuals?" I tore my eyes away to look at Tú.

Patronio blinked in surprise.

Thank you, Discovery Channel.

"Very close, Detective," Tú replied. "We are not true siblings, but our families are related and come from the same village in Vietnam. They immigrated to New York during the Vietnam War. Each of us was born female or male but transformed into 'intersexuals' as you called us."

"I'll grant you, most people wouldn't understand your differences, but Va^n killed Cha^a and Lisa Taylor. He needs to be caught. The police

54

will be respectful."

"Detective Steckler, intersexuality isn't the issue. They don't want their *gifts* to become public knowledge," Patronio interjected.

"Then don't use them. I sure as hell won't say anything." I turned a corner, no longer thinking of them as *tricks*.

"That isn't possible for us, Detective Steckler," Tú said. "We can hide our faces from others, hope to remain calm so our pheromones do not overwhelm people, and avoid touching another's skin, but that is all."

"The fugue happens every time someone touches you?" I verified my understanding.

The four hooded figures huddled in the doorway hissed. Tú calmed them with a raised hand.

"We are not used to sharing information about ourselves with outsiders," Tú explained. "But I see that if we do not, events could go very badly for us." I wasn't sure if Tú was talking to me or the others.

"Our scent entices people and makes them want to approach us. Our gaze stills. To touch us gives euphoria and turns you into our slave for a time, willing to do anything we request. Lying with us will enslave you for life."

I couldn't hide my shudder, but forced my thoughts back to the crime.

"Then how did Va^n kill Cha^a?" Patronio asked, not as bothered by these ideas as I was.

"He wouldn't look at Cha^a's face, and kept his distance," I answered. "This probably helped as well." I stepped forward and picked up the vial.

"I knew I caught a whiff of smelling salts," Patronio said. "Va^n must have dropped it. Apparently, he's been experimenting based on what he learned from us. He used them to resist and have enough willpower to shoot Cha^a."

"Why did Va^n take Cha^a's robe?" I asked, pointing to Cha^a's nude body. It had bothered me since Va^n ran away, but no one answered. "What's with the robes, besides the hoods?" I persisted and frowned at each robed person.

"Our skin changes when we transform. It becomes hyper-sensitive. Wearing anything else is very painful to us," Tú explained.

That didn't make sense given the rough texture of the material I saw. Perhaps it was lined with silk or something else soft.

"The transformation affects us in less obvious ways as well. Our affection for our old lives and families is lost and we become dispassionate. We seek out the company of our five siblings and psychically connect with one another, protect one another. Like a pack of wolves there is one alpha. New siblings vie for a place and, if they are strong enough, become the alpha and direct our actions. Cha^a tried but could not displace me."

"That doesn't explain why Va^n took the robe." I pointed out. Tú tried to distract me and failed.

"Va^n said there is always six," Patronio added.

"Va^n will be the next one to transform," I answered my own question.

"Yes," Tú confirmed. "And maybe the next Alpha."

5

Patronio and I faced the five remaining siblings over Ch^a's body. The city air, scented with rain and jasmine blew into the back hall of the bar.

"Va^n is going to change into … an intersexual?" My stomach lurched.

"I hope it hurts, a lot," Patronio said.

"It is painful," Tú replied.

"Good. Will it kill him?" Patronio sounded hopeful.

"No," one of the robed figures in the back answered.

I turned expectantly to Tú and waited for a rebuke.

Tú nodded. "Bi`nh serves as our historian."

"How long does it take?" I couldn't stop the image of a cocoon from flashing across my mind.

"Three to five days," Bi`nh answered.

"When will it start?" Again, an image of a cocoon hanging from a tree came to me.

"In the next twelve hours," Bi`nh answered.

"How do you know Va^n will be the one to change?" Patronio asked good questions. He was insightful and intelligent and under different circumstances, he would have made a good detective. I decided to let him keep the lead for now.

"The gift runs strong in his family. I was his aunt before my change. Hao was his elder cousin." Bi`nh pointed at another robed figure.

"And he has spent a great deal of time with us," Tú added.

"Does that matter?" Patronio was using the situation to learn as much as he could about the siblings.

"We think it increases the chances," Bi`nh answered.

"Is that why you asked me if any of my relatives were gifted?" Patronio continued his interrogation of Tú.

"Yes," Tú answered. "We think spending time with gifted blood-relatives increases the likelihood of a person becoming gifted. It encourages mutations in a person's genes and brings out the latent gift."

"Like a virus?" Patronio pressed.

"No, more like a person with a specific gene being repeatedly exposed to radiation is more likely to develop specific cancer," Tú answered.

"As fascinating as the biology lesson is, we still have Cha^a and Lisa's murders to deal with," I reminded them. "I'm still calling more police in."

"Detective, what do you think will happen if more people find out about us?" Tú gave me a curious look.

"Most would think you were freaks and your 'gifts' are a trick," I answered.

"What about those who realize our gifts are real, regardless of our freakishness?" Tú said, amused by my choice of words.

I thought for a moment. "It wouldn't be pretty." Great, now I was the one who made understatements.

"The last time knowledge of our 'gifts' spread beyond our family, half died protecting us," Bi`nh answered.

"Willingly?" I remembered Tú's comment about enslavement.

"Is that why you came here?" Patronio spoke at the same time.

"Yes to both questions," Tú answered.

"Why?"

I silenced Patronio with a look.

"We use our gifts to help them. In return they protect us and serve as our eyes, ears, and hands in the world," Tú answered.

"How do you help them?" Patronio jumped in.

"People cannot lie to us when we touch them; therefore, we serve as a court of last resort rendering judgment on disputes. We also ease pain," Tú answered.

"This still doesn't change my mind," I said.

"Detective, I know you're an expert at catching criminals. I've done my research — you have an impressive record and don't need anyone's help. If the government learns about the siblings they would be guinea pigs at best or, more likely, killed out of fear," Patronio tried to convince me. "The same would happen to me," he added quietly.

"People will forget. They always do," I replied but didn't believe it.

"Detective, no one with a gift would be safe." Patronio looked me in the eye to send a message.

"I'm not sure what you're trying to tell me but I don't believe in government conspiracies," I answered, confused.

"Detective, you have as much to lose as we do, should our gifts become common knowledge," Patronio said, less certain this time.

"What are you talking about?" I tired of pointed looks and muttered hints.

"If they find out about any of us, they'll learn about *all* of us," Patronio answered.

I looked at him, baffled and annoyed.

Patronio's eyes opened wide and he took a step away from me. He knew I was angry. "Nothing, never mind." His answer confused me.

I tried to think through a way out of this mess. There wasn't one; every path led to a dead end. If I was lucky, I could escape the siblings but would lose the case. They'd refuse to cooperate after more police were involved. If the siblings overcame me, I'd be their slave. I shuddered; that was not an option.

"Detective, I appreciate your dilemma. You must either help us find Va^n and compromise your position as a police officer by keeping our secret or uphold your oaths and try to take control of this situation. One is not possible." Tú sounded logical and not in the least bit doubtful I had no options. I didn't like Tú very much right then; not that I had before.

"Think of it this way, Detective," Patronio injected. "The police won't know how to deal with someone like Tú. *We* know what we're up against."

I was impressed with Patronio again; he wanted to get Va^n and his accomplice. "Have there been other renegade siblings? Or people who killed to become one?" I kept my face directed toward Tú.

Everyone relaxed; they knew I'd reached the logical decision.

"Our lives before we become siblings lose meaning for us. Over the years, people like Va^n, seek to become one of us, but most try to avoid it. We left behind spouses and children; everything. Some were thieves, prostitutes, one was a murderer. After the metamorphosis it no longer matters," Bi`nh said. "But to answer your question more directly, a sibling has never been murdered by family before."

"It is not possible for one of us to be a renegade. Our mind changes as much as our body; we want to be what we are and physically need to be near one another. Our thoughts are regulated by our role among the siblings," Tú added. I remembered Tú's reference to the historian.

60

"If you need to be near one another after the change, then we can just wait for Va^n to come back here, right?" I admitted to myself that would be too easy.

"Perhaps," Tú answered. I thought about his response for a moment and then connected the smelling salts, Lisa's murder, and Patronio's attempted kidnapping. It all fell into place.

"Va^n thought of a way to use Mr. Patronio's gift to counter yours and that's why he tried to kidnap him. He planned on using Mr. Patronio to murder Cha^a or one of you so that he, Va^n, could take your place. After the kidnapping failed and he saw Mr. Patronio and me walk in tonight, he panicked and used his backup plan to kill Cha^a," I concluded.

"Maybe he isn't planning on joining you," Patronio said.

"He must," Tú replied.

"What if he can't or won't?" I followed Patronio's logic.

"How?" Tú asked in return.

"If he planned a kidnapping and a murder, he or his accomplices figured out how to stay locked away," I reminded them.

"What would Va^n gain by that?" Patronio asked Tú who looked surprised by our train of thought and turned to the other siblings. They spoke in Vietnamese. Patronio shrugged when I looked at him; his Vietnamese wasn't any better than mine. To me, Tú sounded scared or angry.

I sighed. If people learned about them, the siblings' lives would turn into a nightmare. They were weird and a little scary, but didn't deserve that. Neither did Patronio. Since this was an ongoing murder investigation, the police were involved no matter what we wanted.

"Fine," I said to Patronio. He quirked an eyebrow at me. "I'll do what I can to keep the siblings out of it and your secret safe."

"It's not just my secret. But thanks."

"Detective Steckler," Tú interrupted Patronio. "We do not know who

Va^n's accomplice could be. We doubt it's a family member. It is too difficult to keep a secret among them."

I had my doubts. "Do you have another place for the five of you to go?"

Tú paused a moment, processing the implications of my question. "Yes, we own several places."

"What's up the stairs?" I craned by neck to peer around them.

"Our living quarters," Tú answered.

"Is there anything unusual about them?" I wasn't sure what kind of living spaces people like the siblings would have.

"No, Detective, we have a beautiful, normal home," Tú said, amused. "Six bedrooms, three bathrooms, one large kitchen and a living room. Despite our more unusual qualities, we lead a quiet life."

"Great. Glad to hear it," I said. "Can you clean it up and make it look like some of the staff stay here?

"Yes, that would be easy," Tú replied.

"Good. If you agree, I can call in additional police and let them take Cha^a's body, I'll do my best to keep knowledge of the rest of you under wraps. It won't be hard for me to keep quiet about your gifts."

"I do not understand why you need to call in more police," Tú challenged.

"A person's been murdered," I reminded him. "My bosses know I came here tonight. If word got out, I'd be toast and your secret revealed. Beside which, we don't know what we are up against here. I won't risk my ass or anyone else's with a murderer on the loose."

"How do you know I will not force the issue?" asked Tú.

"From what I've seen, you could keep me under your control here, but then I wouldn't be of any use finding Va^n or his accomplice." I bluffed, but felt confident. Their gifts had to have limits.

"You are neither stupid nor easily cowed," said Tú "Both admirable qualities."

"Thank you," I answered, pleased.

"They could also be your downfall. What will you do if you catch Va^n?" Tú wanted to know.

I hesitated.

"After the change, if Va^n touches you, all is lost. You could willingly kill yourself or someone else."

"Can Mr. Patronio's gift counter that?"

"My gift only counters their pheromones, not their touch or gaze," Patronio answered.

"You have to touch skin?"

"Yes."

"What about the gaze? How does it work?"

"There has to be direct eye contact," Tú answered.

"Sunglasses, a mirror, anything stop the gaze from working?" I recalled something about a mirror and the story of the Gorgon.

"We do not know. We have not experimented with the limits of our gifts not used in conjunction with one another," interjected Bi`nh.

"Do your gifts work on one another? Can't you fight Va^n after the change?" I hoped to find some way of countering the situation.

"That will depend on how strong Va^n's gifts are. If they are stronger than mine, which I doubt, and Va^n establishes dominance, we will have to follow Va^n's directions," Tú said.

"Even if Va^n's crazy?" Patronio looked incredulous.

"I do not believe that is possible," Bi`nh answered.

"I don't have a plan for what to do with Va^n when I catch him but I'll think of something. For now, our priority is locating him. We may not need to worry about his gifts at all if we do that soon."

"What do you want us to do?" Tú glanced back at the other siblings.

"Gather as many of your belongings as you can and leave in ten minutes. You have Mr. Patronio's number. Call him later today so we know where to find you," I said.

"Should I leave?" Patronio checked with me.

I laughed. "Nice try, but you have to stay. People at HQ know we're here. It will look bad if you left. We'll have to get our story straight."

Patronio quirked his lips at my choice of words.

"We are done here," Artie, the forensic team lead, told me. Patronio and I stood on the sidewalk in front of Rice Queens. It took less than five minutes for backup to arrive but two hours for them go over the scene. The rain let up sometime between.

Artie was a total tech-nerd but a nice guy. He gave me a nervous smile which turned into a grimace as Cha^a's body was wheeled passed us to the meat-wagon that would take it to the city medical examiner's. Artie's shoulder's twitched with a shudder.

"Ugh," was all he said. He gave me another look, glanced over my shoulder at Patronio, and walked away.

"I guess I'm supposed to be the most open-minded one here but I agree, ugh," Patronio said. We watched as the EMTs loaded the gurney into the back of the truck.

"Everything checks out like you said it would." Detective Luddy's eyes darted between Patronio and me.

"Don't sound so disappointed, Luddy." We went to the police academy together. A loud-mouth, bully, and an all-around asshole, he resented my making it to detective using my brain rather than politics.

"I wouldn't expect anything less from a boy scout like you, Steckler," he answered and glanced again at Patronio. "You don't need to be here anymore. Unless Detective Steckler needs you for something." His tone contained contempt and innuendo at the same time.

"I'll have one of the patrolmen drive you home, Mr. Patronio."

He smiled at me and then gave Luddy a frown, "I'll take a taxi, thank you," he answered.

"I think your boyfriend's upset about his she-man getting killed," Luddy commented loud enough for Patronio to hear, then laughed. Patronio ignored him and looked in both directions for a taxi. This being New York City, there were several taxis driving around. Patronio flagged one down.

"You really are a dick, aren't you Luddy?" I walked away before he could answer.

"Sorry about that," I said to Patronio.

"No problem." He avoided my eyes.

"I can give you a lift back if you'd like. It's on my way." Patronio turned and raised his eyebrows at me.

"You're not worried what your friends will say?" He nodded to where Luddy and a few other officers stood and watched us.

"No. Don't let them get to you. They're freaked out by Cha^a, that's all."

"So am I." Patronio had more to say but I was tired and wanted to get back to the precinct and finish the paperwork. Then I wanted to sleep for a week, though my slumber wouldn't last more than one or two hours – this case had me *hook, line, and sinker.*

"I'm leaving now. Do you want a ride or not?"

"Yes, thank you. I didn't mean to be ungrateful, I'm just tired." The bags were back under his eyes.

"Yeah, me too. Come on." I pointed across the street to my car parked in front of a fire hydrant. *Great*, the rain started up again.

After Patronio made me wait while he put on his seatbelt, I pulled onto the road. The streets were mostly empty at this time of the night. As we left, another car drove out of an alley across the street. The rain came down much harder and made seeing difficult, even with the windshield wipers on high speed.

"Thanks for backing me tonight. The siblings were pretty scary there for a while," I said to break the awkward silence between us.

"Can I ask you a question?" Patronio appeared determined with a clenched jaw.

I groaned silently, it sounded like it was going to be a personal one.

"Go for it." I turned off Fourteenth Street and went north on Third toward Gramercy Park. The car from the ally stayed with us. Third Street was a major road. I doubted the car followed us, but didn't believe in coincidences either. The heavy rain made it impossible for me to see the license plate, but it wasn't a police car. It might be the press; Luddy could have called them out of spite. I sped up and whizzed through a yellow light to lose it then loosened my jacket so I could reach my gun.

"You weren't fazed by Cha^a or the siblings. Especially their gender. How come?" Patronio tilted his head.

I blinked. It wasn't the question I anticipated.

"For the same reason you're handling Cha^a's murder so well. So many things happened these past few days; I'm beyond being surprised at this point."

"Bullshit. There's something different about you. I know it and so do you. You're not telling me what and, at this point, you should."

"Is there a full moon tonight?" First Dad, now Patronio; there must be something that caused people to think I kept a secret. Patronio looked confused. "Never mind. I was being a wise ass."

"Just answer my question," he demanded.

I liked Patronio, despite his affectations. He possessed a backbone. "You're right. I was disturbed by Cha^a's, um, differences, but it didn't rattle me as much as it did you and everyone else."

"Why not?" Patronio persisted.

"Because I'm asexual." He looked at me in surprise. We crossed over Twenty-first Street. "I haven't had a sex drive in so long; I don't remember what it was like."

"Wow."

"Surprised you, didn't I?"

"Yes." He fiddled with his pant leg, clearly not sure what to say. "But you used to have one? Don't answer if you don't want to."

The dark car sped up and got closer. I took my foot off the gas and relaxed as it moved into the right lane to go around us. The car pulled even with us. I couldn't see the driver clearly. The street was well lit but the rain made everything shiny and reflective, obscuring his features. I didn't like it and tapped the brake to slow down even more so the other car would pull ahead.

"No problem. Yes, I was a normal teenager, but after my sister disappeared … Shit! Hold on!" I yelled as the other car swerved sharply into us. Patronio swore and I absorbed the impact by turning the wheel in the same direction it was shoved. I pulled my gun, but with the two cars moving, I couldn't get a clear shot and could hit a bystander. Stomping on the brakes, I hoped the other car would shoot past us and threw my cell phone at Patronio. "Call 911!"

"Who is that?" Patronio held on to the dashboard with one hand and dialed my phone with the other.

"It's either Va^n or his accomplice," I said as the cars collided again. "Shit!" I screamed, ran a red light, and swerved to miss cars headed toward us. My phone flew from Patronio's hand.

"Hold on, I'm going to ram them!"

"Good, kill the bastard!" he yelled. I did my best to comply, then spun the wheel toward the car. They smacked together. The rear bumpers caught on one another. The other driver hit the brakes. My car spun as the bumpers unstuck. As we swirled, I saw blue and white lights flash in the distance. Someone called the police. We shot across Twenty-Third Street and stopped after smashing into an oncoming garbage truck, passenger side first.

My head whipped sideways and smacked against the rearview mirror. I felt woozy but snapped into focus remembering Patronio in the seat beside me. The passenger-side window lay shattered in pieces and the door crunched inward, wrapped around Patronio's still body. I panicked and checked his neck for a pulse, but at the same time, Patronio took a shallow breath.

"Jesus! Are you okay? My light was green, you went flying through it! Shit! Is he okay?" A man opened my door and thrust his face into the car.

"Call an ambulance." I pushed him away from me and heard the sound of rushing steps.

"It's on the way. Are you okay, Detective Steckler?" Patrolman Bently peered at me through the window. I recognized him from that first night, when Lisa Taylor lost her life to killers. My left eye felt normal but the right had swollen shut. It started throbbing and I knew it would hurt real bad, real soon.

"Great," I answered sarcastically. "Check on Patronio. He took the brunt of it." I got out of the car and pushed past them. The garbage man caught me by the armpits when my legs gave out.

"I got you. Can you walk? Let's get away from the car in case it blows up." He kept talking as we stumbled toward the sidewalk. I hated the rain but it still came down.

It bothered me to see Patronio hurt, he backed me up when the siblings went for me. Once again, my slow responses and thinking lead to someone else hurt or lost; the story of my life.

My head cleared and strength came to my legs at the same time as the pain in my eye and head grew. I shook off the garbage man's hands.

"Thanks for the help. I'm fine now." I stood up and went back to the car.

"You have a good-sized rip in your skull, dude. Let the other cop handle it."

I frowned and regretted it when the right side of my face flared with pain. The sight of blood on my coat and sleeve stopped me. Head wounds bled a lot.

The blaring sound of an ambulance siren got closer.

"I'd rather check on him. Thanks again." I headed back. He followed me, muttering, but my attention was on the people at my car.

Bently and another patrolman were on the passenger side. They yanked on the door and pulled it open, metal screaming. I hoped it didn't cover the sound of Patronio's screams, or worse, dead silence.

The rain pounded down even harder, soaking us to the bone. The wind picked up as well, stripping us of any of the warmth.

"How is he?" I checked with Bently when his head came up above the car door.

"He's unconscious but coming around. I didn't see anything obvious but he could have internal injuries. He's got a huge egg on the right side of his head and might have a concussion."

"I've got a blanket in the back of my car," I said.

"Use it for yourself. The paramedics are right behind you. Should they look at you first?" Bently wanted to know, after he gave me a careful perusal. I didn't look too good.

"No. Have them check Patronio," I said, but decided to take Bently's advice. Between the rain, wind, and shock from the accident I shivered.

Bently motioned to the EMTs after they pulled next to my car. He pointed them in Patronio's direction. His partner stayed with them. Bently came up beside me and helped push the trunk the final way open. I wasn't in any condition to do it on my own and groaned with the effort.

"I'll get it," he said and grabbed the blanket. I wrapped it around my shoulders but left my head uncovered. The cold rain felt good.

"What happened?"

I didn't have to answer Bently's question, but suspected he didn't care what I said. He wanted me awake and focused until the paramedics could get to me.

"I was dropping Patronio off. We just finished up at–"

"I heard. It's all over the precinct radio. It's not often a half-man, half-woman turns up," he said and shuddered. "Patronio has some freaky friends." Another shudder.

"True."

"Sorry, go ahead."

"When we left, another car followed. I thought it was a reporter and ignored him. They rammed into my car. We spun and kissed the garbage truck. It was raining too hard for me to see the license plate or make of the car. It was a four-door sedan, black or dark green or blue. The front and driver's side should have enough damage to be noticeable. From the size of the car, I'd guess it was an American make."

Bently nodded and called the information in. An all-points bulletin would go out to New York, New Jersey, and Connecticut.

Another ambulance pulled up next to Bently. Additional police cars arrived in a show of support which I appreciated.

"Which of you is hurt?" A deep voiced, large man climbed out of the back of the ambulance and looked at us. My head throbbed as I craned my neck to look up at him. He sounded cheerful. I took that as a good sign about Patronio.

"That would be me." He turned a flashlight on my face.

"Yeah, I see that now. Can you make it to the ambulance so I can take a look at you, or do you want me to get a stretcher?" He scrutinized my face.

"I'll walk; it's just a cut on my face."

"Sure. Let's take a look at you in the ambulance."

Now he sounded like we were going to a picnic. It made me nervous– I must have a good-sized gouge. Images of Lon Chaney and Boris Karloff in their monster movie roles flashed through my mind. I started to laugh.

"Hmmm. You may have a concussion too," the paramedic added.

I laughed again.

"No, I have an odd sense of humor. Let's go. How is Patronio – the other patient?" I looked away. "I'm a Detective." Frustration rose at my own stupidity. I should have anticipated this despite how rare attacks on police officers were.

"The patient's got a lump on his head and bruises up and down his right side. He needs to be checked for internal injuries."

"Good. Thanks," I grunted and pulled myself up into the back of the ambulance.

"I'll go check if Patronio's awake and aware before the ambulance leaves. Maybe he caught some details on the car. Headquarters sent the tow truck for yours," Bently said then left.

The paramedic, Earl, his name plate declared, looked me over in the bright lights of the ambulance. "You've got a deep cut that goes from scalp to eyebrow. Luckily it missed your eye. I'll clean and tape it but it needs stitches, otherwise you're gonna have a bad scar. Get x-rays to make sure your skull isn't cracked."

He wanted to take me to a hospital. Normally I'd refuse, but I didn't have a ride at the moment. And though I wasn't vain, or interested in sex, the Frankenstein look wasn't for me either.

"Let's go," I said. "Which hospital?"

"Beth Israel. Now sit back and let's get started." Earl gave the driver the go-ahead. As Earl shut the ambulance door, Bently grabbed it and leaned in.

"Patronio insisted I give this to you." He handed me an envelope with my name written on it.

"Thanks." Bently nodded, about to say something but shut the door when he saw Earl's face.

"Later," Earl said firmly and took the envelope from my hand. "I'll give it back when I'm done. Now lie back and let me do my job."

"We're done," Doctor Gould, a plastic surgeon, said. I arrived at the beginning of her rounds, otherwise an intern would have learnt to sew on my face. I sat up to make sure Patronio was assigned a guard – he'd had two attempts on his life already, but she stopped me.

"Stay put for a few minutes. You've got thirty stitches. They're very small and, if you follow the instructions, the scar should be almost unnoticeable."

"Great," the sarcasm dripped from my voice as I looked at the chunk of hair on the table next to me. They had to cut it to sew the wound. I'd shave the rest to even it up. "How's the guy who was in the car with me?" I asked, then groaned while sitting up.

"Fine," she frowned. "Call my office and make an appointment for next week." She pushed aside the curtain and left.

I got up from the hospital bed, held tightly to its railing, and fought off the dizziness. The throbbing in my head faded and I stood without fear of falling.

Clothes. I had a vague memory of taking them off after they gave me painkillers. They were in the locker next to the bed. My shirt, covered in blood, lay in a crumpled mess at the bottom; no way would I put that back on. The trench coat, in better shape because the rain washed most of it away, could be salvaged. I took off the hospital gown, struggled into my pants and got the coat on. All were damp but I didn't care; better damp in my own clothes than walking around with my ass showing.

Past my curtain, a patrolman stood outside a curtained-off section.

"That Patronio?" I indicated the space behind him.

"You Steckler?" He took in my odd appearance. Good. I was glad he was cautious.

"Next time ask who I am rather than give me the name to use to get past you," I admonished.

"Officer Bently told me to keep an eye out for a tall guy that looked like Frankenstein," he laughed.

I rolled my eyes but stopped when a stabbing pain went through my head. "Great," I answered with a gruesome smile and changed the subject. "How's Patronio doing?"

The patrolman shrugged. "I'm not sure. He's not been awake since he got here. Doctors and nurses cycled in a few times the last hour or so. They're waiting for an open room."

I stuck my head through the curtain. Patronio appeared to be sleeping. He didn't respond when I called out his name. I turned back to the patrolman.

"You'll guard his room until the end of your shift?"

"Yes. Why?"

"Call me when he wakes up. Ask your replacement to do the same." I gave him a damp card from a pocket in my overcoat. My next purchase would be a plastic card holder to protect them.

"Will do. You going home now?" He gave me the once over again and didn't like what he saw.

"Not yet. I want to complete the paperwork at headquarters, otherwise it'll never get done."

"Yeah, I hear that." He sounded sympathetic.

"Where's Tony Patronio?" A loud female voice called out. The patrolman and I turned. Given her coloring and nose, she could only be Patronio's mother. Behind her were three men, one older and two younger—a clear family resemblance. I approached them.

"Excuse me, who are you looking for?"

The woman eyed me with suspicion. Given my scar, open coat, and exposed chest, I couldn't blame her.

"Anthony Patronio; I'm his mother," she answered with an Italian accent overlaid with New Jersey.

"Hello, Mrs. Patronio. I'm Detective Steckler. I was driving the car when we were hit." I nodded to the men clustered behind her.

"How is Tony?" One of the brothers, almost Anthony's twin, but more muscled and in conventional clothes queried. I made a mental note to check their criminal records. The Patronio brothers dressed very nicely for run-of-the-mill bricklayers.

"I think he'll be okay. You should ask the nurses to page his doctor." I gestured at the nurses' station behind them.

"We'll do that." Patronio's father took his wife's arm and led her away. He exchanged a meaningful look with his sons.

"Tony was attacked again?" Patronio's near-twin looked at me with raised eyebrows.

"Detective Carl Steckler. You are?" I held out my hand.

"Vito Patronio. This is Pat; we're Tony's brothers." I shook their hands. They were rough and calloused.

"Was it the same ones that killed Lisa?" Pat wanted to know.

"I'm afraid I can't answer that, being the lead investigator in Lisa's death and the attack on your brother." They might have pressed harder but eyed my stitches.

"Do you know who did it?" Vito sounded as though he wanted to take action on his own.

"We're following some strong leads." I evaded the question. The way they looked at me, Vito and Pat would get involved in this.

"Are they still after him?" Vito nodded at the patrolman in front of Patronio's curtained-off bed.

"We don't know. We're keeping an officer here as a precaution." I wondered if a patrolman would be enough to stop someone with *gifts* from harming anyone.

"We'll keep an eye on him from now on," Vito said. I was certain he carried a gun.

"He's awake," the patrolman called out over his shoulder and closed the curtain to Patronio's room.

Vito got his parents and they gathered around Patronio's bed.

I asked the patrolman to call a car to bring me back to the precinct.

Patronio's mother and father fussed over him and his brothers clasped his shoulders. He looked bruised and shaken with a few small cuts but, overall, not too bad.

"Do I look as bad as he does?" Patronio pointed at me once the hug-fest subsided.

"No, he looks way worse than you do." Patronio's father patted him lightly on the shoulder.

"Thanks." I frowned at him. "How are you feeling?"

"Like I was hit by a truck," Patronio answered.

"Technically, we hit the garbage truck." I smiled.

"Whether the pitcher hits the rock or the rock hits the pitcher." Patronio shrugged then winced as he did so. I laughed along with his family. Probably a line from a song or show, one he quoted often.

"Well, I'm glad you're okay. I've got to go back to the precinct and get another car," I said after an awkward moment of silence. They waited for me to leave. "I'll call you tomorrow to follow up about what happened tonight."

"What about the guard?" Vito checked before I left.

"Right. Sorry, I'm a little out of it," I answered, tired and achy everywhere, especially my head. "We have a guard posted outside your room. We'll have a squad car by your home after that until things are under control."

"Thank you," Patronio answered, then fiddled with his bedsheet. "Did you get the envelope I gave the EMT?" I looked at him in puzzlement then recalled the paper Officer Bently handed to me and reached into my overcoat. It felt a little soggy but not as bad as my card had been.

"Yes, right here. I haven't looked at it yet. I'll read it now.

The patrolman stuck his head through the curtain. "Detective Steckler, there's a car waiting for you at the emergency entrance. They'd like you to hurry. It's busy out there tonight, despite the rain."

"Okay." I slid the envelope back into my coat, nodded at Patronio and his family, and shuffled out of the room.

6

With a groan, I sat down at my desk. The painkillers wore off half an hour ago and my whole body felt stiff, sore, and swollen. The doctor gave me a prescription for more but I held off taking them to keep my wits about me. Luddy, Dwayne, and a couple of other detectives huddled in a corner. They nodded but said nothing when I entered the squad room, poured a cup of coffee, and sat down. Something was up.

I opened my desk drawer to take some of the aspirin and looked down. There was a printout of Cha^a's body spread-eagle and naked. I flinched and the guys laughed. As I grabbed four tablets and swallowed them with the lukewarm coffee, they walked over.

"Holy shit! I didn't know you were hurt! You should be home!" Dwayne eyed my face, then dropped his gaze to the floor, embarrassed now for taking part in the joke.

"Did you do that before it died?" Luddy sneered. He had no problem giving me a hard time, no matter what my condition. The others watched my reaction, curious in a morbid, suspicious way.

"Cha^a was a person like anybody else. He, she, or it, didn't ask to be that way anymore than you asked to resemble a large, flabby, ass." I enjoyed Luddy's frown and the other's laughter, but felt guilty about the picture. Cha^a was different but didn't deserve people laughing over his corpse.

"Getting a chub looking at that?" Luddy looked down at my crotch. Dwayne and the two other detectives, Hines, and DelRay shuffled their feet, uncomfortable with Luddy's question but they wanted to know – Luddy must have stirred up trouble again. I'd been on the job for a long time, went through the academy with Dwayne and Luddy. Not once in all those years had they seen me with a woman. I'd never gone to strip clubs or participated in bachelor party antics with them. They were uncomfortable with my distance, but Luddy was obsessed with turning the others against me.

I growled, ready to go toe-to-toe with Luddy and stood up. My shirt pulled away from my back, wet with perspiration. Pain stabbed my head and I grabbed Luddy's arm.

He pushed my hand away but I was in too much pain and too exhausted to deal with him right now.

"Show some respect for the dead and get rid of the picture." I handed it to Luddy and shoved back from my desk.

Luddy opened his mouth but was interrupted.

"That better not make it to the internet or it'll be your ass in a sling," Captain Perez told Luddy. "Don't you people have work to do? If not, I'll find some. Luddy, wipe your nose, it's bleeding." She took the paper from Luddy who glared at her. The others looked chagrinned. Luddy grabbed a tissue and they went back to their desks pretending to be busy.

"Steckler, you look like shit. Why aren't you in the hospital?" She ignored the incident moments before.

"They gave me the Frankenstein look and said I was good to go." I liked Captain Perez; she was a no-nonsense woman who wanted to solve crime and make a difference, despite the odds.

"They lied. Go home and get rest or you'll frighten the perps." Perez softened the comment with a smile.

"My car is wrecked, I need a replacement." The paperwork was secondary. Even in the best of times, I avoided public transportation.

Perez snorted. "You wreck a car and whine to me about it. I'll authorize another car given Patrolman Bently's report, but not for another day or two so you recover. No car tonight, that's for sure."

"Fine." I hated to agree but knew not to drive. "You've got an officer watching Patronio?"

"Yes, but don't know how long that will last. We've got budget issues."

"We'll catch the bastards before it raises any flags with the bosses," I assured her. She didn't respond but her eyes flicked to my bandage-covered face.

"Bently already completed the paperwork, if that's what you came in for. We didn't expect you here tonight, or tomorrow for that matter."

"Luddy knew," I pointed out.

"It was stupid luck you showed up so soon with them here," she contradicted me and glanced at the picture in her hand. "You met him, or her, or whatever, before the murder; what was he … or she like? Wow, the gender thing is so difficult." She, at least, tried to think of the right term.

I thought before answering. "Still human. Cha^a's clothes were androgynous, so until this happened, I just assumed Cha^a was a man."

"You don't seem to have much of an issue with it."

"I don't. Like I said, Cha^a *was* human. I didn't know him, or her, or whatever, well. It's creepy and different, but doesn't matter to me."

"Then you're a better human than me," she said with a shudder. "Now go home. One of the patrol cars will take you. Don't come back until you look better than three-day-old roadkill."

The patrol car pulled up in front of my condo building.

"Thanks for the lift," I told Bently and got out of the car. The sun lit the city for the coming day; the masses woke and crowded the streets. Normally I enjoyed the smell of the city after the rain, but I was too exhausted and the aspirins had worn off. I wanted to take a few pills and crash for two days.

"Get some rest. You look like a cadaver after the autopsy," he laughed. I waved and shut the door with more force than necessary and he laughed again before pulling away.

Bently was right; I crossed the sidewalk to the building without dodging sideways once; people edged away or skirted around me without meeting my eyes.

"Wow, are you okay, Mr. Steckler?" Tim, the building maintenance man, pursued me after I pushed open the entrance door. He spent his time in the building's foyer and watched people or stood outside smoking. His intentions were good though. Tim hurried over to help me but there wasn't anything to do but hover, so he pushed the elevator button and held the door open. "What happened? Were you in a raid or something?"

I didn't want to talk or be rude and liked our occasional brief chats. He kept a key and opened my condo door for repairmen or deliveries when I worked – I didn't want to screw that up.

"A car chase and accident, but it looks worse than it is. The doctor went over-the-top with the stitches." The elevator door opened.

"Let me know if you need anything."

"Thank you." It was empty. I pressed the button for my floor and sagged against the wall when the doors shut.

I fought to keep my eyes open. The closer to home the harder it was to stay awake. I stumbled out the doors and fumbled for my keys.

"Yes, I look like shit," I told Denise's picture and bolted the door. I groaned and shrugged off my overcoat. A paper-crunching sound reminded me about Patronio's envelope. I'd read it after my shower.

I stripped, then threw my dress shirt and the hospital bag into the trash. The blood ruined it. I hoped my overcoat could be dry-cleaned.

What I saw in the bathroom mirror shocked me. I wouldn't have gone to the precinct had I checked my reflection: The Mummy crossed with Frankenstein with a bad haircut confronted me.

Using scissors from the medicine chest, I cut the tape that held the bandages in place. It was against the doctor's orders which were in the bedroom with Patronio's envelope. The cut on the right side of my face started above the eyebrow and went an inch into my hairline. The stitches, small and neat, reminded me of embroidery.

It was stupid, but the gap in my hair annoyed me more than the long cut. I might not care about sex, but did about how I looked, especially my thick, blond hair. Seeing it ruined pissed me off. Despite my exhaustion, I shaved the rest of my head with a trimmer, then showered and put antibacterial ointment on the stitches.

I popped two painkillers left over from my last dentist appointment, took two over-the-counter sleeping pills, and set my alarm for ten. Climbing into bed, I remembered Patronio's envelope but decided to let it wait and slid into a deep sleep.

The phone rang again, jarring me awake. I sighed and picked up the receiver.

"Detective Steckler? Precinct dispatch. Hold for Captain Perez." I squinted at the digital clock on my dresser; it read 8:23 PM. I'd slept through my alarm. Panicked, I sat up, but the spiking pain in my face stopped me.

"Steckler, is that you?" the Captain sounded as happy as I felt. I only managed a grunt. My mouth tasted like I ate rancid meet and rocks.

"Steckler, I know you're out of it, but that can't be helped. Someone stole Cha^a Chung's body from the morgue!"

"Hold on a second." I put my cell phone face down on the pillow, braced for pain, and shoved into an upright position. Who cared if she heard the groan? I rubbed the gunk out of my eyes and yelped when I jostled the stitches.

"I'm awake now."

"I just got the call from the Head M.E. It wasn't a clerical error. Nobody knows or can remember what happened," Perez said. A sinking feeling filled the pit of my stomach when I thought about the siblings and their gifts.

"Did they check the security tapes?

"They're doing that now. Do you think Patronio knows what's going on?"

"Doubtful, but I'll go to the hospital now."

"He checked himself out with his brothers and gave the patrol officer the slip."

"Great."

"He isn't answering calls. We've left messages. I've canceled the protective order for now. If he doesn't want it, why spend the money? Have you heard from him?"

I stood to check my cell and home phone, and groaned.

"No calls or messages on either phone. I'll try his numbers and see if he's been to the gallery or with Lisa Taylor's family."

"Good, I know you're injured, but if we don't find Chung, someone will leak it to the press. If that happens, the bosses won't be happy and we'll both be screwed."

"I'll start working on it now," I said, unable to keep the weariness out of my voice. The initial shot of adrenaline faded.

"Do what you can to find out what Patronio knows and get back to me. Don't overdo it." She sounded only a little sorry for dragging me out of my sick bed.

"No problem, I'll call you when I've got something."

"Good," she said and hung up.

I got up out of bed with another groan and groped my way to the bathroom. Between the scar over my eyebrow, my naked scalp, and the bruising on the side of my face, I looked like a skinhead who'd been on the losing end of a fight.

"It'll grow back," I told myself firmly and turned on the hot water for a shower. It took me a lot longer than usual to pull on a pair of jeans and dress shirt. I looked longingly at the bottle of pain killers but wanted a clear head when speaking to Patronio.

Patronio's number went directly to voicemail. I swore and threw my cell phone back on the stand beside my bed. It knocked the envelope Patronio left for me to the floor.

I picked it up; it had dried overnight. Perfume and the gritty smell of the city wafted from the paper. Inside was a single folded sheet. On the blank side was written, in a neat script, 'Detective, I thought you would be interested in this.'

On the flip side was a contact information form businesses would use to keep track of customers. Most of the fields on the form were blank, but the completed fields held my undivided attention. Name: Denise Yardley-Pham. Credit Card: Amex 9807. Last Purchase: Rescue Me. There was a picture of a woman in her late twenties or early thirties. Despite all of the years since, I knew her: Denise.

At first, I just rocked back and forth, and tried to process what I saw. Pham, the same last name as Kim, the other girl who disappeared. No address, but a credit card with what was likely its last four digits. I suspected Patronio's perfume gallery computer could provide me with the complete number. It could be traced.

I asked Tim to hail a cab and redialed Patronio's number, willing him to answer on the way down to the building's entrance. Tim gave me a look of concern but I went directly to the waiting cab.

When we arrived at the perfume gallery, I threw a handful of bills at the driver. He muttered something but the only thing I cared about was finding Patronio and making him talk to me about Denise.

Lights from the gallery still lit the sidewalk. I arrived just in time; the posted hours on the door said they closed in fifteen minutes. Two sales people, one talking to a customer, stood behind the desk. Both wore white shirts and jeans, Patronio's signature look. I approached the one standing behind the desk. "Eric" proclaimed his very discreet name badge.

"Eric, where's Patronio?"

"I'm sorry, sir, but Mr. Patronio isn't here at the moment, is there something I can help you with?" he said politely but backed away. I didn't care if I looked like a psycho skinhead.

"Bullshit. He's here," I said loud enough for the employees and customers to hear. They turned with an alarmed look. I grinned and showed all my teeth.

"You're Detective Steckler, right?"

I nodded.

"There were police officers here earlier today. They went through the lab as well as Mr. Patronio's home. He wasn't there then and he hasn't come home since. I would know." Eric looked nervous.

"Bullshit," I repeated louder. "Patronio, you said you weren't going to run anymore. You wouldn't leave your gallery or home unprotected." I searched around the area above the desk for the disguised security camera. "How long have you been laughing at me, knowing Denise was still alive?" I spat at the camera in the wall and leaned forward to say more when the desk phone buzzed.

Eric hurried to pick it up as if it would protect him from me. "Mr. Patronio? I didn't know you were here." He held up his palm as if to swear an oath. "I'll send him up." He hung up.

"The computer is supposed to tell us when the building doors open and close. According to the software, they never opened." Eric looked panicked. Maybe he thought I would attack him. At that moment, it was a definite possibility, but I had bigger fish to fry.

"Don't worry about it, Eric. Mr. Patronio is full of surprises and secrets. Isn't that right, Patronio?" I glared into the camera.

Eric walked over to the back room door and opened it for me. "The stairway is through the door on the right." He pointed to a door opposite the "exit" and waited while I went into the storage room, shutting the door behind me.

As I walked through the room where this all started, I thought of how I'd started to respect Patronio while he laughed at me the whole time. My head and stitches throbbed in time with my angry heartbeat. A buzzing sounded and I opened the door to the stairway, pounding up the steps despite the additional pain.

I stopped at the landing and looked around trying to find Patronio. The stairway continued upward. The hallway on the left led to three doors; one closed and unmarked, the other made of glass, revealing what could only be the lab, based on the equipment. The last door stood slightly ajar. A light gleamed into the dark hallway from within.

"Where are you, Patronio?" I called out.

"In here, the light is on," a voice called out. It sounded like Patronio's brother, Vito. I regretted not bringing my gun but, given my injuries, I hadn't wanted to risk anything. As I walked into the lit room, I hoped not to regret the decision.

I found an enormous L-shaped room — bigger than my entire condo. The door opened into the smaller section of the "L." A wall full of books stretched around the entire space had a seating area with couches and chairs, a small bar, and pool table. Patronio sat at a large, antique desk. Probably French, I guessed, covered with all the ridiculously ornate swirls and gilt. He wore a white suit with a white tie and shirt. The bruise on the right side of his face spoiled the image. Patronio's brothers, Pat and Vito, stood on either side of the desk. Each had a hand inside their suit coats.

"Hello, Detective Steckler. There's been a misunderstanding." Patronio watched as if he hadn't met me before. I didn't look my best.

"You seemed to have recovered." There was a trace of bitterness in my voice.

"I have an egg-sized bump on the side of my head and my right side is bruised. Apparently, I was luckier than you," he replied and pointed at the stitches on my face.

"Where is Denise?"

"I have no idea, Detective. Honestly."

"Yeah, right." I stepped closer to the desk, fists clenched.

Vito intercepted me. Patronio shook his head sadly.

"Detective Steckler, until you barged into my gallery, I half-suspected you knew all about your sister and manufactured her disappearance to protect her and her gifts." Patronio watched me from around his brother's shoulders.

"Tell me what you're talking about," I demanded.

"I've only met two people who had gifts like mine," he reminded me. "Before we met the siblings, that is." He glanced at his brothers; apparently he told them about his gift. "Tú was one. Your sister was the other."

"How do you know she was gifted?"

"When she came into the gallery, I introduced myself. Our hands touched and there was a weird popping feeling, like a sudden drop in pressure. She twitched, but then smiled and looked at me carefully. It was like she found the answer to a question or finally remembered something. Then she pretended nothing happened.

"At first, I was too afraid to say anything. I'd never met anyone else with a gift before. Then she laughed when she looked at a particular perfume but didn't ask to sample it." Patronio turned his gaze back to me. "It was a gift for her brother."

"What was it?" I leaned forward.

"Perfume from my Motown line, called 'Rescue Me'."

Hearing that felt like a punch in the gut.

"Detective, I misunderstood the situation. I would have told you sooner. I thought you were hiding her to protect her."

"How did she look?"

Patronio opened his mouth to speak, then shut it again. He seemed to choose his words with care. "Very good, like she was twenty-one. Her plastic surgery was excellent. She has money if she can afford my perfume."

"You have the rest of her credit card number on file?" I checked, not ready to accept she was rich and free enough to buy freaking perfume.

"Of course. It's all on the computer."

I nodded, already working out how to track down Denise. Anger bubbled up. Why hadn't she contacted us for over twenty years if she "looked fine?" Thoughts of her "gift" were pushed aside when I remembered there was police business to talk about with Patronio and a murderer on the loose. I'd have to put off finding Denise for another day.

"What happened to Cha^a's body?" I surprised him with a change in subject.

His eyebrows went up nearly to his hairline. "Excuse me?"

"Do you know where Cha^a's body is?" I repeated.

Vito and Pat exchanged glances. I wasn't sure if that meant they knew something or they didn't want to learn anything else about their odd brother.

"Detective Steckler, I have more trouble communicating with you than I do with my cousins in Italy – and they don't speak English. What are you talking about?" Patronio pursed his lips, annoyed.

I looked at him, then at Vito and Pat, hoping he would understand. We made a deal not to tell anyone about him, the siblings, or their gifts. Up until last night, I kept my word and my oaths. Patronio understood my unspoken question.

"Detective Steckler, my brothers know about my gifts, about Tú and the siblings, and that someone, most likely Va^n, is trying to kill me. They want to protect me." He sounded surprised and pleased by the idea.

"Great." Now Patronio, the siblings, and Patronio's brothers knew about what happened at 'Rice Queens'. At the moment, I didn't care, I wanted to find Cha^a and Va^n and hand them over to the District Attorney. Then I'd work on tracking down Denise. If any of the Patronio family tried to use the information against me, I'd smear the ground with them.

"What happened to Cha^a's body?" Patronio turned the question back on me.

"Someone stole it from the morgue. Was it you?" Patronio's look of disgust told me the answer. "What about the siblings, would they take it?"

"I don't know. We haven't spoken since that night. I wanted to talk to you before calling them."

"Call Tú now." A wave of exhaustion swept over me.

"I will in just a moment. Sit down. You look awful."

Pat brought a chair for me from beside the desk while Patronio picked up a phone as overwrought as the desk. He shook his head at me – voicemail. "Tú, its Anthony. We've got another problem. Call me." Patronio put the phone on its cradle.

"I didn't want to leave any details on the voicemail."

"Good thinking." I smiled at the irony. If the story unraveled, and headquarters learned the siblings left the crime scene, I'd be lucky if they didn't throw me in jail.

"Were you here when the patrolmen came in?" It bothered me they missed him.

"Yes," Patronio answered with his own smile.

"How'd you avoid them?" I tapped my nose.

He laughed and shook his head. "I'm not going to answer that, but it had nothing to do with this." He tapped his nose. "You were right; I'm full of secrets of all sorts."

Pat and Vito smirked. Patronio pulled a computer from under the desk. He typed something, then turned to the printer on a shelf behind him. After waiting while the sheets emerged with a soft whooshing sound, he handed a printout to me. It was the same information about Denise, but with the complete credit card number and date of purchase – almost three months ago.

"Thank you."

"You're welcome. Have you learned anything about Va^n since last night?"

"No, I've been laid up."

Vito and Pat chuckled.

"Are you the only police officer the department has?" Patronio returned.

"Point," I acknowledged. "Sorry, I woke up with the news about Cha^a. Then I opened your note." I let that sink in.

"I have to go to the coroner's office now." I stood up, managed to contain a groan, kept my hand on the chair to be sure I didn't fall over.

"Did you drive?" Patronio exchanged glances with his brothers.

"No, I took a cab. The car's totaled. It's evidence anyway." My grip tightened on the chair as I swayed dizzily.

"You haven't eaten either, right?" Patronio frowned in disapproval.

"No, I can eat later. Besides, I've got to get going."

"Sit down. I'll call for a cab and then get you something to eat while you wait." Patronio picked up the phone.

"Great," I answered, and meant it this time.

The lobby of the city's morgue, or if you wanted to be official, the Office of the Chief Medical Examiner of New York City, depressed me. Dismal yellow paint and tattered brown couches welcomed visitors.

"I'm Detective Steckler. Is Dr. Lukishna in the building?" I approached the security guard while flashing my identification.

"You here about the missing body?" My appearance didn't seem to faze him. He must be used to seeing a lot of odd characters.

"Yes, I'm here about M ..." I paused to think how to say it. "Cha^a

Chung, if that's what you mean."

"Let me call him. He was expecting a visit from one of you guys sometime this evening." Then muttered, "Just not from Frankenstein."

I refused to look in the window at my reflection.

He picked up the phone on his desk, checked a list of names, then dialed a number. "Detective Steckler is waiting for you," he said once someone, presumably Dr. Lukishna, answered. "I'll let him know." He swiveled his chair around to face the clock above the doors to the interior of the building.

"He'll be down in a moment. If you'd like to have a seat …" He pointed to the pair of grungy couches by the doorway.

I ignored the scuffed-up magazines on the table next to the couches and sat down. Just as I did so, a figure pushed into the waiting room wearing an oversized pair of jeans, a sweatshirt with the hood pulled up and a pair of sunglasses. Something about the figure struck me as familiar, and given I couldn't tell the gender, thought it could be a sibling. But the only skin showing wasn't ivory white, nor did I smell jasmine, and my shoulders relaxed. I continued to watch the person and decided it was a woman based on gut instinct.

She walked up to the security guard, leaned forward, and held out her hand to shake his. He stood and I leaned forward, curious. What visitor shakes the security guard's hand? His look of surprise changed into a smile. It was more of a leer. I wrinkled my nose in disgust; who hits on visitors to the morgue?

A dark-haired man in a lab coat opened the door behind the guard, frowned, and said, "Detective Steckler?" Then he spotted me. I stood up with a groan, muscles stiff, and walked toward him, past the security guard, and who could only be his girlfriend.

"You look like you should be on one of the gurneys," he said to me by way of an introduction.

"I feel like you've already done work on me," I said and he surprised me with a deep laugh. "I'm Detective Steckler." We shook hands.

"Stan Lukishna, Supervising Coroner on this shift." He smiled and held my gaze just a little longer than necessary, then looked beyond me and frowned. I turned to see the couple hadn't moved yet, but the girl now had her back to me.

"Ron, are the tapes from this afternoon ready?" Ron kept staring at the girl. "Ron? The security tapes?" he said more loudly. We both were staring at them now.

Ron dragged his gaze from his girlfriend. "They're in your office. I sent them up earlier," he answered, his eyes turned back to the girl.

"Good. Thank you." Dr. Lukishna frowned, shook his head again, and opened the door leading to the rest of the building. There was a long, dark hallway on the other side. Once the door closed behind us, he asked, "Is there a full moon tonight? Everyone is acting so oddly."

I started to laugh.

"What's so funny?" He smiled, puzzled.

"I asked the same thing just last night. It's been that kind of week." As he smiled up at me, I became very aware of my shaved head and stitches.

"It certainly looks that way," Lukishna stated, then his voice took on a serious tone. "I've never had a body go missing before, especially like this one." We walked down the darkened hallway.

"Do you think it's really missing or just lost in the building or system?"

"If the body was in the building I'd know by now. There isn't a person on staff who hasn't been asked about it."

I wanted him to use Cha^a's name, not "it," but knew in their job, like mine, emotional distance was a necessary habit.

We reached his office, a plain, utilitarian space with a desk, computer, phone, and two chairs. A long wall, comprised of glass overlooked a small yard and the sidewalk. He took the seat behind the desk and motioned me to the other.

"Even though I knew better, I called the other offices throughout the city to check. All our other bodies are accounted for. This body is missing," he concluded, sitting back in the chair frustrated and unhappy. "It came in on the first shift. None of us thought about going into 'VIP body' mode. We've had famous remains here before."

"How do you think it happened?"

"I don't know," he answered, clearly frustrated. "No one remembers anything out of the ordinary. They don't remember anything at all."

A bad feeling came over me. "What do you mean?"

"When I asked where they were during the beginning of the shift, from three to four, many people had a blank spot." He saw my puzzled look and added, "They remember being in a room or the hallway, or somewhere, but then they suddenly found themselves somewhere else with no recollection of the time between."

I looked away so he wouldn't see my lack of surprise by his description.

"No one saw anyone they didn't know or recognize," he added. He opened a desk drawer, took out a computer disk, put it in the computer and turned the screen toward me.

"I asked two senior technicians to go through the security footage. Separately. They spotted the same things." He clicked his mouse and an image of the back entrance, where the bodies were brought in, appeared on the screen. A vehicle that looked like an ambulance, but I knew was used to transport bodies, pulled into the garage after a large door opened. A small, hooded figure in jeans entered at the same time and walked up to the vehicle as the driver got out of it. My eyes widened in recognition. The walk was familiar but it had been over twenty years since I last saw it.

"Kim Pham! She's the one with the security guard!" I stood, ignoring the sudden tilting and swaying of the room. The way the security guard reacted when she touched him told me she was one of the gifted.

Dr. Lukishna stared at me in alarm. "What's wrong?"

"She's at the front desk right now!" I pointed to the screen. "Call security and tell them there's a dangerous person in the building."

He lifted up his phone and dialed. "She has some kind of drug on her hands or skin that affects the people she touches."

"Are you sure?" He waited for someone to answer.

"No, but I'd rather be wrong now than sorry later." I started for the door, unable to stop the wince or my groan.

"What are you going to do? Scare them? You're in no shape to do anything."

Before I retorted, someone picked up on the other end.

"Bill, this is Stan Lukishna. We have a problem. I think the body snatcher is back. She was with Ron at the entrance desk a few minutes ago. A detective from NYPD is with me and thinks she's using some kind of drug on people she touches. Is she still there?" He listened to a voice I could almost hear.

I wished I had my gun.

"Bill can see Ron on his security cameras," he told me. "Ron's still at his desk but alone, staring at nothing, not answering his phone. There's no sign of the girl." Dr. Lukishna shifted back and forth, eyes moving around the room as if searching for answers. "What is going on?"

"I'm trying to figure it out," I answered him honestly.

"If it isn't the lesser Steckler," a voice I hadn't heard in twenty years said behind me. A chill went down my spine when I saw the small woman in the doorway. She held a gun in her hand, pointed at me.

7

I stood in the coroner's office, staring at a woman who disappeared with my sister more than twenty years ago.

"Kim?" Her hood fell back and she took off the glasses. She looked the same as I remembered her. Exactly the same. No wrinkles, even around her eyes or mouth. Not a single gray hair.

At that moment I didn't care about Cha^a's body, Lisa's murderer, what Kim looked like, or the gun in her hand.

"I should've killed you when I had the chance. But the old man thought you still had the potential for the gene to express. Besides, Denise would never forgive me," Kim replied.

One part of me processed what she said, sifted for information to use to find Denise and Pham. Irrationally, another part felt stung; back then I thought she liked me.

"Tough to tell me with your mouth full that night, right?" I snapped, then shook my head at my idiocy; I wasn't seventeen anymore. From the look on his face, Dr. Lukishna felt the same. "Kim, where is Denise? Why did you disappear?" I felt the pain of her disappearance as if it happened yesterday.

"She's fine," she answered. "No thanks to you."

"What did you do with the body?" Dr. Lukishna looked back and forth between us.

Kim turned her gaze to him, eyes dilated wide. She scrutinized Dr. Lukishna; a faint smile on her face. Then Kim turned to me; her head cocked sideways. Her smile faded, replaced by a puzzled expression.

"You want him, I can see it," Kim told Dr. Lukishna who turned bright red.

From the way Kim said "see," I knew she referred to her gift.

"Don't waste your time. Something's wrong, he's got nothing for you," she said to Dr. Lukishna. "I've never seen anyone without a sex drive before. What happened to you? You had one that night I–"

"Kim, give me the gun and I'll tell you all about my life. Then you can tell me all about old man Pham." I made a guess about his name, hoped she'd give me new information and struggled to keep my face still when it worked.

"Yardley would kill you if he heard you call him that." Kim smiled, and for the first time I was reminded of the girl my sister befriended in high school. Her grin faded. "Seriously, what happened to you?" It was as though she forgot why she was here.

I kept her talking for as long as possible and hoped the troops arrived before she escaped. But I did have a new name now, Yardley Pham.

"Who knows, Kim? It worked that night with you." I watched her face show surprise, and then what I thought was guilt. As fast as she changed gears before, Kim's breathing sped up again and her eyes lost focus.

"Yardley wanted your sperm for the reason he wanted the he /she body. Another stupid experiment. Just like Va^n. He'll kill us all one of these days." I wasn't sure she answered mine or Dr. Lukishna's question from before.

"What do you want, Kim?"

"The disk with the video. Where is it?"

Dr. Lukishna's eyes slid to the DVD slot on the side of his computer.

"Thank you." Kim laughed. "Stupid Puppy was supposed to take care of this. I had to save the day. Again." She leaned forward and took the DVD from the computer.

Puppy, a nickname or a derogatory term?

"The meathead at the front desk already deleted the originals," Kim added.

"If you're so interested in Cha^a, you should ask Carl about the other five he/she freaks. They watched while Cha^a was shot." She cackled and brandished her gun at me.

When word of that gets to HQ, my ass is grass. If either Dr. Lukishna or I live that long.

There was noise from down the hallway. "The cavalry has arrived," Kim said after she looked out the doorway.

I jumped up to knock the gun out of her hand, but my injuries made me slow. Kim snorted and fired, missed me and shattered the window. I ducked and Dr. Lukishna whimpered.

Kim pointed her gun in the direction of the noise and fired two shots down the hallway. The lights went out. People yelled and scrambled to get out of the way.

She turned back to where we stood frozen in horror and laughed again. "Sorry to disappoint you but I only shot at the lights to scare them. I'm not yet crazy enough to murder people on the old man's say so. Now get out of the way!" She swung the gun back at us and we dropped to the floor. The gun went off three more times and I heard pieces of glass break behind us.

She put the DVD in her jacket pocket, then grabbed my chair and used it to knock out the remaining shards. Kim dropped the chair and swept the contents of Dr. Lukishna's desk off at the two of us, scared the doctor, and caught me on the hurt side of my face. She kept the gun trained on us and stepped onto the windowsill.

Dr. Lukishna made a move to grab Kim, but I stopped him.

"Don't touch her! Remember!" I kept my hands on his shoulders.

Kim stopped then and pointed the gun at me. "Don't look for Denise. It's too late now." Then she jumped to the ground and ran off.

I just pressed the elevator button and the doors started to close when a familiar hand shot out to stop them.

When I thought my day couldn't get worse, Luddy walked into the elevator and the doors closed. My head pounded from the car accident and stitches, as well as the drubbing I got from Captain Perez. It was the first time I'd seen her pissed in the five years we worked together. The fact I refused to explain myself hadn't helped any. I wanted to talk to Patronio first.

Luddy smirked. "Thank you, Steckler. Watching Captain Perez ream your ass was fun."

Despite my exhaustion, I wouldn't give him the satisfaction of seeing me that way. I stood up straight despite the pain in my side.

"I should have known you were lurking around somewhere from the smell. I kept checking the bottom of my shoes."

"Funny, Steckler. You got caught screwing a bunch of freaks and you're pissing off one of the few people on the force who can help you.

Not that I'll do anything but laugh when they yank your badge and pension."

"Luddy, the day I turn to you for help is the day I resign from the job. But, for the record, this thing is a big misunderstanding that will clear up and blow over."

"Steckler, that's what they all say. You're gonna need your union representative when you meet with Internal Affairs."

I groaned silently, knowing he was right.

"There's no way it'll go that far. And no matter what, you won't be anywhere near these meetings," I bluffed with confidence.

Luddy shook his head. "You're in the union, Steckler. It'll be involved in anything that happens. There's no choice."

"And you'll grease the skids to help me fall, right Luddy?"

Luddy was moving into new territory; he'd actively tried to turn other officers against me but had never worked the system.

"You betcha!"

"Maybe I do need your help. Is what they say about 'Muddy Luddy' true? Are you for sale?" I goaded him and got an idea for a way to throw a wrench into his plans.

"Steckler, I am so gonna enjoy watching you fall."

I'd hit a nerve.

"It isn't going to happen. But I still want to know my options. Having you and the full weight of the union behind me might be what could turn the tide." I let my shoulders drop in defeat.

"You don't have that kind of money."

"Don't be too sure, Luddy. I own my condo outright and no kids to spend my money on."

"What happened to not turning to the likes of me?"

"I was pissed you overheard everything but I'm a practical man. I don't want to lose my pension or benefits. The medical coverage alone is worth it."

"I'll think about it."

"Perez is talking about a meeting with Internal Affairs by the end of the week and putting me on indefinite unpaid leave! After that, who knows?" I pretended to be panicked. "What's it gonna take?"

"Twenty-five grand. Cash." His eyes glinted with greed. I tried not to grin; Luddy swallowed the bait.

"What'll that get me?"

"The union will throw so many lawyers at the department it'll take months for them to do anything."

"Isn't the union supposed to do that anyway?"

"Not if I don't say so." He smirked.

"You'll do your job if I pay you twenty-five grand?" I gave him a wide-eyed stare.

"Yup." He licked his lips, hungry for the money.

"Excellent." I smiled. "I can't wait to play the tape of this conversation at the next union election meeting." I held up my hand and showed him I had something in it. It was my cell phone, but he couldn't see it with my fingers curled around it.

"Steckler, you're a bastard!"

"Not really. You're just a moron." I laughed as the elevator doors opened.

Rather than go home right away, I went back to my desk and ignored the inquisitive looks from the other detectives. The news of my getting chewed out by Captain Perez had spread like wildfire – I'd never been in the "doghouse" before. The look I gave them combined with the cut on my face kept them away from me.

I straightened my desk, filed old case notes, and threw away scraps of paper with scribbled numbers or addresses I didn't need. Dwayne took my files on older open cases we worked, most of them not likely to be closed, especially with only Dwayne working on them. Dwayne was a good detective and definitely a man I'd want with me on the more physically dangerous investigations but he wasn't a go-getter on older cases.

As I gave the files to Dwayne, I noticed an English language dictionary on his desk. It stopped me. Yardley was an English name. How did someone from Vietnam get an English first name? Probably a Vietnamese father and an English mother. In Vietnam, like other Asian cultures, that racial combination had to be rare. An Englishman or another foreigner likely fathered a child with a Vietnamese mother. If that were true, Yardley was likely from England originally.

Dwayne glanced up from his work. "I've seen that look before, you've thought of something. But you're on leave, right?"

I nodded and logged onto the police databases again and, this time checked Interpol for a Yardley Pham from England. Nothing. I tried Yardley Pham from France since Vietnam had once been under their influence. Then a few different combinations of names and countries. Still nothing. What about Yardley as a first name? It was a man's name and English in origin. "Yardley" and "English" together gave me a list of hits. A village called Yardley Gobion caught my attention. The White Pages from the U.K. with Pham in Yardley Gobion provided a hit. A lead.

"Steckler," Captain Perez said above my head. "What are you doing here? I gave you a direct order and now you're using police databases while you're supposed to be on sick leave." My satisfied smile fell; I was in serious trouble. Captain Perez couldn't let me get away with ignoring her orders or the other detectives would walk all over her.

"In my office. Now," she said and slammed the door behind her.

I shook my head at my own stupidity despite the pain; this research could have been done from home. Luddy's smirk annoyed me. I closed the door behind me and turned to face the music.

"You found something, didn't you? I saw your face." She frowned from behind her desk.

"It's only the beginning of a link. I need to keep working on it to be sure."

"Is it something Dwayne or Luddy could work?" I worked hard to keep my face neutral. Dwayne wasn't good on a computer and Luddy wouldn't work period. Perez read my expression.

"I didn't think so."

"Does it involve the Chung case or just your sister?"

"Both, there's a name that connects the two. Yardley Pham."

Perez shook her head.

"You're a pain in the ass, Steckler. Why didn't you do this where I couldn't see you? If I don't smack you down for this, the others, especially Luddy, are going to start testing their boundaries with me as well.

"You're on leave without pay for the next two days. Look contrite on the way out and don't show up here. If your instincts weren't so good, I'd take your badge and gun and make an example of you. But I won't check the usage statistics on the databases for the next two days either. Now leave."

"Thank you, Captain." She turned her back to me. I was dismissed.

No stopping at my desk: time to get while the getting was good.

Despite being in a boatload of trouble with Perez and my hurting head, the clue put me in a better mood. My phoned declared the time just after midnight but with no rain at the moment, there were plenty of taxis. One driver saw me and stopped before I hailed him. While he took me to Patronio's address, I sat back and tried to get my thoughts in order.

My worry over the job and lost benefits paled in comparison to the joy I felt knowing Denise was alive and well. Her circumstances were still a mystery but it was clear she was with Kim and Yardley Pham, and more "gifted" people were involved.

I wanted to talk with Patronio and Tú; maybe they knew something about them. Perez hadn't given me time to check Pham out while at the precinct. My home connection provided access to only the most limited of police databases so they were my best bet for now.

Tú needed to know word had gotten out about them, and that Yardley Pham was behind Va^n's murders as well as Cha^a's missing body.

Something Kim said bugged me. I suspected she was one of the "gifted" people based on the security guard's reaction to her touch. Initially, he'd been dazed but gradually came out of it. He'd told the EMTs he felt fine but couldn't stop thinking about sex; it was like reliving the best sex of his life. It absorbed him, made it nearly impossible to think about anything else. If Kim could do that to him just with a touch, what could she do with sustained contact?

Before Denise "disappeared" I was a normal, horny teenage boy. The weekend before they vanished, I went to a party at a friend's house. Kim and I spoke a few times at their softball games. She was cute in a boyish kind of way. At the party, Kim flirted with me, laughed at my lame jokes, stood close and touched me whenever she had an excuse. There were no adults at the party and the alcohol flowed like water.

Denise spoke to us a few times but left angry when Kim gave her the cold shoulder. At first, it upset me, but the more I drank and the more

Kim touched me, the less I cared about Denise. Kim and I made out in the living room in front of everyone, but they were as drunk and sex-crazed as we were; no one mentioned the tent I pitched. We wound up in an extra bedroom with my hand up her shirt – she was flat-chested. She wouldn't let me in her pants. Each time I made a move to go there she stopped me with a kiss or a hand under my belt. After ten minutes, frantic for something more, and scared by the intensity of my need, I knew I would to go any lengths to satisfy it. My body pressed against her with the urge to plunge myself deeply and violently into her.

"Easy there, Steckler, I don't want you that much, but you'll still love me in the morning." She laughed at her own joke but I didn't care. She reached out and unzipped my pants then pushed them down.

"Nice one," she commented and took me in her hand. She leaned forward and used her mouth on me. I saw colors and felt sensations I'd never heard of, even in the most lurid porn magazine. Within minutes, I was close to finishing, my balls high and tight. I almost cried when she stopped, reached into her pocket, and took out a packet and opened it.

"What's that?" I stared, curious. The shape wasn't right – too wide.

"A mouth rubber," she answered, and rather than putting it over me as I anticipated, she put it in her mouth, and then took it out. "Let me give you a kiss you'll never forget and finish you off." I nodded, grateful for the pause which gave me back some measure of control. We kissed, her tongue slipped into my mouth, and I could taste myself on her. I felt an incredible rush and thrill; all of my focus in the kiss. If I didn't end it, I'd be embarrassed. Kim chuckled, pulled away from me and slipped the rubber into her mouth. Then she pushed me back onto the bed and slid down to my crotch.

Her hand gripped firmly and her mouth covered me. All my thoughts and feelings focused on what she did. As I finished, I felt as though my very soul left me.

Kim gave a throaty growl after I shifted my body to return the favor.

104

She stopped me and took the rubber filled with my sperm out of her mouth, tied it off like a water balloon, and put it back in her pocket. I was too dazed to think how odd that action was.

"Don't bother, Steckler, this was just an assignment." She got up and left the room without another word. I spent the next few days wondering why she did that.

Then Denise disappeared and everything changed. I don't remember feeling desire of any sort after that, and sometimes wondered if what happened with Kim had anything to do with their disappearance. Now I thought maybe it did, since, as Dad had claimed, they were a couple. Now I realized Kim had caused it.

I dug my phone out to call Patronio. It surprised me when it rang: I didn't recognize the number but answered anyway.

"Detective Steckler?" It was Dr. Lukishna.

"Is everything okay?" I realized I cared. It was rare for me to like anyone so quickly. First Patronio and now Dr. Lukishna. I told myself it was from being injured and tired and not from getting old, weak, and soft.

"Yes, I wanted to apologize. I didn't realize you'd get in trouble for what I said about there being more of the hermaphrodites."

"Bet you thought you'd never say that." I enjoyed his laughter. "And, you don't have anything to apologize for. Kim told you that specifically to get me in trouble."

"I don't enjoy being used by anyone to cause trouble. I do that on my own, without anyone's help." I remained silent. "That was my attempt at a joke. I do feel bad."

"You shouldn't, you told the truth. I didn't and got caught. That's my problem, not yours."

"Still, I wanted to apologize." He took a deep breath. "And make it up to you. Can I buy you lunch?"

"Umm ... sure," I answered and leaned forward to look in the taxi's rearview mirror. Yup, I still looked like a walking cadaver.

"I also wanted to thank you for saving me," he said, the words running together.

"I hardly saved you, Dr. Lukishna. Kim was on her way out; she would've just knocked you down. I didn't want you to touch her."

"I heard what Ron went through. I'm glad it didn't happen to me."

"Ron looked pretty happy to me," I said.

"Trust me, Ron looked happy to anyone who saw him standing up." We both laughed.

"Are you sure you want to be seen with me? I'm in a lot of trouble and may lose my job."

"I have ulterior motives."

"Ha! I knew it!" I said and waited for him to explain.

"I'm curious about the hermaphrodites. I'd love to meet a live one," he told me. "I took samples before the body was stolen. I've run tests and got odd results."

"What kind of results?" I couldn't help but asked.

"Got you now!"

"Okay, let's have lunch," I said as the taxi pulled up to Patronio's perfume gallery.

"How about tomorrow night at ten? I'm on the odd shift again so that's my lunch hour. Meet me at the morgue and I'll take you to an undiscovered and excellent Italian place around the block."

"Sounds great. Looking forward it."

"Me too. See you then," he said and hung up.

I paid the driver, got out of the taxi, and called Patronio.

The street outside the perfume gallery bustled with people despite the hour. I gave up long ago trying to figure out the pattern.

"Come on up," Vito said after he unlocked the door to e-Scents. I waited while he relocked them, resetting the alarm system. When he was done, he pointed to the back door of the gallery. The silence between us grew awkward.

"Something tells me you've got some antiquated ideas about Pasquale and me, Detective," Vito said suddenly. My face must have given my thoughts away. "I'm sure you've checked us out – we're not in the system, are we?" By the smug way he asked it, I was sure he wasn't. I shrugged but wouldn't admit to not having a chance to check yet.

"Back in the days when our father came over from Italy, you had to be a tough guy, connected, to make it. That's not true anymore. Pasquale and I didn't have those kinds of problems. We own a successful masonry business, that's all."

I pointed my chin at his waist before climbing the stairs to Patronio's office. "Do successful businessmen usually carry guns under their jackets?"

"The ones I know do," he answered. When we reached the top of the stairs, Vito stopped me. "Detective, I'm serious. Pasquale and I can protect Anthony from street thugs and the average person because they look at us and see mobsters. The stuff that's going on now is beyond us." He looked scared.

"We've got a serious lead to follow during the next few days," I placated him.

"Pasquale and I have kids. We have families to worry about. What if it takes longer?"

"Take a longer trip to Italy." I was serious. Then I walked into the office. I didn't have any other answers for him.

Patronio looked first at me then his brother as we entered the office. He must have heard us talking. Pat, or Pasquale as I had just learned, stood farther away with his back to us and spoke quietly into a phone.

"Hello, Detective Steckler, how are you feeling?" He gave me an appraising look.

"Tired, Mr. Patronio, very tired. But I'm also excited about Denise." I couldn't help but smile at the thought of Denise alive somewhere. All I had to do was find her.

Patronio returned my smile.

"I learned a lot today and want to talk to you about it." I glanced at Pat and Vito.

"That's our cue to leave," Vito said, moving back toward the door and motioned at Pat who was still on his cell phone.

"No, you stay here. I've set a conference call up in the lab for the two of us," Patronio told Vito and stood up from his desk.

"Good, I want to call Gina and tell the boys goodnight," Vito said. The menace he and Pasquale projected when I first met them wore thin and revealed the family men I almost believed they were.

"Why don't you guys go home tonight? I'll be fine. Detective Steckler is here. He'll keep an eye on me," Patronio told his brothers. Vito snorted and Pat chuckled.

"He might scare them with his looks, that's about it." Pat spoke to me for the first time. His voice rumbled an octave lower than his brother's.

"Thanks a lot." I laughed and they joined me. "He's got a point. I've not got much juice left. You may want them to stay."

His brothers were the next best thing to the NYPD, for tonight anyway.

"Just until tomorrow morning. I'll come up with something else or hire bodyguards. You have families and work," Patronio said. "And thank you, again," he told them.

"We got your back, Tony, don't worry about it," Vito said.

"That's right," Pat added.

Patronio smiled and gestured for me to follow him. We walked into the laboratory and closed the door.

"Nice place," I said gesturing with my hand to encompass the steel and glass enclosed room that was a combination chemistry lab, old-fashioned apothecary, and hipster coffee shop. One wall was all shelves with thousands of small bottles and test tubes in all sizes, shapes, and colors. Each was labeled but too far away to read.

"Thank you." He saw where I looked. "Each one of them was distilled and cataloged by me," he said with pride. "If I haven't smelled a particular scent before, it's unique and uncommon. Don't forget I tracked down the essence of a giant water bug." He picked up a small vial from the counter next to him and held it up.

"Yes, I know. Good work."

"Thank you," he said, pleased. "Believe it or not, I brought you here for more than listening to me brag." He pointed to a camera mounted in the corner of the lab. It was larger and more complicated than the other cameras mounted in the back room of the gallery and stairway. He pressed a switch on the wall behind him and moved a computer monitor forward to the edge of the counter. The monitor light came on and an empty chair appeared.

"Tú, are you there?"

"Yes, Anthony. Have you told Detective Steckler what we're doing?" Tú's voice came out of the speakers on the walls.

"I figured it out," I said and looked away from the monitor.

"Detective, you don't have to turn away. We learned that Tú's gifts don't work over the web. Neither does mine," Patronio said. I heard a faint hiss from Tú over the webcam. Patronio leaned toward me and whispered, "You have no idea how long it took me to convince them to try this. Tú preferred for us to meet in person, but I insisted we do it this way."

I turned to face Patronio and carefully kept my focus away from the monitor. Out of the corner of my eye, I saw Tú sit down.

"Don't look at me, look at him," Patronio laughed and pointedly turned his face to the monitor. "See? No problem."

My curiosity got the better of me and I looked directly at the monitor. Tú's face was centered in it. I braced myself for a reaction but nothing happened. His lips were still a deep red, skin white, and hair pulled back in a bun. I thought of a geisha.

"Are you wearing makeup?" I asked Tú without thinking.

Patronio laughed and even Tú smiled.

"No, Detective, this is my natural coloring. Cha^a looked exactly the same."

"Sorry, I don't remember that particular detail," I said.

"There was a lot going on that evening," Tú agreed.

"There is quite a lot happening now," Patronio reminded us.

"Such as?" I asked.

"Va^n's transformation has begun," Tú said.

"How do you know?" I dreaded the answer.

"It is difficult to explain, but my siblings and I sense Va^n's thoughts. The pain of the transition comes through."

"Good," Patronio muttered.

"Anything else?" I didn't want to get off track again. Exhaustion set in. What little energy I had wouldn't last long.

"Lisa's funeral was today," Patronio added. I nodded sympathetically.

"We've met with our family. None are Va^n's accomplice. We think he is somewhere in Suffolk County," Tú said. I heard hissing and Tú glanced at someone off the screen and frowned. Apparently, that was news to the other siblings.

"Those are my old stomping grounds. I grew up on Long Island," I said. "Do you know where yet?"

"No, we're still asking questions," Tú replied, again surprised hissing in the background. "Will you check addresses when we have them?"

"No," I answered shortly. Captain Perez's rebuke still stung.

"Are your injuries that bad?" Patronio frowned and scrutinized my head.

"No, I've been put on administrative leave." I filled them in on what happened. I did my best not to be surly or angry about it.

"This is unfortunate. I'm sorry we put you in an awkward position. We will do what we can to mitigate it, so that you can get back to work with the full force of the NYPD behind you," Tú assured me.

I heard a trace of sarcasm but didn't pursue it.

"Thank you, but that will get me in more trouble. I'll be in the dog house for a few months, that's all." Patronio and Tú exchanged determined looks so I distracted them with more bad news. "I'm sure Mr. Patronio told you that Cha^a's body was taken from the Medical Examiner's offices."

"Yes, another unfortunate event, one that we are not responsible for," Tú replied. "I have no need of Cha^a's body, although I would prefer to have kept it to prevent others from learning about us."

"I know you didn't do it. While I was at the morgue, I ran into an old friend, another gifted person. She took Cha^a's body. A man named Yardley Pham told her to take it."

Tú became very still while the others off-screen reacted with loud hisses. "Yardley Pham? You're sure she said that?" Tú's words sounded rehearsed, eyes moving quickly from me to several points off camera and back again. The emotions Tú showed were real. Trembling hands couldn't easily be faked.

"Yes. Why? What do you know about him?" I wanted to know what could scare these people.

"Yardley Pham was the reason we left Vietnam. Half of our village and two siblings died so the rest could escape. One of them was my mother before she changed," Tú said, and I saw the first discernible reaction from a sibling – hatred. Apparently not all emotions and feelings fade after the transformation. Behind Tú, other siblings came into view. Each laid a hand on a shoulder or arm as if to give Tú comfort. As a group, their white pallor, black hair, and clothing reminded me of a nest of spiders. They spoke to one another in Vietnamese and ignored Patronio and me. I wondered if we would be caught in their web.

"This just gets better and better." Patronio looked as concerned as the siblings.

"Kim says he's behind Denise's disappearance as well." I told him.

"Who is Kim? You said she's an old friend." Patronio said.

"She was a friend of Denise's when we were in high school. She is definitely gifted."

"How do you know?" Tú had stopped talking with the other siblings.

"She touched the security guard and sent him into some kind of psychotic sex dream so she could get past him." I couldn't keep my voice steady as a wave of anger swept over me.

Patronio tilted his head and leaned forward. "What else did she do?"

"I'm not sure." I answered despite a growing suspicion.

"Did she touch you?" Patronio wanted to know.

"Not this time." I felt my face turn red.

"When? In high school?" Patronio was persistent.

"Yes. She blew me." My face and neck heated to the boiling point.

"I thought you didn't like … oh! That's the one you told me about?" Patronio stopped when he saw me wince and made a gesture at his crotch instead. "How do you know?"

"I'm just guessing," I said, and noticed Tú and the other siblings were listening.

"Detective Steckler has no sex drive. A gifted person may have taken it away. Can you could fix it?" Patronio pushed forward toward the screen to stare at Tú. I cringed again but paid careful attention to the answer. At this point in my life, I wasn't sure I wanted it back. At

112

middle-age, what good would it do me?

"We would have to experiment," they answered. They were back to talking in unison. The news of Yardley Pham rattled them.

"Thanks, maybe I'll take you up on the offer. For now, we need to focus on finding Va^n."

It'll be a cold day in hell before I let them experiment on me … probably. I surprised myself; an image of Dr. Lukishna flittered around my head. Maybe Dad wasn't wrong about Denise after all.

"If Yardley Pham is behind the kidnapping attempt on Anthony and killing Cha^a, we will need additional time and resources." Tú said, no longer in unison with the others.

"What kind of resources?" Patronio and I asked simultaneously.

"When he tried to capture us, he had an armed force of one hundred men and the support of the Viet Cong. He also had several gifted people." Tú told us.

"When was that?" I wondered if any of them were old enough to have been there. It was impossible to guess their ages.

"It began in 1967. The siblings escaped in 1968. The remaining family joined us during the next two years." I think it was Bi`nh, the apparent historian, who answered.

"You fought him off for two years? That's a long time for the five of you to hold out," I said.

"Our family numbered more than five thousand. Nor did we need to conceal our gifts or our wealth there," Tú said.

"How many of them made it to New York?" Patronio beat me to the question.

"Less than a thousand. The others died." Tú answered.

"Because of Pham?" Patronio swallowed loudly.

"As well as the war. But mostly because Pham hunted them down to reduce our source for new siblings," Bi`nh said.

"That was nearly fifty years ago. Pham is an old man now and you're

not in a war-torn country. He can't come after you with an army here."
I tried to calm the fear I saw in Patronio's eyes.

"He would use different methods, but don't underestimate him. And
he may be older but he's found a way to hold off aging," Tú said.

I remembered the picture of Denise; how she looked years younger
than me, how Kim looked exactly as I remembered her from more than
twenty years ago. "Pham's gift is being able to keep people from aging?"

Patronio's looked up at that.

"We don't know what Pham's gift is. He fought the siblings with a
group of gifted people. He was able to control them. Perhaps by bribing
them with the gift of youth. That would be hard for anyone to resist,"
Tú said.

"What did Pham want with you – the siblings, I mean?" Patronio
asked. I wasn't the only one who was confused about how to refer to
them.

"To dominate us, then use our gifts as he saw fit," they answered in
unison – a little too dramatic for my taste.

"How do you know? Did he send you a note?" I suspected they were
putting on a show.

"Sarcasm doesn't become you, Detective," Tú said. Either the siblings
had calmed down or Tú was miffed enough to leave their mind-meld
thingy.

"Whatever. How can we track down Va^n and Pham? Is there a way
for us to counter their gifts? And how are we going to get Denise away
from Pham?"

"We can't say at the moment. We hoped Pham long dead," Tú
replied. The wording struck me as evasive.

"We need to know more about what it means to be gifted," Patronio
said. "You said Pham had other gifted people with him. That's the first
time you've mentioned knowing other gifted people. How many are
there?"

The siblings hissed at one another. Patronio and I looked at each other, glad we weren't there.

"That we know or know of?" Bi`nh tried to clarify the question.

"Know, know of, alive, dead, or somewhere in-between," I demanded, again sensing evasion.

"Several thousand." Bi`nh answered.

Patronio and I blinked in surprise.

"But the majority were from Asia and are long dead."

"How many do you know of, or suspect, are alive in the New York metro area now?" My voice had a definite edge.

"Several hundred, at least, possibly one thousand."

"Jesus! That's not good," I said.

"Excuse me?" Patronio narrowed his eyes at me.

"Hey, I've gotten mesmerized by Cha^a and possibly neutered by Kim. I know you're all the good guys ... people, but still."

"Good point," he conceded. "You look exhausted. Sit." He grabbed a chair. I took it gratefully.

"What do you mean, exactly, by gifted?" I tried to understand what I was up against.

"Gifted individuals possess the potential to develop extraordinary mental or physical abilities." Definitely Bi`nh this time.

"Great." I closed my eyes and longed for a simple murder to solve. "Does that mean some of them can fly or shoot fire from the hands?"

"No, nothing that extreme. The abilities we've seen are focused on the five senses, thoughts, and feelings as well as biological processes. Gifts are mostly limited to the gifted-one's body, but some affect other humans or can impact other living things including plants and animals." Bi`nh sounded like a university professor.

"If there were that many super-people running around the city, everyone would know about them," Patronio commented.

"If all 'gifts' were as extraordinary as ours or yours, Anthony, we

115

would agree. Most are not," Bi`nh said. "They're like any other skill or capability. Just like any person can sing, only a minuscule percentage become famous because of how well they do it."

"Detective, you should go home, you're falling asleep. You can stay here if you'd like." My eyes snapped open.

"Soon," I agreed. "How many people in New York are super-duper gifted?"

"We don't know. We suspect the number is growing more rapidly each year. We are concerned."

"Why?" I couldn't keep the fear out of my voice.

"There is a high correlation between the extremely gifted and severe mental illness. Anthony and we are among the exceptions," Bi`nh said.

"Great," I said, not entirely sure I agreed with their assessment. Then I decided Patronio was right, I was done for the night.

Patronio called a cab and I was home twenty minutes later. It was too late for Tim to be up and haunting the front entrance. I felt a flicker of gratitude, not having the energy to talk.

Despite my exhaustion, I kept going over what Kim and Tú said about Yardley Pham. Denise was involved with bad and weird people. Patronio said she looked good; she'd been able to freely walk into his gallery and buy perfume. If she could do that, why couldn't she call me?

I unlocked the condo door and hung up my old overcoat. My favorite was still covered in blood. I would drop it at the dry cleaners, but doubted it would get clean. It covered me a long time and deserved another chance.

I glanced up at Denise's picture. "Whatever." I went to bed.

This time I answered the phone ready to hurl it at the wall. Why did people insist on calling me when they knew I would be asleep?

"Steckler, it's Captain Perez, hang up again and you're fired." I brought the phone to my ear and pretended I hadn't hung up three times already. It was a good thing she spoke first.

"Wonderful to hear from you again, Captain. I'll record your voice for my alarm clock." It was ten in the morning. Today the right side of my face felt like someone hit me with only a sledgehammer instead of a truck.

"I don't need any crap right now, Steckler." I got a call from Commissioner Cast. He wants the two of us in his office at noon. Do you have an idea what this is about?"

"No idea. Has Cha^a's body turned up?"

"No."

"Do you want me to meet you at the precinct or 1 Police Plaza?"

"1PP. I'll meet you in the lobby at 11:30. We need to go over what to say. Wear your dress blues." She hung up.

8

I groaned and went to my closet to check on my dress uniform. Thankfully, it was there, still in the plastic bag from the dry cleaner. I'd worn it a year ago at a retired cop's funeral.

Usually I enjoyed seeing myself suited-up and looking good, but it wasn't possible with a shaved head and Frankenstein sutures surrounded by purple and red flesh. I shook my head, immediately regretting the motion and stopped before putting my hat on.

I ignored Denise's picture on the way out the front door.

After hailing a cab, I pondered what the topic of the meeting with Commissioner Cast could be. Permitting witnesses to leave a crime scene was a serious matter, but not enough to make it to his calendar this quickly.

What reason could I give? Nothing plausible, even untrue, came to mind. Perez didn't ask during our last discussion only because she'd been too busy yelling at me.

He pulled to the curb and I waited for the receipt. If the Commissioner wanted me in his office, the Police Department could pay for it.

"Good morning, Detective Steckler. You look especially formal," Patronio's now familiar voice said behind me.

"You could have lied and said 'dashing'." I turned. He wore a different white suit, tie, and white cashmere overcoat.

"I don't lie." Patronio's smile faded. "And Detective, I may be gay, but even I don't use 'dashing'." We laughed. "You do look good, Detective, despite the gash on your head." I said nothing and he laughed again. "You're blushing!"

"Nice limo." I motioned to the large car and equally big chauffeur. Another stood right behind Patronio. I realized he was with Patronio. "What's with the security?"

"Half the siblings' relatives died protecting them from Pham. Two of the siblings died as well. I have to protect myself."

"What about your brothers?"

"They know how to look tough and take on small-time thugs, but this is out of their league," he reiterated what his brother said the night before.

"Good call." It was almost half-past eleven. I walked to the building's entrance.

"You're behind the meeting with the Commissioner?"

"I made a few calls and was invited."

"Did the siblings set it up?"

"Probably."

I shook my head. This couldn't be good.

"What did they do?"

"I don't know."

"Steckler," Captain Perez called as I neared the entrance. Patronio and his escort slowed down to give us space.

"Captain Perez," I greeted her, my tone neutral.

"What's Patronio doing here?"

"Same thing we are," I replied.

"Are the two of you behind this meeting? If so, you'll be lucky to be walking a beat in the Bronx by the time I'm done with you." Her voice echoed loudly in the entrance-way.

"Captain Perez, I don't know any more about what's going to happen at this meeting than you do." My conscience winced at the true but carefully chosen words.

"Fine. But if your screw-up gets me in trouble, you're going down no matter what."

"Detective Steckler, I'm not sure where the Commissioner's office is, do you know?" Patronio checked with me as he approached.

"Yes, just follow us." I turned to him. He smiled and winked.

"Hello, Captain Perez. Nice to see you again." Patronio leaned around me to shake her hand.

"Yes. Hello, Mr. Patronio," Perez replied, her voice flat. "I see you've hired your own security."

"It didn't feel right to use New York City's finest as guards when I could hire my own," Patronio answered. "Especially given how they treated me," he said, his voice equally hostile.

"Detective Steckler must be treating you well if you gave him a lift this morning," Perez said.

"I'm grateful; Detective Steckler saved my life the night those morons tried to kill us." He smiled at me, and this time, I wished he didn't. As if he read my mind, his smile widened. "But we just happened to come at the same time."

"We need to hurry or we'll be late," I told them.

We entered the building and waited to pass through the metal detectors. Patronio and I went through first as we had no weapons.

120

Captain Perez went next, showing her ID and badge. Patronio's guard went last. It took him awhile with three guns. The cops at the desk would have given him more trouble except Captain Perez was with us, providing tacit approval.

It was a quiet elevator ride. Captain Perez fumed, pissed we couldn't talk before the meeting. As we got off the elevator, Patronio tensed up. When we neared the Commissioner's suite of offices, I smelled it too, jasmine. Patronio looked scared. I was too. A sibling with the Commissioner of the New York City Police Department was a scary idea.

After opening the glass door, I held it while they all tromped in. Captain Perez's glare could have frozen the Hudson River. Instead of looking at her, I watched Patronio's guard scan the area for threats. It wouldn't do him much good if a sibling was here.

It was a typical u-shaped office, with the administrative aid's desk at the open end. On the wall to the left were a series of rooms, most of the doors shut. The back wall, which was the longest, held only one door – the Commissioner's office. The glass panel that made up the right wall contained two doors. Outside were three Asian men who were a cross between private security guards and street thugs. Their wide shoulders blocked the view of the people in the meeting room behind them.

I leaned forward and spoke to the Administrative aid, "Captain Perez, Detective Steckler, and Mr. Patronio here to see the Commissioner."

"I'll let him know you're here." She smiled politely at us. If his attire puzzled her, there was no indication of it on her face. When she opened the door and went into the meeting room, the smell of jasmine grew stronger.

"That's a surprise," Patronio said and glanced at me.

"What is?" Captain Perez asked.

"There are a few people here other than you and Detective Steckler," Patronio answered and Captain Perez frowned.

The aid came back. "Please go in," she told us. "Mr. Patronio, once your security guard has checked the room, he should wait outside with the others."

"That's fine," Patronio said after his guard nodded in agreement and we waited while the security man entered. He returned a moment later. The scent of jasmine came out with him. His eyes didn't look dilated. Patronio glanced at me as if asking my opinion. I shrugged, then winced, forgetting again about the stitches in my head.

It was a standard, but sumptuous, meeting room: windows and floor-to-ceiling curtains on one wall, an HD TV on another, a small counter with a coffee urn and cups. In the center of the room stood a long oval table with plush leather office chairs.

The Commissioner stood near the door and waited to greet us, smiling. I hoped that was a good thing. He shifted and the man behind him turned around from prepping his coffee. It was Mayor Silvan. Next to him were two figures in black burqas.

"Detective Steckler, good to see you again." The Commissioner surprised me and shook my hand. We met at a press conference some years before after I broke a years-old murder case and captured the press' attention. Commissioner Cast stood tall, thin, with red hair just beginning to silver. His deceptively soft blue eyes misled people; there wasn't anything soft about a man who could make it to the Commissioner's office. A dark blue business suit, white shirt, and red tie made sure everyone knew he was in charge.

"Thank you, Commissioner. I'm glad I could make it."

"Yes, you look like hell." He laughed. "But you're protecting our good citizens," he said in a loud voice and smiled at Patronio, then looked behind him at the two dark-clad figures. "You must be Anthony Patronio. Chris Cast," he introduced himself.

"A pleasure, Commissioner Cast," Patronio replied, his face neutral as they shook hands.

"Thank you. Before we go any further, I want to apologize for the incident you experienced. I pride myself on my police department's ability to work with the gay community, but old, foolish, prejudices are slow to change."

"Thank you, Commissioner, I appreciate that," Patronio replied.

Commissioner Cast turned his attention to Captain Perez.

"Captain Perez, welcome."

"Commissioner," the Captain said, and they shook hands. It was the type of minimal greeting exchanged by old enemies or close friends. If I ever returned to the precinct office, I'd have to check the rumor mill to find out which.

The Commissioner turned to the Mayor who walked over to us. Two of the siblings were together, facing the other way, I could hear them speaking softly to one another in Vietnamese. One turned to face us, covered from head to toe in black canvas material, eyes covered by extra-large, dark sunglasses. A quick look told me gloves, made of what looked like black latex, covered his hands.

"Tony, how are you? I'm so sorry about your friend, Lisa. I remember her from your gallery reopening last year." Mayor Silvan shook Patronio's hand and grabbed his shoulder in sympathy.

"Thank you, Charles. Grace's check for Lisa's children's college fund was very generous," Patronio answered. He smiled and looked more relaxed; apparently he liked Mayor Silvan.

"It's the least we could do," the Mayor said, then turned to me. "You must be Detective Steckler. Charles Silvan." Not that he had to introduce himself; his face was on the television and in the newspapers at least once a week.

"Nice to meet you, sir." We shook hands. Tall, good looking, and impeccably dressed in a pair of khaki colored dress pants, a blue blazer, white shirt and blue tie, he competed and won against the Commissioner for dominance. I wondered why Patronio liked him and hoped it was more than his attractiveness.

"My good friend, Tú Chung, has explained to me what happened the night of Cha^a's death," Mayor Silvan said smoothly, and backed-up to allow Tú to join our circle. The smell of jasmine tickled my nose.

"Ah, yes, it was a very unusual night," I said.

"My remaining siblings and I are grateful to Detective Steckler for allowing us to leave, even if it meant leaving our beloved Cha^a's body behind," Tú said with a Vietnamese accent that hadn't been there before.

"Hello, Tú. Again, let me say how sorry I am about Cha^a," Patronio said.

"Thank you, Tony; I'm glad you were able to join the Mayor and the rest of us at our impromptu meeting. Especially under such trying conditions," Tú answered.

"Why exactly was this meeting called?" Captain Perez asked. She didn't sound pleased at being left out of the loop.

"I'm sorry; I do not know enough about the uniforms in the United States, you are?" Captain Perez froze; she knew a slight when she heard it.

"My apologies, Tú, this is Captain Perez. She is Detective Steckler's superior officer," Mayor Sylvan explained. Captain Perez held out her hand but Tú simply bowed slightly in her direction.

"Have you visited the Third Precinct headquarters lately? You were talking to a dispatcher the same day Mr. Patronio and his friend were attacked," Captain Perez slid the question at Tú like a knife. I filed that away to think about later. It was Tú's turn to freeze.

"You must be very proud to have such a fine Detective working for you, Captain Perez. Undoubtedly, due to your leadership." Tú avoided the question. The smell of jasmine became more distinct. I watched Captain Perez out of the corner of my eye to see her reaction. She visibly relaxed and even smiled.

"Yes, Carl is one of the city's best Detectives. He's solved some very difficult cases," Captain Perez replied. "As much as I like him, though, we didn't need a party to confirm it."

We all chuckled, but I didn't miss her glance at the other black-clad figure who stood off by the coffee. Like me, she wanted to know why we assembled here.

"My siblings and I wanted to show our support for Detective Steckler. We learned he was in trouble because of us," Tú answered the Captain's unspoken question.

"Detective Steckler didn't follow established procedures at a crime scene," Captain Perez answered. "You shouldn't have left. He was wrong to let you do so."

"We didn't give him a choice," Tú answered.

"You threatened him?" Captain Perez's voice grew soft; not a good sign. At five foot, six inches tall, she towered over Tú. I had another six inches over that.

"Captain, I'm sure you know by now that my siblings and I aren't like most people."

"Yes, I'm aware of your differences."

"You only know of the most obvious ones. In addition to what you know, we are extremely photosensitive. We are also so allergic to some common substances that if we were to come into contact with them, we would be dead within a few short minutes. We are prepared now, although there is still some risk. If we stayed the night of Cha^a's murder, I am convinced more of us would have died due to our allergies."

As Tú explained, the scent of jasmine became more intense. I looked at Patronio for help; I couldn't sanction Tú mesmerizing the Captain, even if it was on my behalf. Patronio nodded slightly and I smelled a faint trace of oranges. It was hard to tell with the burqa and sunglasses on, but I think Tú looked at Patronio. The smell of jasmine faded.

"Captain, I've known the Chung family for years. What Tú says is

125

true. I've never seen them out of their protective clothing and I've been there when one of them was overcome by dust," Mayor Silvan added. "They rarely are out in public for fear of how people react as well as their health."

"They own a drag bar and were in it the night of the murder," Captain Perez commented dryly. Even though this was for my benefit, I couldn't help but admire her guts to stand up to the Mayor. Neither the Mayor, nor the Commissioner, looked pleased.

"Our family is quite wealthy, Captain. My siblings and I believe it is our duty and privilege to provide a place for others like us to gather and feel they are not alone," Tú said. "We meet friends in the apartment above the bar, but we do not visit the bar when it is open. Our health will not allow it."

"What happens if the press gets a hold of this?" Perez asked. "It can be construed as a cover-up."

"Annotate the reports stating that the Chungs were all present, but they had to leave due to health," Commissioner Cast replied.

"Officer Bently will interview each of the Chung siblings about the night's events and add the notes to the report," I added; the siblings would present a unified testimony.

"We can do that as long as it is arranged in advance and this Officer Bently doesn't wear certain fabrics and fragrances," Tú injected. "Otherwise, we will have to wear our protective clothing which we weren't wearing that night."

Mayor Silvan nodded in approval.

"You can see the position that Detective Steckler was in," Commissioner Cast said. Captain Perez looked from the Commissioner to the Mayor, then to me.

"Yes, I can imagine. He made the best decision he could under difficult circumstances," she said after a moment. She wouldn't have made Captain if she couldn't recognize when it was time to go along to

126

get along.

The Mayor and Commissioner smiled.

Tú nodded.

I looked down, uncomfortable. I was a cop, a crime solver, not a politician.

"Yes, I'm glad we could clear this up. We owe Detective Steckler a debt of gratitude," Tú said. "If there's nothing else for us to say, we should be going." Tú turned and gestured to the other sibling. "Ladies, gentlemen; It's been a pleasure. Good day." Tú bowed slightly in the direction of the Mayor and Commissioner and gave Patronio and me a nod on the way out the door. The other sibling hadn't said a word.

After they left the room, Commissioner Cast smiled and said, "I'm glad we had the opportunity to settle things." He turned to me and Patronio and shook our hands. "Gentlemen, always a pleasure to see you." We were dismissed. I said my good-byes and walked out of the room as quickly as possible. Patronio was right behind me.

"Captain Perez, wait just a moment, please," Commissioner Cast said. "The Captain will be out shortly if you'd like to wait." He shut the door behind us.

"I've got to wait, you don't."

"I'll stay if you want me to back you up with your Captain," Patronio offered. I shook my head. He stared ahead to the hallway; it was empty. "Tú and the other sibling smelled different today," he tried to sound casual.

"How so?" I asked, knowing it was somehow important.

"Charcoal," he said and I wrinkled my brow in confusion.

"What for?"

"I don't know yet," he admitted. "But I thought I'd let you know."

"You don't trust them?" I wouldn't blame him. He shrugged.

"It's hard to say. Tú is much more focused than when we first met," he said.

"A family member was murdered and another was the one who did it. That would affect anyone," I said.

"I should leave, the Captain will probably want to talk to you," Patronio lowered his voice to sound evil.

"True. I'll call as soon as I learn anything," I tried to laugh and failed at his attempt at humor.

Patronio nodded, gestured to his security guard, and the two of them left me with nothing to do but pretend my Captain, Mayor, and Commissioner of the New City Police Department weren't in a room talking about my fate.

It wasn't long before they came out, the Commissioner and Mayor nodded and walked to the Commissioner's office. Captain Perez exited to the hallway and remained silent while we waited for the elevator. Once we were on and the doors shut, she turned to me.

"You have very powerful friends, Steckler."

"Yes, I guess I do."

"People like that make dangerous enemies if you're not careful."

"Captain, I had no idea they would do this."

"Too late now."

"I guess so. What's going to happen?" I hated hearing the anxiety in my voice.

"You're off unofficial leave. Nothing goes on your record or in your file."

"Great, thank you, Captain."

"Don't thank me, yet."

"I know I'm off the case, Captain," I said.

"No, you're still on the Chung case."

"Even with my sister involved?" That went beyond unusual and into against regulations.

"I explained all that to the Commissioner. He wasn't concerned. The Chungs want Cha^a's body found along with the murderer. They told

128

the Mayor you have special insight into this Yardley Pham because of your sister. Is that true?"

I almost denied it, but given my sister was apparently "gifted", maybe that would help. "Yes, I think so."

"Good answer," she said with a chuckle. "Make sure you arrange for Bently to conduct the interviews with the Chung family and annotate that report as soon as you can."

"I'm sorry you're involved in this mess, Captain."

"Good. Don't make *me* sorry for it."

Captain Perez gave me a lift back to the precinct. We kept our discussion to minor office politics and city traffic. As we relaxed, the conversation turned to the case.

I thought about it last night and decided to frame the facts in a way people who didn't know about the gifted would understand.

"Yardley Pham is an anti-gay religious fanatic," I told her.

"The Chung siblings are intersexual. Are they gay as well?" Captain Perez's face twisted a bit at the end.

I shrugged, winced, and wished I remembered the injury before I did it. "I have no idea and don't want to know. Being what they are, Pham hates them either way."

"Who is Yardley Pham? What do you know about him?"

"Not much yet. Patronio never heard of him. I started checking at the precinct after Cha^a was killed. Tú said the Pham family were political rivals in Vietnam, but that they'd not had any dealings since they came to the States," I told her and stuck as close as possible to the truth.

"You knew this yesterday?" Perez's voice lowered, a veiled accusation in her question.

"Not until last night. I spoke with Patronio and Tú Chung after I left the precinct." She frowned but hadn't told me not to talk to people, just that I was on leave.

"The Mayor and Commissioner would like this case solved quickly and quietly. There is no upside to this getting out to the media or public."

"No, I don't think so either. And I've never been a media hound," I added.

"I wasn't implying anything. Just giving you the parameters. You may want to tell Patronio that as well."

"It's not like he asks me for advice. He just appreciates that I didn't get him killed that night," I told her.

"He and the siblings seem to want Taylor's murder solved pretty badly. Is there a connection to Pham?"

"Maybe Pham got her caught up in his religion, or cult, or whatever it is," I answered her but shook my head, knowing it was a stretch.

She made no comment. "So, you don't think the murder was a love triangle thing with Patronio, Cha^a, and Va^n?"

"No, Patronio wasn't lying. He hadn't met the siblings or been to Rice Queens until a few weeks before Lisa Taylor was killed. Pham recruited Va^n before that. Va^n either didn't like Patronio or saw an opportunity to impress his new boss by kidnapping him."

"What's in it for Va^n? What's his motivation?"

"He got tired of being the low man on a very weird totem pole and Pham used that to build the hate. I only saw him for a few minutes the night he killed Cha^a. He muttered something about there being six siblings. He wasn't going to be an owner of a bar with that many people in line before him."

Captain Perez waived to a police officer outside the precinct parking area. She pulled into her parking slot and we got out of the car.

130

"I'm going to change," Perez told me in the entrance to the precinct. "You should do the same, just to keep Luddy off the scent." She chuckled.

If Luddy saw my dress blues, he would sniff around to find out what happened. I was headed to the locker room when Captain Perez stopped me with a hand on my arm.

"When you have something on Pham, Lisa Taylor's murder, or the Chung body, let me know. Don't do anything on your own. You're one of us and we'll back you up when it comes down to it, even Luddy."

I smiled.

Captain Perez's laughter followed me down the hallway.

I spent the rest of the afternoon researching Yardley Pham, the Chung siblings, Va^n, Kim Pham, and even Denise Pham but found nothing new on them. Yardley Pham owned the Pham Corporation which was incorporated in New York, but the only address I could find was a post office box in Uniondale. It was fake.

Old man Patronio had arrests from the sixties, but no convictions. All for small-time racketeering. The sons were clean. That meant what Vito and Patronio told me was true; they were all show and no real malice.

Thankfully, most of the crew I worked with were either out or on another shift. Another confrontation with Luddy or any questioning glances from the rest of them would only end with me in more trouble.

By five o'clock, exhaustion set in. Since I was going to meet Dr. Lukishna at ten, I went home to get some rest.

A cab stopped for me as soon as I left the precinct. It would be a long stop and go ride. Cars were backed-up in both directions, and with the return of the rain, I knew it would take forty-five minutes to go the three miles to my address. I flashed my badge at the cabby and told him to wake me up when we got there.

After I paid a ridiculous amount of money to go where it took me thirty minutes to walk, I ran into Tim.

"How ya' doin' tonight?" He stood in his doorway but didn't answer. Less than ten feet away, there was no way he didn't hear me. "Tim, you okay?" I asked louder. He blinked and looked as if he saw me for the first time. "Tim?"

"Carl, ah, sorry," he said and rubbed at his eyes.

"You just wake up?" I grew concerned. Tim never drank, it gave him bad headaches.

"I must have dozed off. Too bad I woke up. I was dreaming about a girl I knew in the Navy. Man, she was smokin' hot!" He laughed. Something bothered me about his expression.

Exhausted, I shrugged the thought aside and pressed the button for the elevator. "Go back to sleep! Maybe you'll catch her!"

Tim laughed again.

The elevator doors opened. I looked back, but Tim was gone. His dazed expression bothered me.

After the elevator arrived at my floor, the doors opened, and I crossed the hall to my condo. I unlocked my door, pushed it open, and walked in.

"Always one step behind, Steckler!" A voice said.

I felt a blinding pain in my head and the world went black.

9

ET, the family dog, snuck into my bedroom again. She licked my face, wanting me to wake and play. I lifted a hand to pet her then froze. ET died a few years after Denise disappeared.

My eyes flew open to see the face of a young man. He had the largest brown eyes and longest tongue I had ever seen. His dark, reddish brown hair hung long and shaggy. He smiled around his tongue and licked the wound on my face. I lay there dumbfounded for a split second, then tried to attack him. That's when I realized my hands and feet were bound.

"Get off me!" I yelled and tried to buck him off, twisting and arching my body. My head felt like a sharp spike drove into my temple.

"Ow!" He rubbed his forehead. "Wait. One more lick." He leaned on my shoulders with his hands, blinked his chocolate eyes at me and smiled, straddling my waist. My anger and fear faded for no reason. I felt more annoyed than anything else. A cut on the bridge of his nose caused a small trickle of blood to descend to its tip. He extended his long tongue, covered his nose, and shrugged. The cut was gone. He smiled and licked me again despite my wriggling. Gratefully, I realized we were both fully clothed.

"There, all done," he told me, tongue out, and panted. He cocked his head at me, just like ET used to when she wanted something. At least his breath smelled better.

"Get off of him, Puppy," Kim said as she came closer to the bed. The man straddling me looked at her and back to me again. His eyes grew even bigger and he bowed his head.

"Okay." His bottom lip trembled as he struggled off me, then the bed. While hard to guess from my prone position, he appeared my height with another thirty pounds of muscle. He wore an "I 'heart' my Golden Labrador" sweatshirt, and a pair of running pants.

"He has bruises on his side, should I make them better?" The eager way he said it made me think he was developmentally delayed.

"No, Puppy. Fontain, Trainer, and I have got to do our thing with Captain's brother and get back home before Pham knows we're gone."

I looked at Kim and Puppy and tried to figure out what the hell was going on. Puppy's expression went from petulance to fear at Pham's name.

"But he smells just like Captain!" Puppy whined. Kim looked angrily at Puppy but then she shook her head and smiled. Puppy was like a toddler who had done something bad but knew he was too cute to punish.

"Fine, take this out into the living room with you." She took out an undershirt from my hamper and threw it at him. Puppy caught it in midair, smiled at Kim with his tongue out, and then left my bedroom, shutting the door behind him.

My fear and anger returned.

"He fixates on new people he's healed for a few hours," Kim told me as if it explained everything.

"Kim, what's going on? Let me go! Do you realize what's going to happen when the police learn you've got me?" My teeth clenched together in anger.

"Steckler," Kim replied with a sad shake of her head as she sat on the end of my bed. I moved as far away as possible. "No one knows we're here, and hopefully won't learn it from you. Don't yell or I'll touch you, and you know what that means." She spoke more calmly than she had at the morgue. More like the person I remembered.

"Why are you doing this? Where is Denise? Is she with you? Why didn't she come back?" The feeling of helplessness and anguish from Denise's kidnapping hit me all over again and tears ran down my face.

"It's all been a huge mistake." She sighed and looked at me with a black eye. Her hand went up to touch the bruise. "Your stupid sister didn't tell me her plan. She always said you were the key to getting Pham off our back. You were supposed to be our hero."

"Kim, untie me and let's get Denise. I've got enough money we can all disappear until they catch Va^n and Pham."

She shook her head.

"Untie me, Kim, I'll go with you right now and shoot the bastard myself!"

Again, Kim shook her head.

"Doesn't work that way, Carl. Pham fixed us all to prevent that. We're only here because Denise could get around Pham's brainwashing to send us."

"Then help me. Let me go!"

"I can't. But I did tell Denise I saw you. She was so excited – she's waited for you all these years. Then I told her what I sensed about you; that your sex drive was completely gone.

"You haven't had sex since that night, have you?" She looked me in the eye for the first time. I knew what she was going to say before she said it.

"That's what I thought. Denise figured it out the moment I told her. I did it to you, my control, especially with men, sucked back then. Denise hit me before I knew she moved!" She gave a small laugh and touched her bruised eye.

"That's the first time she's lost control in all these years, and all we've been through. She never lost faith in you. Denise knew you had a gift that would set us free; you just had to figure it out. She's left clues with all the gifted people Pham found over the years. Hoping you'd find one and save her. Save us."

"I don't have a gift, Kim." I struggled against the ties and hoped my lack of a gift would deter her.

"We know. If I hadn't screwed you up, we might have been free of Pham years ago. She sent me here to undo what I did to you." Kim wiped away a tear. "I don't know if it'll work after all these years. She still thinks you are the key." She reached out to me.

"Please don't!" I didn't want her hands anywhere near me. "I'll go to a doctor and get it fixed."

"That won't work, or it'll take too long. Pham gets worse each week. His control is slipping; he's killed three of us this year. Last month he nearly killed Puppy. Now be quiet and let me kiss you." I turned my head side to side and struggled against her hands when she grabbed my head and held it still with incredibly strong hands.

"Where is Denise? I'll come get her!" My words sounded mushy because she held my jaw and my thoughts blurred.

"Carl, I would if I could, but I can't. Pham fixed it that way. Come find us. We're giving you what help we can since you aren't gifted like Denise. Don't kill Pham or you'll kill us all, even Denise. Now shut up," she whispered and the world got fuzzy when her lips touched mine.

No light came through the window to reveal my bedroom. I lay there, eyes closed, but leapt out of bed when the memories flooded in. I smacked the switch on and squinted in the sudden light to find the room empty.

Naked. I cringed at what that could mean. Ignoring that, I pulled a lock box from the closet and struggled with shaking hands and fingers to work the combination. Once opened, I loaded my Glock; glad I put it there rather than the other bedroom after the accident the other night.

I opened my bedroom door quietly despite the fact anyone in the living room or kitchen must have heard me. My small condo had two bedrooms and a bathroom off of the living space. The place looked empty. I walked all the way to the kitchen to make sure they weren't hiding somewhere.

My stomach rumbled. I was ravenous, and thirsty as well. When the adrenaline faded, I became light-headed. I took out an unopened carton of orange juice from the refrigerator and drank it, then waited for the sugar rush to hit.

Rather than think about what may have happened, I counted to thirty, threw away the carton, and checked the front door. My odd attackers had locked the door behind them.

I desperately wanted to shower but needed food. Only two unopened packages of processed cheese sat on a shelf in the refrigerator. Unwrapping one slice after another, I shoved them into my mouth, and ate through both packages without stopping. Now there was only pasteurized half-and-half for my coffee and an old brown grapefruit left.

At least the worst of the hunger was gone. Cheese wrappers littered the floor. As I picked up the wrappers and threw them out, I looked at my naked stomach. There was something different about it.

I shook and forced myself to close my eyes, still my mind, and breathe deep. What happened after Kim kissed me? She was a small, thin woman who couldn't have undressed me alone. I shuddered at the image of her and Puppy stripping me. Rather than dwell on it, I looked around for evidence of what happened.

A scan of the living room furniture and floor revealed the condo still clean and neat. I couldn't face my bedroom, so I checked the room that served as my home office. Flicking on the light showed me nothing disturbed, but there was a folder on my desk chair that hadn't been there before – Denise's folder. I flipped through it. *Nothing missing.*

Without any conscious thought, I flung the folder across the room. The papers scattered across the floor.

"Twenty-six years, Denise. Twenty-six freaking years. I wasted my whole life looking for you! Then you send Kim and a bunch of wack-jobs to do God-knows-what to me!" I screamed with ragged breath. To calm myself, I picked up each piece of paper, smoothed them out, and put them back into their folder.

Squaring my shoulders, I went back to my bedroom, but wasn't ready for the bed yet, so examined the floor. They had used electric extension cords to tie my legs to the bed, both of which were still there, wrapped around the legs of the bed frame. They weren't *my* electric cords, which meant they knew what they were going to do to me before they got here.

"Nice. What have you become, Denise?" I forced my anger to rise rather than have my knees shake. In the kitchen, I got a plastic garbage bag, then, because there were no latex gloves in my condo I took a pair of new leather gloves from the closet that Dad gave me two Christmas' ago.

Returning to my bedroom, I unwrapped the cords, and wondered if I would file charges against them. My lips stretched; there wouldn't be anything left of Kim and her friends to arrest by the time I was done

138

with them. Denise wasn't included among them. I threw the cords into the trash bag to preserve them as evidence.

The clothes line they used to tie my hands lay on the floor. Looking at my wrists for the first time, I saw no rope burns or bruises. I flexed but wasn't sore despite how hard I struggled. In fact, I felt no pain or soreness anywhere, despite what hap—

A disaster had struck the room as well, I reminded myself. It needed cleaning. Now.

The clotheslines went into the trash bag. I picked the clothes up off the floor. The white collared shirt, t-shirt, dress slacks and boxers ruined; they used scissors to cut them off. My shoes and socks were in a crumpled pile but undamaged. They joined the others in the bag. I hyperventilated again and forced myself to stop and take deep breaths. It didn't stop the shaking, but I could check that my wallet, keys, and phone were still there. The money remained folded in a tab and my phone unused. A text message waited for me but I didn't check it, afraid it was from Kim. The digits read half-past ten. That bothered me but I couldn't figure out why.

I was afraid to look at my bed for fear of seeing moist evidence but forced myself to pull the blankets and sheets down. They were clean and unstained. I stripped the sheets and blankets, grabbed my clothes, threw them in the plastic bag, tossed it in my office, and shut the door. I'd worry about tagging things later.

My entire body shook now. Time to look in the mirror, maybe go to the hospital. I chuckled at the irony of me, a man who hadn't had sex in thirty years, getting checked for sexually transmitted diseases. I clenched my jaws again and counted to thirty willing myself not to lose it.

The bathroom had been updated a few years ago with a shower stall instead of a tub. The toilet and sink were new as well as the tiled floor. Dad suggested I put in a full-length mirror behind the door – not for my benefit but to increase the appeal to a potential buyer, especially a woman, should I decide to sell.

I shut the door, took a deep breath, and then turned on the light. Eyes fixed on my torso; I remembered something about my stomach had caught my attention.

As a cop, it was important to stay in shape. I worked out four times a week to keep fit and strong. On the days I didn't hit the gym, I ran. The processed cheese in my refrigerator not-with-standing, I generally ate well. Despite all this, in the past few years, small love handles and a bulge of fat around my belly button showed. A personal trainer explained it was natural for a man's metabolism to slow down at fifty. He recommended three more runs per week. I thanked him for his suggestion and flipped him bird when he turned away but ran a few extra times with no improvement.

The torso I looked at now didn't have an ounce of fat. It was flat with a six pack for the first time since the police academy. My gaze went to my chest and I saw more of the same. My pecs stood out more than ever, like a swimmer's. The bruises that flowered after the car accident were gone.

I was transfixed by my face. The long gash and stitches were gone leaving only a faint line. There was no pain. I didn't look like Frankenstein anymore. My back and backside were all lean muscle. I looked like a celebrity who'd gone through extensive physical training to star in a movie where they had to get naked.

"Wow, Denise, I take it back. I don't know what happened, and I sure as hell don't want it to happen again but ... wow!" I laughed. A part of me knew my reactions were not normal given what happened while unconscious, but another part of me howled joyfully at the moon.

My cell buzzed; a text message. I ran to it, hoped it was Denise; needing to talk to her so badly it hurt. Instead, Dr. Lukishna asked if we were still on for lunch. I controlled my disappointment and managed not to throw the phone across the room. It was a quarter to eleven. I sent a text to put it off for an hour. He agreed and sent me the address for the restaurant. We would meet there.

I looked at my bed again; far more ambivalent about it than I'd been fifteen minutes before. Time to get away from my condo for a while. Meeting Dr. Lukishna would take my mind off things.

Dim lighting hid most of the restaurant but I spotted Dr. Lukishna after he waved. I did a quick jog over to the table.

"Sleep has done you wonders," Dr. Lukishna said as I sat across from him. We met at the restaurant rather than his office to give me extra time to shower and dress. I wore dark jeans, a tight black turtleneck and a ski cap to cover the stitches. Should the upgrade Kim and Puppy gave me be temporary, I wanted to take advantage of it.

"Thanks. You look much better tonight, too." His smile froze and I forced a laugh. "Sorry, that didn't come out right. You looked great the other night and tonight as well. Just more relaxed."

"Thank you." His smile looked natural again. "You look like you lost ten pounds and as many years. What'd you do?"

"Good genes and Botox?"

"Fine, keep your secrets. I warn you, as a medical examiner, I have my ways to get you to talk." He took a sip of red wine and smiled at me over the rim. A glass waited for me as well.

"What do you like to eat?" I blathered. He blinked, then my head caught up with my mouth. "I mean, what's good here?" I brandished my menu to emphasize the point. What the hell is wrong with me tonight? Well, besides getting tied up, licked by a grown man, swapping spit with a psycho, losing twenty pounds, and fifteen years.

141

"Detective, why are you laughing?" he gave me a frown. I clamped my hand over my mouth. Maybe going out tonight wasn't the best idea I'd had.

"Sorry, Dr. Lukishna. It's been a very weird few days."

"Are you talking to my father? I'm Stan."

"Sorry, again. Stan. It's Carl." We clinked glasses.

"I heard you had a rough week."

"From whom?" I spoke more sharply than I intended.

"Relax, Carl. I know Officer Bently. He's worked a few of your recent cases. He was the first officer, besides you, on the scene when Kim, your ex-girlfriend, shot-up the morgue the other night."

"Kim isn't—"

"Dr. Lukishna, are you ready to order?" the waitress interrupted with a smile and put a basket of Italian bread with butter on the table. She looked back and forth between me and Stan.

"I am."

"I'll eat anything. Please order something you think is good," I told him and took a piece of bread.

"Two of my usual, Audrey." She nodded, then winked suggestively at Stan. First Patronio's waiter, William, now Audrey. Are they all matchmakers or just horny-by-proxy?

"Is your week getting any better?" Stan inquired.

"I think it is," I answered, smiling.

"You sound surprised."

"A little. I've not had a lot of experience with positive change."

Stan's eyebrows rose.

"You found something from Cha^a Chung's samples?" I wanted back on safe ground.

"Yes, it's fascinating. I ..." He paused and looked around the restaurant.

Whatever he found, it must be weird.

"We're the only ones at the tables. Besides Audrey, there's a busboy and the bartender. There are three people at the bar. Two of them are drunk. There's probably a cook or two in the kitchen."

Stan's eyebrows rose again and I shrugged.

"I'm a cop; I check places when I enter from habit. What did you learn?"

"I collected tissue samples before the body was stolen, remember?" I nodded. "Fingernail clippings, skin and hair samples, and swabs from the mouth and genitals." Even he stumbled over the last one.

"What was fascinating?"

"They were unbelievable! I wish I could have done a complete examination! Cha^a Chung and the siblings are the most fascinating humans I've encountered."

"I'll give you that. They are fascinating, enchanting, in fact," I agreed, amused at my own cleverness. Stan's eyes zeroed in on mine. I glanced away and began eating another slice of bread.

"That's an interesting choice of words. It's eerily close to what I thought about them."

"What do you mean?"

"There were high levels of dopamine in the skin samples and even higher levels in the swabs from the mouth and genitals."

"Dopamine? The brain's pleasure chemical?"

He raised his eyebrows, impressed. "Yes. The levels were the highest I'd ever seen. I remembered your girlfriend and what you said about the drugs on her hands and her effect on Ron, the security guard."

"I'm not sure I see the connection," I hedged. Again, Stan's gaze snapped to mine.

"I'll explain it, but it's all conjecture." He frowned. "When people touched Cha^a Chung, it was a particularly pleasant experience." He watched for my reaction.

"Because the dopamine transferred to the other person?"

He nodded.

"I don't understand how it works but given what I saw your girlfriend do—"

I interrupted him, "Look, she isn't, wasn't, nor will be, my girlfriend. She was a sexual encounter from twenty years ago. You heard her, she's with my sister."

"Wow. Awkward."

"Whatever, just tell me what else was so fascinating about Cha^a Chung." I hoped that didn't sound like a whine. His smirk told me it did.

"Sorry," he apologized without sincerity. It was my turn to quirk my eyebrows. "Right, back to business. The dopamine levels were much higher in the mouth and genital samples. There were high levels of both estrogen and testosterone there as well. That means if—"

"Yeah, I can guess what that would mean. Please don't say it."

"Squeamish?" He laughed.

"Abso-freaking-lutely." I shuddered.

"I also found something I can't explain. A large percentage of pluripotent stem cells in all of the samples."

This time, I had to admit ignorance.

"Pluripotent stem cells can turn into any type of other adult cell." Stan watched me for a reaction.

I kept my face neutral; that would explain how an adult male or female could transform into a hermaphrodite.

"No comment?" Stan prompted, and I realized I had gone silent.

"This is beyond me, science was my weakest subject in college," I answered. "Did you notice anything about the skin? They've mentioned several times their skin is very sensitive to light."

"No. I didn't have time to run tests, but the skin was thicker than normal – almost leathery," Stan answered.

Audrey brought our food; stuffed baked shells with extra mozzarella. We ate in silence for a few moments. I embarrassed myself by wolfing down the entire plate before Stan even finished two shells.

"Still hungry?" Stan smiled, amused.

"Starving," I agreed, wiped my mouth and checked the basket in case bread was hiding under the napkin. Stan waved to Audrey.

"Please bring another plate of pasta." He pointed to my empty plate.

"And bread, please," I added.

"I love a man with an appetite." Audrey licked her lips suggestively, laughed, and left for the kitchen.

"Do you always eat this much?" Stan glanced at my torso.

"No, I'm recovering from the accident and catching up on a few missed meals."

"Speaking of the accident, how do you feel? How's your head? That cut looked pretty nasty."

"I'm okay. The cut is doing well; I'm a fast healer." I'd planned what to tell him and anyone else who asked.

"Doesn't that hat irritate the stitches?"

"No, it's covered with bandages. The hat hides it."

"That's not a good idea. Cuts need air to heal properly. Why don't you let me take a look at it?"

"I'm good," I told him. Audrey brought the plate of pasta and more bread.

"Thank you," I told her, grateful for more than the food. I started in on the pasta right away.

Audrey smiled, about to reply, but Stan interrupted her. "What are they like?"

"They're delicious," I answered around a mouthful of pasta. Audrey took the hint and walked away.

"Not the pasta, the hermaphrodites."

"They're people, like everyone else," I told him, glad for the change in topic.

"But still, growing up so different from everyone else must have had an impact on their personalities," he said, a question in his statement.

"I didn't do a psychological evaluation of them; I talked to them in the context of a criminal investigation."

"You still must have gotten a sense of what they were like," Stan persisted.

"Not really. I spoke to one who seemed to be the spokesperson for the rest of them," I explained.

"You don't seem very curious," he commented and I shrugged. "How can you not be?" Again, I made a noncommittal gesture. "Come on! You've been in contact with hermaphrodites and now a woman puts men into a sexual stupor by touching them! And you said she hadn't aged!"

I stopped eating, tempted to tell him more but between the freaky night and the trouble I was in, I played it safe.

"Stan you're asking about things that may have a bearing on the body snatching and murder. I'm already in hot water with my Captain, so can we talk about something else?"

"Well, if you put it that way," he said, disappointed.

"I'll figure out a way to introduce you to Tú Chung, the one who speaks for the others." His eyes lit up with excitement and he leaned forward to take my hand.

I froze, not sure how to feel or react.

"You mean that? Thank you!" Then he checked the time. "Wow, I've got to go."

I reached for my wallet.

"No, it's on me," he insisted, and waived Audrey over. He handed a credit card to her. "No, you stay," he said and stood to put on his coat. "Have another plate of pasta if you want."

"Thanks, I just might." I smiled and rose to my feet despite his protest. I waited while he buttoned his coat and accepted the bill.

"Thanks, it was delicious. Next time it'll be on me," I said, and blushed; wondering if I just ask him out. I forced my smile to stay on my face, hoped I looked nonchalant. His hand paused when he finished signing the bill.

"I'd like that. Give me a call so we can plan something."

"I will."

"Now, sit and finish your dinner." He patted my shoulder and walked to the front of the restaurant. Audrey said something and I heard Stan's answering laugh. I hoped that was a good sign and sat to finish eating. I was still hungry.

It was tempting to have another glass of wine, but I felt too antsy to sit or research Yardley Pham at the precinct. Besides, given Stan's reaction and the likelihood of the detectives noticing my lack of stitches, it might be better to skip working at my desk for the next few days.

It turned out to be a nice night. The drizzle stopped and the wind died down. There wasn't a taxi in sight. I wore my sneakers so decided to jog home; I could change my mind on the way and take a cab. The run would bleed off the extra energy and clear my mind.

At my age, it took time for my knees and ankles to warm and loosen up. After the first hundred yards, they felt fine and I increased my speed. I started on Twenty-fifth Street and First Avenue while my condo sat way up in Midtown near Fifty-Second Street and Tenth Avenue. It would be a five-mile run, longer than my usual, but I didn't care. I put thoughts about Denise, the murders, what happened tonight, and everything else aside and concentrated on running around the occasional people on the street and jumping over puddles.

By the time I got back to my condo building, it was after one in the morning. Tim wasn't in the lobby; it was way too late for him to be up and about. There were two women in the entrance hall who eyed me warily as I pushed open the door. I nodded, grinning, realizing I was barely winded. They didn't look thrilled as I joined them in the elevator.

"It's okay. I've lived here for ten years. I'm a Detective with NYPD," I told them, breaking a long-held rule. *I don't tell people I'm a cop when they didn't need to know.* "It's a great night for a run, the rain's stopped and no one's out." I spoke so fast my words ran together. One of the young women reached into her purse – most likely for a can of mace. "No need for that! I'm cool." Luckily, the elevator opened on my floor. "Good night!"

As the doors shut, one of them muttered, "Coke-fiend." I laughed while opening the door to my condo.

"Hey Denise"–I smiled and touched the photo–"whatever you did to me has completely wacked me out!" Part of me was concerned I acted like a drunken teenager but I enjoyed it overall. The obsessed, uptight cynic I had become needed a vacation. I shut the door, threw the bolt, and leaned my head against the wall, suddenly tired.

In my bedroom, I stripped off my shirt, shoes, and socks. As I took off my pants, my wallet fell to the floor and several cards and slips of paper dropped out. Most were cab or store receipts, one was a credit card and the last was my driver's license. I renewed it, and taken a new picture a few months ago. It was the only photograph of me taken in the last five years. Curious, I brought it into the bathroom and turned on the lights.

The face in the mirror and the face on my driver's license were different. The scar above my right eye, which had been faint when I first woke, was now gone. In the photo, my eyebrows had gray hairs among the blond; now they were all blond. The same was true of the beard stubble that had grown in the past few hours. Lines creased the skin under my eyes in the picture. In the mirror, I saw smoothness around

148

my eyes, no crow's-feet.

Kim and Puppy hadn't just healed my cut and gotten rid of a few pounds; they had taken fifteen years off. The only thing about me that still suggested mid-forties were the few gray hairs on my chest.

I sat on the edge of the toilet, hands over my face, entire body shaking in reaction. Questions bounced around my mind like ping pong balls. How long would it last? Were there side effects? How to explain it to people at work? Could I hide it from them? What would I tell Dad about this? About Denise? I don't know how long I sat there; eventually I calmed down then had a shower. When finished, I put on a pair of sweats and a t-shirt, and went into my office. I wanted to spend time at my computer, allow my mind to focus by accessing databases with the new information I'd collected over the past few days. Hopefully, it would lead to Denise, Pham, and Va^n.

The folder I used to keep track of the information I had on Denise was in the second bedroom. Flipping through it, I found a blurry picture of Kim Pham. Wendy, a friend of Denise's and a member of the high school photography club, snapped it during one of their softball games. Wendy gave it to me after Denise and Kim disappeared. Kim hadn't changed as far as I could tell.

Once my computer booted up, I logged on to the NYPD systems. I ran checks on Kim Pham and Denise Steckler again. I'd done this a million times over the years, but never found anything. This time was no different. Then I entered Va^n Chung, Tú Chung, and each of the Patronio brothers. I discovered Vito had been arrested fifteen years ago for a drunk and disorderly, but the charges were dropped.

Nothing came up for Va^n or Tú Chung or, most irritatingly, Yardley Pham. Frustrated, I leaned away from the computer and idly picked up the picture of Kim. They had to have some kind of history, some kind of background if they'd been around for all this time. I went back to the computer and accessed the public records for Suffolk and Nassau

County on Long Island. I ran all of the names again, searching for something, anything that would give me a lead to where Denise would be. Again, I found nothing useful, although I learned that Tú Chung owned a large coastal home in South Hampton – the siblings were very wealthy, that's for sure.

Feeling aggravated, I got up from my chair and paced. I stopped and picked up my folder on Denise, looking through it again, hoping for some inspiration. Getting none, I threw the folder to the ground, scattering its contents for the second time in one day. Shaking my head at my own stupidity, I bent to pick up the papers. I grabbed the two pictures first, Denise's then Kim's, putting one on top of the other. Admitting it was adolescent, I still smirked at the implication of Denise on top of Kim. Then I stood still and thought about it more. Kim said she was in love with Denise. Dad said Denise was a lesbian. I sat down at the computer again and searched for Denise Pham and Kim Steckler.

Finally, a hit – Kim Steckler. She owned an adult entertainment store in Hauppauge, NY. Given her gift, I had no doubt this was Kim's place. The name clinched it. Unusual Gifts; somebody had a sense of humor. I wrote down the address, then searched for which Suffolk County Police Precinct covered Hauppauge. The precinct house was located in Smithtown.

It was three in the morning. There would be a Detective on duty I could talk to about Unusual Gifts, tell me what was on-the-record about the place. But I decided to wait until mid-morning and go in person, using whatever influence I had to learn what was off-the-record.

I had to resist my impulse to go to Unusual Gifts now and confront whoever I found there. It was open twenty-four hours a day, seven days a week. I could feel the adrenaline pulsing through me at the thought and I clenched my hand against the corner of the desk, forced myself to think through the rush. My body may be twenty-something again, but I had four decades of experience. I wasn't going to ignore what that had taught me despite what my renewed youth encouraged me to do.

Patronio could give me his take on things but, again, the time stopped me, even he was sure to be asleep. I considered calling the siblings but knew they wouldn't appreciate being woken up any more than Patronio.

Frustrated, I spent more time looking up Unusual Gifts on the internet and in databases to which I had access. After an hour of searching and finding nothing beyond a few posts on Craig's List about men meeting men there, I gave up.

I felt tired again and decided to lie down. My mind raced with half-formed ideas and thoughts of rescuing Denise or taking out Yardley Pham. Sleep stole over me and I gratefully surrendered to it.

10

For the first time in several days, I awoke with no phone ringing in my ear or strange men sitting on my chest. Lifting the sheet, I looked down with a smile. "Hey there, big man. Haven't seen you up and about in a long time." Apparently, Kim's gift still worked its magic.

Whistling, I got out of bed. It was still early for me, just before ten. A glance out my window showed the sun shining.

I called Perez and told her about Unusual Gifts being a potential lead to the Chung body.

"That is the most disgusting thing I've ever heard of," Perez told me.

"Excuse me?" I blinked. New York City, even after the clean-up in the 1980s, still had more than its fair share of adult entertainment stores.

"Come on, Steckler! What the hell do you think a place like that would do with a hermaphrodite's body?"

"Jesus, Captain, I hadn't even thought of that!" I assumed Yardley would either dissect it to learn more about the siblings or ransom it back to them.

"You really are a boy scout, aren't you, Steckler?"

"I guess so, Captain," I admitted, not embarrassed. There are things I didn't want to think about.

"Don't worry about it. You've got a solid lead. What do you need from me?"

"Can you call over to the Third Precinct in Suffolk County? See if you can prime the pump for me? Also, I need a car."

"You'll do anything to get another car, won't you? Even go to the boonies of Long Island." Perez laughed.

"Careful, Captain, that's my old neighborhood. You should get out there more often, although the shock of fresh air may kill you." Perez chuckled. I was glad to be back in her good graces.

"I'll make some calls and find out who to talk to out there. It shouldn't take too long. Use an unmarked car until we can get a permanent replacement."

"Great, Captain. I appreciate it."

"Do you want another Detective to go with you?"

"That would be more trouble than it's worth."

"Probably," she agreed, surprising me. "Give me an hour before you pick up the car. Then head out to the island. I should have all the calls made before you get there."

"Will do. Thanks again, Captain."

"No problem."

I wished I could trust another cop enough to come with me to Unusual Gifts. If I could get there, find Denise and bring back Va^n's body without other police learning about the gifted, I would. More importantly, I wanted to keep Denise off the official radar.

Patronio could come along with me. On one hand, he wasn't a cop and could be more of a hindrance than a help. On the other hand, he knew more about what we were up against. And he was gifted. But as nervous as I was to face more strangers with gifts, I wasn't sure what to tell Patronio now that Kim had given me "the treatment".

Still undecided, I took a shower and got dressed. I wore a blue blazer, white shirt, and a red tie, with gray slacks and brown dress shoes. It was important to look professional when representing the NYPD to another agency. I secured the shoulder holster and slipped my Glock into it. The "mouse gun," a Union automatic pistol, went under my left pant leg, using a calf holster; an old-school pocket pistol, it used 6.35 ammunition.

As I dressed, I decided to call Patronio to let him know about the new information and what happened to me. If he volunteered to join me, I wouldn't say no.

"Detective Steckler, how are you feeling?" Patronio wanted to know after I identified myself.

"Much better, and twenty years younger."

"Excellent, glad to hear it," Patronio answered.

"I've got new questions I'd like to ask you."

"Go ahead," he said.

I decided against saying anything over the phone about what happened to me. Not being a believer in conspiracy theories and "Big Brother" didn't mean I wanted to take any chances. If Captain Perez learned I'd been assaulted, if she also heard I told Patronio first, she'd be pissed.

"Can I come by in the next ninety minutes or so?" I checked my watch.

"Do you want to meet for lunch?"

"No, I don't have that long, I have to drive out to Suffolk County."

He was quiet for a moment. "Would you like company? We can take my limo," he said.

"Thanks, but I'm on official business. You can ride with me. Do you still have the security?"

"Let me check on something," he said and put me hold. Then he was back. "They'll follow us in a separate car."

"That should be fine, we'll figure out the details later."

"Can you tell me where we're going?"

"Yes," I answered.

"Wait, don't tell me now. Do you have paper and pen?" Patronio interrupted me.

"Go ahead," I told him once I got something to write with.

"It's a secure land line," Patronio said after he gave me the number. "The siblings recommended it after the other night. I can have one set up for you as well if you'd like," he offered.

"It's a good idea, all things considered. I can get one on my own, though, thanks anyway," I said. "Give me twenty minutes and I'll call you on that number. I've got to go to the precinct and pick up a temporary car. Then I'll come get you."

"Sounds good," he said and we hung up.

I shook my head at Denise's picture while leaving. "Secure lines? What in the hell have you gotten us into?"

I nodded to Tim and tried to keep my head down and away from him. Kim must have whammied him last night. That was the only way she and Puppy could have gotten into my condo without me being alerted. I needed to do something about my home security as well as get a secure line, once again concerned about Denise and her associates.

Running across Tenth Avenue, I entered a small convenience store I'd gone to for the last decade.

"Mr. Steckler, good to see you again!" the small Indian man called out from behind the cash register.

"Mr. Sanjiit, how are you today?" I walked up to the counter and looked past him at the wall of electronics, cigarettes, and gift cards.

"I am fine, thank you!" He smiled, squinted, and let out a cackle. "You've had work done haven't you?" Then he gestured at my face, I knew meant plastic surgery.

"Do you like it?" I decided that would be my answer when asked about changes in my appearance.

"You look wonderful! The best work I've seen but don't tell my wife I said that!" He laughed again and I smiled.

"Not a word," I assured him. "Do you have any prepaid cell phones?" I pointed to the phones hanging on the wall behind him.

"Two," he replied and put them on the counter. "This one is fifty dollars with one hundred minutes. This is one hundred with two hundred minutes."

I chose the fifty-dollar phone and paid in cash. While he called to activate the phone for me, I used his ATM to withdraw money. I winced at the fees but the taxis I'd been taking these past few days cleaned out my wallet.

"Thanks, Mr. Sanjiit," I said and walked toward the exit.

"Say hello to the new Mrs. Steckler!" I smiled and hailed a cab.

The traffic was worse than usual. It took me thirty minutes to get to the precinct car lot. I used the time to call Patronio on the secure line to let him know where we'd be going.

The back entrance to the precinct lot was empty, which allowed me

156

to avoid people. I showed the attendant my badge and identification. It wasn't my ego or imagination when she looked up at me and smiled. That hadn't happened in a long time.

"Your picture doesn't do you justice," she said and handed me back my ID. "Take the Charger in the corner. Don't wreck it, it's my favorite."

"I'll do my best," I promised with a wink.

"Ease off there, junior," she said, trying to sound harsh but smiling as she handed me the car keys. I signed the release for the car and shook my head at my stupid behavior. What the hell was wrong with me?

The drive to Patronio's took twice as long as it normally should, thanks to malicious traffic gods. It was nearly one o'clock and the lunchtime crowds brought the roads to a standstill.

I pulled up in front and dialed Patronio. He was at the car in moments. I blinked when he sat in the passenger seat. Dark blue jeans, a black turtleneck, and a brown leather trench coat; I hadn't recognized him.

"What are you wearing?"

He laughed. "Clothes."

"They're not white!" I stated the obvious. A car pulled up behind mine and I recognized the driver as one of Patronio's security guards. "The security team didn't think it was the best idea to always wear white. It's too recognizable and an easy target, right?"

He nodded.

"Good, they're competent." I pulled into traffic and headed for the 59th Street Bridge. It was silent in the car for too long and I used a pause at a red light to look at Patronio.

He was staring at me. "What happened to you?"

"Looks good, right?" I laughed nervously. His eyes were open wide and he flattened himself against the passenger door. "What's the matter?"

"Tell me what happened to you." He took out his cell phone and slid the other hand into his coat pocket. I saw a gun handle.

"What's the matter?" I glanced sideways at him and drove past the green light.

"Just tell me."

"Jeez, relax," I said. "I got a visit from my old friend Kim. She had a mentally disabled guy with her. She did something to me and I passed out. When I woke up, all this happened." I gestured at my face and body, leaving out the part about the guy straddling me and licking my face.

"I'm not sure that's as good a thing as you think." He hadn't taken his hand from his pocket or relaxed. The fear and anxiety I ignored spiked.

"Why, what do you know?"

"I spoke with Tú after you left the other day. One of the ways that Yardley Pham converted people to his cause was to cure them of their illnesses and give them back their youth."

"I can definitely see how that would work," I said with a laugh.

Patronio didn't say anything, just eyed me. "He wasn't there. Kim said Denise sent her to make up for what she did to me back in the eighties."

"You even smell different," Patronio said.

"Is that good or bad?"

"Good, I think, at least for you. You smell more like a man. Before, it was like you were very old. Now, there's a lot more testosterone." Patronio relaxed and the smell of burnt popcorn faded, hand still in his coat pocket.

"What else did Pham do to people?"

"He controlled them. He sent people to his enemies like suicide bombers against the troops in Afghanistan or Iraq. They looked innocent until they were close and then—boom!"

"Tú said 'boom'?" I seriously doubted it.

"Don't be a smart-ass. He said they acted like the Cold War spies who seemed normal then killed people when they heard a code word."

"So, you think they made me a sleeper spy that will come out at just the wrong moment?" I tried to sound incredulous, but was more worried than I wanted to admit.

"I don't know, Detective Steckler, I have no idea what these people are capable of. They killed Lisa and tried to kill us once already." Patronio slumped in his seat. His hand out of his pocket.

"Now you know why I didn't want to talk over the phone."

"Yes, that makes sense."

"Can I ask you a question?" I could see him nod out of the corner of my eye. "How old do I look?"

He turned to examine me.

"Mid-twenties or early thirties at the latest," Patronio answered after a few moments. I expected him to be jealous, but he looked more concerned. "Detective, Tú told me something else as well."

"Yes?" A knot formed in my stomach.

"There were several stories about those Yardley converted using gifted people. None of them turned out very well."

"You mean they did a suicide run or bombing?"

"Or they went really crazy. Like chewing-their-own-hands-off insane."

"Great."

The car ride quieted down after that. I drove across the 59th Street Bridge and pondered how Kim lied to me again and wondered when I would go postal. I was sure Patronio worried about the same thing.

"Do you know anything about where we're going?"

Patronio shrugged.

"I googled it and called friends out there to see if they knew anything. It's got a weird reputation," he said.

"I'll bet," I said, thinking about Kim's gift. "What did they say?"

"The front room is a porn store with all the usual stuff. The back room is what they called weird. You pay to get into it. It's normally only open at night on the weekends. It's got couches and places to stand. It's a sex club." Patronio fidgeted, uncomfortable talking about it.

"You mean like a gay bathhouse?"

"I suppose so, Detective. I've not been to one." Patronio sounded offended.

"Sorry, I wasn't suggesting you had, it's just—"

"Detective, don't finish the sentence. I've friends who go to such places. They're nice people; they just have different tastes than I do. Let's leave it at that."

"Works for me. You said it has a weird reputation. Why?"

"I didn't ask too many questions, but they implied it was the type of place that encouraged its customers to go way beyond their normal boundaries. One of my friends said it was like a 'Fellini film'." Patronio shuddered. I had vague recollections of who Fellini was and what that would mean. I flashed back to Puppy licking my face.

"Anything else?"

"No, I could learn more with time."

"If you can, that would be great. I thought I'd go to Unusual Gifts and scope it out. Then stop at the local precinct house to learn what they know," I said.

"What am I here for?" Patronio squinted his eyes at me. I squirmed in discomfort.

"I'm caught between a rock and a hard place. Law enforcement doesn't know about people like you. I don't have any defense against the gifted except long range weapons. That won't help with the investigation. Also, my sister is involved somehow.

"You don't want her arrested or even connected to it and I'm the next best thing to a long range weapon?" Patronio sounded pleased.

"You also have a lot more experience with the gifted than I do."

"Not much, I only learned about others like me a few weeks ago."

"Weeks longer than I have."

"True," Patronio answered. The traffic lightened and we made better time. In a short while, we neared the Queens-Nassau County border. The close-packed houses and buildings became trees separated by manicured industrial parks. Patronio passed the time identifying different plants by the scents that came through the vents.

"How does it feel?" Patronio startled me with a question. I wasn't sure he asked me the about the gifted, my sister, the assault by Kim and Puppy, or its effect. My confusion showed on my face.

"How does it feel to be young again?"

I couldn't tell if he was wistful, jealous, or curious. "I'm not sure yet. It confuses me when I catch my reflection in the mirror, but I'm more energetic, less cautious. It hasn't been a huge change."

"The cut is healed too?"

"Yes, even the scar is gone."

"What about the problem that Kim, um, gave you?" Patronio waved his hand at my crotch. "I can smell a lot more testosterone on you than before."

"Kim fixed it. Now I'm more aware of people and sexual innuendo than in years. People notice me more too." I laughed.

"I'll bet they do." Patronio smiled. I wasn't sure if he agreed with or patronized me but didn't want to know. Then I remembered what bothered me since he mentioned the espionage angle Kim or Yardley Pham could be running.

"If Pham is using me the way Tú mentioned—"

"You're delivering me to them," Patronio finished. "I thought of that as well."

"So why are you still here?"

"Because you didn't tell me to leave the security guards."

"Ah." I wondered if they'd be any help against the gifted. Patronio must have read my mind.

"The guards aren't gifted, but they do have long-range automatic guns," he said with a smile.

We drove the rest of the way in silence. The sun came out and shone on the new light-green leaves budding on the trees. This far out on the island, industrial parks gave way to solid walls of foliage. Spring finally arrived.

"I forget what the countryside looks like. I miss it."

"Me too," Patronio said. "Although my hometown is more like a small city than the country these days."

"Metuchen, right?"

"Yes, been doing your homework on me?" He quirked an eyebrow.

"Of course," I said.

"Good, I wouldn't expect any less. How long until we get there?"

"We're almost there. It's off the highway, near the county government buildings, in amongst a bunch of warehouses." I handed him my cell phone to use to find directions.

"I got it," Patronio said. "We're at the exit we need."

For the next twenty minutes we negotiated side roads between the expressway and the actual address. The streets were mostly tree-lined and residential interspersed with strip malls and chain restaurants. Then we were surrounded by big blocky buildings with windows that didn't open. It was the type of personality-sucking architecture I hated, built during the nineteen-sixties, surrounded by vast, full, parking lots for the drones who worked there.

"What will we do once we get to the store?" Patronio wanted to know when we were a block away.

"Maybe nothing. We might just sit and watch who goes in and out, to see if we know anyone. I'll write down all the license plates. It might lead us to Denise and Pham."

"We're not going inside?" Patronio stared at me, surprised.

"I don't want them to see us. They might spook, disappear, or worse, think they don't have anything to lose and go nuts."

We pulled into a parking lot that surrounded a series of connected businesses. The sign at the entrance listed six companies in alphabetical order. Unusual Gifts was last. We circled the building and found it in the back. There were fewer cars on that side. Patronio called the security team, telling them to park within sight of our car.

I backed the Charger into a space across the lot from the door. Tree branches dipped low over the car and hid us from view. We could see the short stairway that led to the door discreetly marked "Unusual Gifts".

"Now what?" Patronio reminded me of a kid playing 'Cops and Robbers'.

"We wait and watch," I told him.

"That's boring."

"Welcome to the glamorous part of police work," I said and handed him my notepad and a pen. "If you want to keep busy, write down the license plates, make and model of all the cars."

"I'm the one with the super powers here, Detective." Patronio quirked his eyebrow and smirked.

"Yeah, so?"

"You're supposed to be *my* sidekick." We laughed.

"Keep dreaming, Mr. Patronio."

We sat in the car for an hour. Patronio wrote down the information about each car parked as well as those that showed up afterward.

"Will their names be added to a list somewhere?"

"Yeah, with all the men who like porn. I'll use the phonebook as my starting point."

Patronio laughed but persisted.

"I'm serious. What will you do with the information? I feel like a fascist."

I couldn't stop my eye roll.

"I'll see if the plates belong to either Pham or Steckler. If there isn't a connection, I'll toss the names and information."

"Who's that?" Patronio pointed at a blue mid-size sedan as it pulled up near the stairway to the store entrance. At the same time, another car backed into the space next to our car on the passenger side.

Two men exited the car near the store. The one on the passenger side was large and dark-blond: Puppy – he stood, stretched, and scratched his butt as he looked around the parking lot. His mouth hung open and tongue stuck out. The other man made Puppy look small. Bald, African-American, his skin-tight black t-shirt barely contained him. Puppy moved around in a grizzly bear kind of way. The other man reminded me of a professional wrestler – only bigger. Large really didn't accurately describe him; his body rippled with hyper-muscles like a cartoon steroid user. The car frame rose three inches when he got out.

Patronio pressed the button to lower his window and inhaled deeply. His nose wrinkled. The two men walked up the stairs and were about to enter Unusual Gifts when a man got out of the car next to us. The car door shut and drew Puppy's attention.

"The blond one's familiar but doesn't smell right, just similar to the man with Va^n," Patronio said and noticed me watching Puppy. I stayed silent and leaned forward to start the car engine.

At the same time, Puppy stood up straighter, his eyes became focused, and the vacuous expression transformed into shrewd intelligence. He even stood differently, leaning forward aggressively. I knew this was important but not why.

"Did he say anything that night?" I put the car in drive. Puppy's massive companion took notice of us as well.

"Yes, but it was in Vietnamese. I told you that," Patronio said. He ignored the man from the next car who checked us out.

"I didn't get the impression Puppy could speak Vietnamese. He's developmentally disabled or something." The muscle freak must have figured out who we were; he grabbed the railing. It bent while he snarled.

"The man with Va^n wasn't developmentally disabled. He knew exactly what he was doing," Patronio said. He stuck his head out of the car window and inhaled deeply. "That's one of them!"

The muscle-head jumped over the railing. Puppy tripped at that moment and the muscle man's foot caught on Puppy's shoulder and both went down.

"We're out of here." I floored the pedal, screeched out of the parking spot and past the two entangled men. The steroid freak screamed at Puppy crouched down next to him, arms held out to protect himself from the other man. Puppy looked up and held my gaze as I drove by.

"We're not going after them?" Patronio almost yelled.

"No! Did you see what that guy did to the railing? We can't fight that without backup, but this confirms we're at the right place. Besides, you're a civilian. I don't want you getting hurt again on my watch."

"That's sweet of you, Detective." I ignored his sarcastic tone.

"While you go to ground again, I'll check with the Suffolk Country cops to see what they know about the place. Did you get their license plate?"

Patronio wrote down the numbers on the pad before he forgot them.

We drove to another parking lot down the road and waited for Patronio's security to catch up. We'd pre-arranged the location on the drive out.

"Don't let the glamor of police work fool you, Mr. Patronio," I told him as he got out of the car. "There are days when it's a real grind."

He shut the car door with a laugh.

11

I watched Patronio get in the back of a black Mercedes sedan. His security team better be worth the money he paid them. They seemed competent, but I wondered if they knew what they were up against.

The guards guided us back to the expressway, but where they turned west toward the city, I stayed on Route 111 and crossed into Smithtown to the precinct house. Pricey condos, stores, and restaurants appeared as soon as I crossed the town line.

I lost time finding the precinct house, it had been years since I'd been out this way. Holding a phone, figuring out the app, while driving was still new to me. It was a small, one-story building. There were many open parking spaces. Sometimes I missed life in the suburbs; the spaces in the city were gone by six in the morning.

Sitting in the Charger, I organized my thoughts. Unusual Gifts was sure to be on the cops' radar. Places like that, in a town like this, wouldn't be welcome.

The siblings exerted their influence over Mayor Silvan. I wasn't entirely certain of it, but my instincts told me the siblings used traditional tactics, meaning money, rather than their gifts to sway him. Yardley Pham and Kim didn't strike me that way. Neither would hesitate to use their gifts to extract themselves from a law enforcement encounter. It didn't matter: I would find Denise and do whatever was needed to get her out of this mess.

The entrance-way where I came in took up an entire wall. Small and empty, the police station lobby looked like all the other suburban ones I'd been in. The couches and chairs, standard government-issue, but clean and new; the benefits of a wealthy neighborhood. They lined one side of the room below windows that overlooked the parking lot and my car. A thick-plated glass window over a long counter faced the outer windows. Next to the counter, a solid door, secured by a keypad lock, kept casual visitors away from seedier side of law enforcement. I leaned into the microphone embedded in the bullet-proof glass protecting the dispatcher who sat behind it.

"Good morning. I'm Detective Steckler." I flashed him my badge and an "I-mean-business" look. A young man with broad shoulders, he filled out his dispatcher uniform nicely.

"Hello, Detective. Detective DeNali told me to expect you sometime this afternoon. Let me tell him you're here." He leaned back to grab his phone and released the intercom button. I watched as he spoke then hung up.

"He'll be out in a moment." His smile suggested he knew I noticed his build.

"Thank you," I mumbled, embarrassed and almost wished Kim hadn't flipped the switch or whatever she did.

"Detective Steckler? George DeNali." He stepped through the secure door between the dispatch window and the chairs. Standing five foot, eight inches tall, with a stocky build and brown, his crew-cut hair faded to gray. Black slacks, a white shirt, and a dark blue tie – the detective's uniform. He wore his gun and holster at his waist.

"Nice to meet you. I'm Carl." He squeezed my hand just hard enough to hurt, then stopped.

"George," he said and his shoulders relaxed. Some cops had issues dealing with cops from outside their department. I noticed the dispatcher watching us and felt the urge to take control of the situation – to show off. I blinked and pushed the thought away. Just because I got my dick back didn't mean I had to act like one.

"Let's go to a conference room." George turned to the door and looked at the dispatcher who reached under his desk. There was a buzz and George opened the door. "Do you want coffee or something to drink?"

"Bottled water would be great." I reached for my wallet. They would have a vending machine here somewhere, just like my precinct, a bottled anything wouldn't be free.

He waved off my offer. I would have done the same. I was a guest in his "house" and he'd treat me that way until I showed up more than twice, or if I ran an operation on his turf.

"Thanks."

He nodded and pointed to an open doorway at the other end of a corridor lined with doors on the left and work cubicles on the right. "Go in, I'll join you in a second." George walked down the other corridor behind the dispatch desk.

Several men and women seated at their workstations looked at me with curiosity as I approached the meeting room. The same would have happened in my precinct. We didn't get many voluntary visitors.

I took off my coat and hung it on a chair in front of the table. Another gesture to put George at ease. The more comfortable and relaxed he was, the more likely he'd tell me any "off-the-record" information about Unusual Gifts. I suspected there'd be more of that than any documented infractions.

"Thanks," I said again when George returned. He shut the door and handed me my water. We sat down and I put my notepad and pen on the table beside me and left them there. I wanted to demonstrate I was prepared but would share information before asking any formal questions.

"You've got an impressive record of arrests, not to mention your reputation for solving cold cases." George let me know he'd done his homework. "It's a shame you didn't come last week, you could have met Sergeant Ray. He's solved even more cold cases than you." George smiled.

I grinned back at him without showing too many teeth. Law enforcement people can get a little hung up on numbers and records – who had the largest poundage of marijuana in a drug bust, who solved the most murders, break-ins, whatever. You name it; someone had a plaque to show for it.

"Sergeant William Ray, right?" I asked and George nodded. "I've used his manual on forensics so often I've had to buy two of them in five years. Sorry I missed him."

George leaned back in his chair. I passed his second test; the first had been if I'd offered to pay for the water. There'd be one more before I got the information I wanted.

"Yeah, Bill retired last week. We're still recovering from his send-off party," George said and we chuckled. "You're here about Unusual Gifts. My Captain said yours called to grease the wheels but didn't tell me about your case. What's it about?"

Test number three. I gave him the official story on Lisa Taylor's murder, Patronio's assault, and Cha^a's murder and body theft. When George shuddered, I knew I passed. He'd tell me what he knew or suspected about Unusual Gifts.

170

"Tell me about Unusual Gifts and the owner, Kim Steckler."

"Officially, there isn't much to say." He confirmed my suspicions. "She is paid-up on her license, keeps the place clean, and supposedly doesn't allow sexual activity in the place or parking lot. There's no evidence of prostitution. She pays her taxes and even contributes to the policemen's benevolent fund."

"What about unofficially? What have you heard?" I leaned forward and made sure the door remained closed. I wanted to appeal to his desire to gossip in case he was anything like Luddy.

"Nothing we've been able to prove officially."

I pushed my notepad and pen further away.

"A couple of years ago we received complaints from the surrounding businesses. They claimed people were having sex in the parking lot." Now he leaned forward and glanced at the door. "But it wasn't the run-of-the-mill blowjob or handjob. Or even a quickie in the back seat. The neighbors said it was like an orgy, groups of men and women, even animals."

"Animals! Wow." I felt sick but wanted him to keep talking.

"When the guys investigated, they found nothing. They interviewed the business owners, went into Unusual Gifts, and came out with nothing. I was there when they came back to the precinct house. They were dazed and couldn't remember much. The next day the other business owners withdrew their complaints."

"None since?"

"Nothing anyone is willing to put on paper. There's been rumors of people gone missing after they went there," he said. "I've heard other weird stuff about it; anything from the best psychedelic drugs to Satanism and human sacrifice."

I feigned skepticism but was afraid they were true.

"Yeah, I know. If anything that weird were going on, we'd be all over it." He shook his head. "There are other porn stores in the precinct.

They draw their share of kooks, but mostly draw men on the 'down low' looking to hook up. The stories I've heard about Unusual Gifts are way beyond that. It wouldn't surprise me if they stole your dead hermaphrodite and are taking turns with it in the basement. But I doubt you'll be able to prove it."

"Why's that?" I got a chilled feeling and knew I was onto something here.

"Anyone who gets near the place, or any of the players there, comes up dazed or quickly becomes disinterested."

I stood and took my jacket from the back of the chair. The conversation was over. George remained seated. Puzzled, I waited.

"The owner's name is Kim Steckler. Any relation?" George leaned back and tried to sound casual.

"I hope not!" That was true.

"Your sister disappeared with a young woman named Kim, didn't she?" I looked at him in surprise. "We can do research here too."

I kept quiet.

"This is personal?"

"Maybe."

"Let me give you a word of advice, off the record." He nodded at my notepad. "If you get something you can use on them, bring in the Feds. I'm not proud of it, but that place and those people scare us. And the people that disappear from that store, well, let's just say no one misses them. If the cops here learn you're going up against them, we may just call in sick."

"Can't say I blame you. I wouldn't do this if I didn't have to."

He handed me a folder he'd carried into the room.

"That's all the complaints we have on Unusual Gifts. It's not much."

"Thanks." I took the folder from him; it was very thin. He stayed in his seat as I left.

I flipped through the papers in the folder. There had been three complaints about Unusual Gifts. The reports described them but they could wait until later for me to read in detail. It was nearly four o'clock; the ride back would take three hours rather than two if I didn't leave now. The files provided no new names or addresses associated with Unusual Gifts. The address used for the license was a post office box.

Driving west on the expressway, I tried to piece together a plan to get into Unusual Gifts and find Denise. The information that came from Patronio and the siblings felt trustworthy. Anything else was based on information from Kim; an unreliable source. Usually notes helped me keep track of things but this was the first time I had to process what I knew unaided. Maybe later I would have time to write it down.

First and foremost: Denise lived and still involved with Yardley Pham and Kim. Pham had a gift he used to control people and to stop Denise from escaping or contacting me. Denise tried to reach out and get me to help her despite Pham. Denise was gifted but I didn't know how or if that would help.

Kim Steckler, horribly enough, became my long-lost sister-in-law. Great. She could drive men and women into sexual catatonia and turn their sex drive off and on. In addition, she owned and operated an adult porn store with a back room that scared the local law enforcement. To make matters worse, she and Puppy broke into the city morgue, stole Cha^a Chung's body but botched the job. Kim blamed it on Puppy and had to go back for the evidence.

Patronio, who got me into this mess, manipulated trace elements to affect olfactory senses. I considered him an ally targeted by Yardley Pham for his gift. Va^n and an unknown man attacked Patronio and killed Lisa Taylor during an attempted kidnapping.

Tú and the other siblings reminded me of the spiders in the old cartoons with the spiders and flies. I hoped I wasn't the fly caught in their web. No one beyond the siblings themselves knew all of their gifts or their extent. I knew to stay upwind of them and to avoid their gaze and touch. They were terrified of Yardley Pham. But Tú also hated Pham. Tú and the siblings would back me against Pham with their gifts and money as long as it served their goals.

Va^n Chung was a murderer and wanna-be/soon-to-be sibling. He killed Lisa Taylor and Cha^a Chung. Neither his family nor the siblings knew much about his personal life, only that he wanted to be the next sibling. His motivation for killing Lisa or Cha^a was unclear. He had a large, unknown accomplice with him when he killed Lisa and assaulted Patronio, perhaps Puppy if Patronio's nose could be believed. Va^n may be acting in collaboration with Yardley Pham but there was no definitive connection.

Va^n puzzled me but Yardley Pham defined enigma. No information existed about him in any database to which I had access. Tú said Yardley tried to capture the siblings in Vietnam during the war. He decimated their numbers and village and killed Tú's mother. Had he been in his twenties during the Vietnam War, that would make him, at least, seventy-five now. I suspected he used whatever happened to me, to keep himself young. According to Tú, Pham wanted to gather people with gifts, but didn't know for what purpose. Kim implied Yardley led the group but his control slipped at times. Maybe he had one facelift too many?

Puppy somehow fit in with this crew. His gift, I shuddered, healed and possibly rejuvenated others. From what little I saw of him, he might be developmentally disabled. Patronio said Puppy smelled familiar, but wasn't Va^n's accomplice when Lisa Taylor died.

Kim mentioned two others, Fontain, and Trainer. I suspected the

174

man who got out of the car with Puppy could be one of them but not Va^n's accomplice. Patronio would have said something about his size and muscularity.

Satisfied with my understanding of most players in this game, Yardley Pham still eluded me. He had to be connected to the murders. Now to prove it while keeping Denise out of it.

Traffic slowed to a standstill at the city line. Time to let my subconscious percolate on the cast of characters; it sometimes made missing connections. Leaning forward, I tuned the radio to a top-forty station and enjoyed the rest of the ride.

It felt strange to pull the Charger into the parking space in the garage next to my condo building. The sun still shone, so I had time for a run. Close to my building entrance, I put on my ski hat in case Tim smoked in the doorway. He would notice the changes in me, especially the healed injury. With his powers of observation, i.e. nosiness, he would've made an excellent detective.

Tim stood in the doorway speaking with another man whose back faced me. Good, he'd be too busy to notice anything.

I walked up to the door and kept my head down. Before I could open the door, the other man turned to me. My father. So much for *my* powers of observation.

"Carl"–he looked at my hat-covered forehead–"how are you?"

"Hi." I gave him a quick hug and moved to his side, out of the light. Dad hugged me so as to barely touch; we rarely displayed affection. "Is everything okay? Did something happen to Barbara? What are you doing in town?" I sounded concerned and annoyed. We never showed up at the other's house without calling first.

"Yes, everything's fine. I was worried about you."

Tim studied his shoes with a great deal of intensity. "I'll leave you two alone and let you visit." He avoided my eyes. "Good night, Everett. Carl." He scrambled back to his condo door.

I watched in silence as he entered his condo. "Is Barbara with you?" I looked up and down the block for his car.

"No, she stayed in Brooklyn."

"Then let's go up. If you're hungry, we'll have to order in. I've got nothing in the refrigerator."

"That's fine." Dad kept his eyes on my face as he held the door for me. I kept my face away as I passed. What should I say to him? Should I tell him about Denise? What parts should I tell him, especially about my sudden change in appearance? He would see it as soon as I was in normal lighting.

The elevator door opened as soon as I punched the button. We went in and I kept my back to him.

"Are you paying Tim to spy on me?" I took the offensive.

"Your personal life is so boring, I'd be wasting my money."

He scored with that one. "I deserved that," I said by way of apology.

"Yes, you did. And no, I'm not paying Tim. I've called you several times over the last few days. You didn't answer or return my calls. I met Tim when you bought the place and called him to check on you. He said you'd been in an accident and hurt your face." There was recrimination in his voice.

"Why didn't you call my cell or work?"

"I lost your cell number, and those morons you work with wouldn't tell me anything. They said they'd take a message but that clearly didn't work. So, I called Tim and here I am. Why the hell didn't you tell me were in an accident? And why won't you look at me? What are you hiding?"

The elevator reached my floor. I waited until we got into my condo before replying, "Sit down." I pointed to the couch, went into the kitchen and came back with two tumblers of scotch and ice. He took one. Then I carefully extracted the paper from Patronio with Denise's picture on it from my pocket.

"I found her." I handed him the paper with shaking hands.

He looked at me, then the paper, knowing I spoke of Denise. Hesitantly, he read it. Tears ran down his cheeks.

"Carl, this can't be her. Look at her, she's too young. It's someone else." He glanced up from the paper to me and his eyes widened. "What happened to you? You look different." He scrutinized my face. His hands trembled. I redirected him to Denise.

"It's her. I haven't seen her but I saw Kim."

"Kim? Her girlfriend?" He sounded bewildered.

"Yes, that Kim. They're both alive. They're living somewhere out on the island."

"Carl, she's dead. You have to let this go, it's made you crazy and that's killing me." Tears ran down his cheeks.

Pressure and pain built up in my temple. I stood and picked up the lamp on the table and threw it over his head. The electric cord snapped and the lamp exploded against the wall.

"You idiot! You gave up all these years when we could have found her! You always take the fucking easy way out! Shut up and listen to me! I told you she was alive and I found her!"

He cringed on the couch and stared at me as if I were a stranger.

Just as suddenly as it came over me, the rage was gone, leaving me feeling empty and depressed. The pain behind my eyes eased at the same time.

"I know, I'm so sorry I failed you." He looked away from me now.

"Jesus, Dad, I'm sorry. I don't know what the hell I'm doing." I sat down and rubbed my head. *What's happened to me? I've never thrown*

177

something at someone in anger.

"Are you sure? Please Carl, if you're not sure, tell me. I can't go through this again. I won't." He stood with legs shaking so hard I could see them tremble through his pants.

"Yes. I'm sorry, really."

"Where is she? Where has she been? Why hasn't she called us?"

"I don't know anything for sure. She got involved with some pretty bad people; Kim being one of them."

Dad frowned. He knew I wouldn't talk about my work, especially if it involved anyone we knew.

"Why did she leave us? Why?" Dad yelled.

I handed him a scotch and put my hand on his shoulder.

"Here, drink this. Hell, I could use another one." I finished my drink.

He did the same and followed me into the kitchen. I poured us another round while he watched.

"Carl, what's going on? Tim said you had a big gash on your forehead. You don't. There's not a mark on your face. Even that scar on your cheek is gone. You look different, younger. What happened?"

"I don't know. Kim is involved in a case I'm working. She showed up at a crime scene and let the news slip about Denise. After she escaped, she showed up here with friends, assaulted me and doused me with drugs. Since then, my face healed. The drugs were some kind of hormones."

"Drugs? Did you go to the hospital?"

"I don't need to. The cut was healed and my face looked better. I'm fine."

"You threw a lamp at me."

"You've got a point," I admitted and took a sip of my scotch.

"What now?"

"Denise is mixed up with some bad people who have murdered twice. I don't know how, or if, she's involved."

178

Dad shook his head and downed the scotch in one long pull. He poured himself another one. Normally he was a teetotaler but I didn't blame him tonight.

"I'll have pizza delivered." I dialed my favorite place and ordered three large pizzas, two with extra cheese and pepperoni, and one with anchovies. The anchovies were for him; I couldn't abide them.

"That's a lot of pizza," Dad commented.

"I'm starving."

He went to the small closet in the corner of my kitchen and took out a broom and dustpan.

"I'll clean up. I'm the one who threw the lamp." He looked at me a moment, shrugged, and handed me the broom and dustpan. "Why don't you sit in my office so I can move the furniture around in the living room? The pieces are going to be all over."

"Good idea." He shuffled away with his drink. The news about Denise still sinking in. He hadn't been shuffling when he got here.

I grabbed a garbage bag from the box under the sink and went into the living room to pick up the pieces.

The pizza delivery arrived just as I returned from the dumpster in the back of the building. I threw the lamp pieces out and used the time to calm down, unnerved and frightened by my anger. After Denise disappeared I trashed my bedroom, but those intense feelings faded after a month or so. Afterward, I suffered through black periods of depression but eventually it lightened to what Dad and Mom had referred to as my "happy Boris Karloff (but still Boris Karloff)" mood. I was afraid my newfound youth may have something to do with my sudden lack of control.

After I paid the delivery woman for the pizzas, I went into the kitchen and grabbed plates, napkins, and the bottle of scotch. I put them all on top of the pizza boxes and walked into my extra bedroom-come-office.

Dad sat at my desk with his back to me. His glass placed in front of him, empty. When he spun the chair to face me I saw an old photo album on his lap as well as the tears in his eyes.

"Do you think she's been in New York the entire time?"

"Maybe." I opened one of the boxes of pizza. It had anchovies on it. I put two slices on a plate and handed it to him.

"Why didn't she call? Was she sick? Brainwashed? On drugs?" Tears flowed but I heard his anger and anguish as well. I pointed to his pizza. His words were slurring – I didn't want him to pass out.

"Maybe she couldn't. Kim implied they were controlled by someone else. He may be slipping, so Kim was able to talk to me." I grabbed a slice of pizza and started eating.

"You said she assaulted you. Why?"

"She's unstable – one minute she sounded crazy, the next, normal."

"What are the rest of the cops doing about this?"

"It's my case." I hoped to avoid the next question but he knew me too well.

"Don't be evasive. Are they helping you find Denise?"

"No. Denise is an adult woman who disappeared a long time ago. She isn't a kidnap victim if she went with them willingly and stayed with them."

Dad shook his head in frustration; this had been a big issue when Denise first disappeared.

"Is she the murderer?"

"No, I don't think so, at least not directly," I threaded through the truth.

"Could she be charged with anything?" In a flash of anger I almost told him I could charge her with assault, but managed to keep my mouth shut and handed him another slice.

"The murders are just the tip of the iceberg with these people."

"Why didn't they take you off the case if Denise is involved? They can't expect you to arrest your sister."

"They tried, but the victim's family is pretty influential. They wanted me on the case."

"Are you going to arrest Denise?" He was incredulous.

I didn't answer, having no idea what I'd do if it came down to it. It depended on if she hurt other people.

"You said someone was controlling her. Who is it?"

"I don't know for sure." Even with Denise involved, sharing information about a case went against the grain.

"Carl," he demanded.

"Yardley Pham. His name is Yardley Pham," I answered him around pizza.

"What kind of name is that?" He wrinkled his nose.

"Vietnamese."

"Is Kim Vietnamese?"

"I think so,"

"They related?"

"No idea."

He looked at me with his jaw locked and lips pressed together then reached for another slice of pizza. "I know you'll do your best to get this guy and bring Denise home," Dad said, his face now smooth and voice calm.

I was puzzled by his change in demeanor but didn't pursue it.

We ate in silence. Much to my horror, I finished both of my pizzas. When Dad said he was done, I even finished the remaining slices with anchovies.

"I'll be back." He left for the bathroom.

I grabbed the empty boxes, plates, and glasses and brought them into the kitchen. After rinsing the plates and glasses and I put the pizza boxes in another garbage bag. They'd go to the trash bin later. Another round for each of us and then I'd put the scotch bottle away; we'd eaten enough to sober up.

"You okay?" I'd waited in the living room for a few minutes for him to come out.

"In here." He called from my bedroom.

I hadn't heard him move but wasn't surprised. Growing up, he often snuck up on Denise and me to scare us and laugh. Mom always said he had a gift for sneaking around. Dad rummaged around in my closet.

"What are you looking for?" *Maybe he was drunk after all.*

"The sheets. I came out the wrong door, saw your bed stripped and decided to make it for you." He definitely had too much to drink if he wanted to do housework.

"Thank you, but you don't have to make my bed."

"I was just trying to be nice." Dad sounded defensive.

"Thanks, but I'll do it. Do you want another scotch?"

He nodded and took the glass from my hand.

"What are those locked boxes in your closet?"

I laughed at the suspicion in his voice.

"Sorry to disappoint you but they just have my guns and paperwork in them. No body parts, blow up dolls, or gay magazines."

"That isn't what I thought!"

I laughed.

"I'm messing with you."

"I hope you have a more difficult combination on those locks than you did at home. We all knew it was your birthday," he said. "Denise constantly pilfered money from your stash." He laughed, then became serious after mentioning Denise.

"No comment. And, yeah, I knew Denise ripped me off; I stole it back from her." I laughed again but got choked up at the memories.

"I remember," Dad said with a smile on his face. "Where do you keep the sheets?"

"In the other bedroom closet," I answered.

"Well, I don't want to sit here and drink all night." He finished his drink. "Let's go for a walk while it's not raining."

"Good idea." I swallowed my own scotch, and went to my bedroom for a sweater. On the way back, my cell phone rang.

"Detective Steckler?" It was a voice I knew but couldn't immediately identify.

"Mr. Patronio?" I guessed but it didn't sound quite like him.

"It's Vito Patronio," he said.

"Hello Vito, what can I do for you?" He must have gotten my number from one of the cards I gave to his brother or his parents.

"Tony is missing."

12

"I've got to go."

"I could tell that from your conversation," Dad answered with an understanding nod. "What happened?" He followed me into my office. I answered him carefully while I opened the safe and took out my Glock and ankle holster.

"I'm not sure. Someone I'm working with has gone missing."

"Is Denise involved?"

I hoped the way I phrased it would make it sound like she wasn't.

"Never mind. I can tell from your face that she is."

"I don't know that for sure."

"Are you going to take your extra guns with you?" His question surprised me.

"No, why?"

"I just want you to be safe." He gave me an unexpected hug.

"I'll be fine. Don't worry."

"I know." He took my jacket off the back of the chair and handed it to me. "Go. Stay safe and keep Denise safe too. I'll stay here for a while, though. I've had too much to drink to drive yet."

"That's fine. Just lock up before you go."

I stopped in front of Denise's picture. "Patronio's a good guy; don't hurt him." As I shut the door behind me, I saw Dad looking at Denise's picture with hope in his eyes for the first time in years.

With no time to waste, I skipped the elevator and ran down the stairs to the first floor. I waved to Tim as I went out the front of the building and ran to the garage.

As I pulled into traffic, I thought about what Vito told me about his brother's disappearance. It wasn't much. Patronio's security men had called their boss about an hour ago. The last thing they remembered was Patronio getting into their sedan near Unusual Gifts. Someone called or stopped the car afterward, but they weren't sure who. They had no recollection of what happened to Patronio. When they woke up, came to, or whatever, it was after six and they were in their car in a parking lot near the Expressway. I told Vito to call the boss back and send the security team to Patronio's.

Pham had to be behind Patronio's disappearance, but I wasn't sure how he'd done it. Puppy and his companion had seen us, but they hadn't enough time to organize a response before we left. I used a car no one knew was mine; Patronio even eschewed his beloved white to avoid notice.

What I could do about it? If they were able to get past Patronio's defenses, they could get past mine.

The loading zone in front of e-Scents was empty, so I parked in it. I entered the gallery and walked up to Eric who sat at the desk. There weren't any customers in the store. He scrutinized my face as I approached.

"Hello Detective." He reached under the desk to buzz me into the back room. "Go on up."

"Thank you." I ran up the stairs to find Vito and Pat waiting for me. Both men paced, anxious frowns on their faces, but stopped when I entered. They looked very out of place in Patronio's French rococo-inspired room wearing carpenter's overalls splattered with cement. They must have come directly from a job.

"Any news?" I shook first Vito then Pat's hand. They glanced at my forehead and face but said nothing about my lack of stitches or scar.

"No. The security men should be here soon," Vito said.

"Not that they did Tony much good," Pat added.

"I'm not sure any security force, even the police, would have done much better," I said.

"I doubt that," Pat replied, making me wonder if he or Vito knew what their brother, and the others like him, were capable of.

"What did their manager have to say?" I asked, changing the subject.

"That they'll commit their resources to finding Tony," Vito answered. I again wondered if Patronio had told the security team about the existence of gifted people.

"That's good news; they may have additional information sources and manpower," I told them.

"You can't call more police in?" Pat wanted to know.

"I'm not sure that's a good idea."

"Because he's gay?" Pat leaned in toward me. Vito put a restraining hand on his shoulder.

I would have to see how much they knew about the gifted. Hopefully they had a clue, otherwise, they'd think I'd lost my mind.

"No, that makes no difference to me or anyone else on the force." Few cops approved of the gay community, but that wouldn't impact how they'd react to a kidnapping.

"Then why?" Vito jumped in with a warning glance at Pat.

"Has your brother told you anything about his"–I hesitated for a moment–'gifts?'"

"If you're talking about making the room smell like perfume or burnt pizza, then yes. So what?" Pat threw his hands up in frustration.

Thanks, Patronio. He hadn't explained the full story to them. That made me wonder again how much he had told the security team.

"That's not the only thing he can do. He got away from his attackers the night Lisa Taylor died by filling the room with ammonia and bleach," I explained.

"That's poison, right? "Pat raised his eyebrows in surprise.

I nodded.

"Good for him. He should have killed the bastards."

"Is that what this is about, his gift?" Vito gave his brother a quick, nervous glance.

"I think so," I answered.

"Who wants him, the government?" Pat swallowed loudly.

"Not the government," I answered, reluctant to share the details of the case with them. "There's a group of people who are gifted like your brother, but in different ways. I think they're trying to coerce him into joining them."

"Why? What's the point?" Pat threw his hands in the air in frustration again.

I shrugged and shook my head. "I wish I knew."

"You said they had gifts different from Tony. In what way?" Vito interrupted his brother with the question. I guessed he was the peacekeeper in the family.

"I don't know that either," I told them, but their look of disbelief prompted me to give them what little information I had. "Some of them can influence how you think or behave. Or put you into a kind of trance for a while." I thought of the security guards.

"Jesus! How did Tony get involved with people like that?"

"They found him," I corrected.

Patronio's desk phone rang. We looked at each other; none of us wanted to answer the white and gold phone. Vito sighed on the second ring and picked it up. I noticed Pat's sad, slight smile; I was sure they'd faced similar situations in the past in Patronio's mansion. *Real men answer black phones.*

"Send them up. Thanks, Eric," Vito said and hung up. "The security guys are here. Their boss is with them." We faced the door, hearing the sounds of footsteps on the stairs.

"Rick Beam." A short, dark-suited man entered and held out his hand to Pat. He appeared about fifty years old with short, dark brown hair just beginning to gray. The material his suit was made of caught my eye. It was thick, like canvas. I'd seen that type of fabric before on the siblings. Being in a lighter color it made it easier to see. Beam and the siblings wore "bulletproof" garments.

Behind him stood the security guards from the car with Patronio earlier today. They physically towered over him but despite that, Beam was clearly in charge. They looked no worse for whatever happened to them.

"Pat, Tony's brother. That's Vito, the other brother." Vito stepped forward and shook Beam's hand. Beam eyed me. While I respected a man who could command a room, I kept my distance.

"Detective Steckler, NYPD." I stayed put and nodded my head at him. "Are these the two guards who were with Mr. Patronio when he 'disappeared'?" I knew the answer, but wanted to let Beam know this was my show without whipping out my badge or anything else, metaphorically speaking.

Beam held up his hands to forestall the men behind him from speaking.

"You're very young to be a detective," Beam challenged me and tried to establish control.

Great, a Napoleon complex. I stopped my annoyed eye roll when he reminded me of my new look. The Patronio brothers turned back to me at his statement.

"It's amazing what they can do with plastic surgery nowadays. I was in an accident recently. Despite my good looks"—I grinned at Beam. Thank you, Mr. Sanjiit—"I've got twenty years on the job."

"That's wonderful!" Beam exclaimed with a fake smile. "It was my understanding that Mr. Patronio wanted to keep this a private matter, rather than bring the police into it. But your experience will be a great addition to my team." Beam returned my grin.

"I'm well aware of Mr. Patronio's wishes, Mr. Beam. I'll do my best to honor them. But this is serious business. The people who tried to kidnap him the first time killed two others and made an attempt on my life."

Beam's smile faded only slightly before he replied, "I know the circumstances, Detective. Understanding such things is a fundamental part of my business."

"Glad to hear it." I nodded and moved past him to the men standing behind. "What happened this afternoon?" I kept my tone neutral without accusation. They glanced at Beam.

"Go ahead. Maybe Detective Steckler can shed some light on the matter," Beam said from behind me. There was sarcasm in his voice, but decided it didn't matter.

"Most of it's a blur," the man on the left said, eyes dropping. He swallowed twice. Despite that and the fact I hadn't spoken to him before today, he struck me as a man not used to failure.

"You were at the Commissioner's office?" I thought he looked familiar.

"Yes." He stared at me without expression. His eyes were wider than when I saw him last.

"Carl Steckler." I held out my hand to him. Both of them were freaked out by what happened to them. Time for "good cop".

"Steve Morgan." He shook my hand and his shoulders relaxed.

"Doug Stone," the other guard said as he offered me his hand. Both nodded to the Patronio brothers now they were out of their "guard" characters.

"What do you remember?" I wanted to bring us back to business. They didn't tense up this time but were uncomfortable.

One more "good cop" gambit before I took off the gloves. Some people responded better to the stick than the carrot.

"I know you're pissed off and embarrassed by losing the man you were hired to protect. I've dealt with the people responsible for it. They're pretty strange and have access to drugs that twist you up. They've used them on me as well."

That got the guards' attention. Beam and the Patronio brothers had moved around to face me.

"Some were no worse than a shot of vodka and a Viagra. Others, worse. With longer lasting effects." I thought about what Kim did to me.

The two men shifted uncomfortably.

"I don't know what you went through this afternoon, but I've been through something similar. Even with your training and weapons, you couldn't have done anything to prevent it."

The two men exchanged glances, and then looked at Beam who gave another slight nod.

"We're sorry that Mr. Patronio has gone missing." Morgan apologized to the Patronio brothers, upset.

Pat said nothing.

Vito replied, "Thank you, we appreciate it. Please tell us and the Detective everything you remember."

Morgan nodded.

"We followed Mr. Patronio and Detective Steckler out to Long Island. We circled around the businesses and parking lot and parked on the side opposite them. The spot was out of sight of people entering or leaving Unusual Gifts but we could still see Mr. Patronio. Our baseball caps, glasses, and lack of ties helped us blend in. We stayed alert; no one saw us. Then we followed the Detective and Mr. Patronio's car out of the lot when they left. When we stopped, Mr. Patronio got in our car, in the back seat."

This jived with what I knew, but didn't provide new information. Given how careful he'd been in the Commissioner's office if they had been spotted by any normal means, Morgan would have known it.

"Go ahead," I encouraged Morgan when his pause continued. He and Stone exchanged looks.

"Mr. Patronio told us to bring him back to the gallery. We pulled out of the parking lot. You followed us for the first few miles. The next thing we remembered, we were pulled off a few blocks down the same road and Mr. Patronio was gone."

"You remember anything else?" I addressed them both.

"Just the smell of flowers," Stone added.

"Flowers? What kind?" I tried to get more information but he only shrugged.

"I'm not a big flower guy, sorry."

I frowned with frustration but wouldn't have been able to answer the question either. If Patronio were here, he'd figure it out. I filed the information away and asked another question.

"We left Unusual Gifts early in the afternoon. What time did you come to?"

"It was 6:01. I looked at the clock," Stone answered.

"Yeah, that's right. I looked too," Morgan added.

"You woke up at the same time?" That seemed odd to me.

"Yes, I think so," Morgan answered.

"Were you groggy, sluggish, or hung over? Anything like that?" I tried to think of the usual side effects from being drugged.

They shook their heads.

"Some of the people involved in this case stole a body from the city morgue. They used a drug or something that left the security guard stoned, dazed, and horny. Is that how you woke up?"

"Not at all," Stone said. Morgan agreed with him. This didn't sound like Kim's gift.

"Were you on the shoulder of the road?" Beam stepped in closer.

"No, a parking spot right off of the road. In front of another set of businesses," Morgan answered.

"It doesn't sound like they pulled them off the road with a gun or without a plan," Beam answered my unspoken question.

"How so?" I wanted to know Beam's reasoning.

"The Mercedes was armored. Guns wouldn't have gone through the doors or the windows. Neither of them would have stopped if there was a problem or danger," Beam said. Stone and Morgan nodded.

"So, they or Patronio know the person who's got him?" That would make sense to me.

"Maybe. Or maybe Mr. Patronio left on his own," Beam answered.

"Hey," Vito growled and stepped closer to Beam. Pat was right behind him.

Beam didn't move. "Maybe he got away to keep them out of the line of fire," he said nonplussed.

"Oh." They both stepped back.

"We should explore as many possibilities as we can think of," Beam explained.

"Why are we wasting time asking each other questions! We should go to this porn store and kick some ass! They know where Tony is, I know it!" Vito said.

I felt all eyes on me. Beam waited for an answer as well, testing me.

"It would do us no good." I didn't want to say more yet. "They've got drugs and tools at their disposal we're not ready for."

"So, we shoot first and ask questions later! We should go! They've got Tony!" Vito's anger and frustration were plain.

"Vito"–I patted his shoulder–"you're worried about your brother. We are too. Rushing in could get us and your brother killed."

An idea formed, but just then the phone rang again. It was Patronio's private line. We looked at one another in surprise, then Vito picked it up.

"Hello. Bring it up." He hung up. "Eric signed for a package for you, Detective Steckler."

Only the police department knew I was at Patronio's. Them and whoever took Patronio. The department wouldn't send me anything.

We were silent as Eric came up the stairs. I wondered if anyone told him what happened but from his worried look, he knew. He stood back, but didn't leave as I opened the package.

It was letter-sized, but not completely flat. My name along with the gallery's address stood out on the front. There were no other markings or a return address.

"Are you sure you should open that? Could it be a bomb?" Vito's eyes were wide.

"Good question but I doubt it. Who delivered the package?" I turned back to Eric who, along with everyone else, took another step back and looked more nervous.

He shrugged.

"One of the bike messengers that work around here. He's delivered packages before. Wears the weird bug clothes like they all do," he added.

"Then I doubt it's a bomb. It may have gone off before it got here." The fear in the others' eyes told me they weren't reassured. "I'm going to open it. We don't have time to send for a hazmat team." The moment I said that, an earlier idea solidified.

"I'll open it, he's my brother," Pat said and reached for the envelope, but I moved it out of his reach.

"Just to be on the safe side, why don't you all wait outside in the hallway? I'll call you after I've opened it." I held each of their eyes with mine in turn until they blinked. Vito handed me scissors from Patronio's desk and I waited as they filed out of the room. Beam shut the door behind him. We all knew who ran the show.

"I really hope I'm not wrong about this." That's as close to a prayer as I'd gotten in years. I stopped believing in God. *Another thing Denise cost me.* I shook off the train of thought and opened the envelope.

Nothing happened when I clipped off the top. I looked inside and gingerly slid out the piece of paper. Along with the single sheet came a gold crucifix.

"Come back in!" I called out and unfolded the paper. It was a handwritten note with an address in Central Islip, New York, a rough town out near Hauppauge, on Long Island; near Unusual Gifts. My heart sank when I realized the handwriting was familiar to me – Denise's.

"That's Tony's cross," Pat said and pulled out an identical one from under his shirt.

"We each have one." Vito showed his as well.

Everyone ignored the tears in his eyes.

"What's the point of the message? There's no ransom note or anything?" Beam took the paper from my hand and gave the cross a cursory glance.

"It seems pretty clear to me. We have to go get him," Pat said.

"Anyone know anything about Central Islip?" Beam glanced at each of us in turn.

"Only that it's become a pretty bad neighborhood over the last decade with one of the highest murder rates in the state," I answered. Even growing up, we'd avoided Central Islip.

"So, what do we do?" Vito sounded scared but wanted to do something. I admired his courage; he was ready to rescue his little brother no matter what.

"Leave it to the professionals like the Detective and my team," Beam answered him. I nodded.

"It was your team that lost him in the first place." Vito leaned over the smaller man.

"And we're the team that will get him back safely," Beam answered calmly, neither blinking nor acknowledging Vito's threatening posture. Vito immediately deflated.

"You're right, you know more about this kind of thing than we do," he admitted. Pat nodded his agreement.

"So, what are you going to do?" Pat pushed us for details.

"Make some phone calls," Beam and I said at the same time.

"Why?" Pat didn't look impressed with our answer.

"To find out anything we can about the address," I answered Pat without looking at Beam. "Do you have any people out in that direction?" I checked with Beam.

"No, the furthest out I've got anyone is Queens. They'd get out there just about the same time we would," he answered. "What about you?"

"A few," I answered vaguely.

"Why can't we call the police out there and have them get Tony?" Pat paced with impatience.

"Because we don't really know what's going on yet, and your brother asked us to not bring in more police," Beam answered.

"And it wouldn't do your company any good if word got out that you lost Tony," Vito added.

"That's true but not a factor. If I thought it was the best thing to do, I'd be on the phone to the police myself." Beam didn't miss a beat in his reply. I almost believed him.

"Why don't we take a few moments to call our sources and see what we can dig up?" I didn't want to waste time with finger-pointing – at least until after we had Patronio back, safe and sound.

Beam nodded in agreement.

"What should we do?" Vito wrung his hands. He had caught some of his brother's impatience.

"Hold tight until we're done," I answered and handed him his brother's crucifix. "Keep this safe until you can give it back to him." I gave his shoulder a pat. "I'll make my calls from the hallway," I told Beam; we would want to keep our sources private. He nodded. Eric followed me out.

"I'll go back to the gallery in case anything else gets delivered."

I nodded but doubted we'd be getting anything else.

Eric stopped at the top of the stairway.

"Mr. Patronio is a great guy. He's done nice things for a lot of people and never made a big deal of it. I can't shoot a gun or fight but I can carry stuff and drive a car. If there's anything you need, let me know." His hands trembled, but he clearly meant it. My estimation of him went up a few notches.

"I may take you up on that, Eric. Thanks." He nodded, and went down the stairs.

I dialed Detective DeNali's number.

Twenty minutes later I was ready to go back and lay out the plan I worked out while DeNali confirmed my suspicions with his contacts in Central Islip. The local cops wouldn't go near the address. I wasn't sure anymore if it was due to fear and unease or whether one of the gifted had gotten to them; I hoped it was the latter.

I grinned while pulling the Charger back into the parking space by my condo. The look on Beam's face when I told him my plan had been priceless. It was eventually replaced with resignation and admiration. Beam said he would get everything we needed and meet me with his team in Central Islip. The Patronio brothers agreed to remain in the city and call in backup if they didn't hear from us within eight hours.

The prospect of seeing Denise again made me rock back and forth with energy. A young body didn't help me keep perspective.

The whole way up the elevator I whistled and ignored Tim as he scuttled back into his condo. I'd settle up with him being my father's spy eventually. My whistle petered out when I opened my condo door and saw Dad passed out on my living room couch. I shrugged and ignored him. He'd wake up in a few hours and go home shamefaced. Neither of us wanted to be drinking buddies.

I went into my office and opened the closet door. Old clothes and suits as well as neatly stacked boxes of folders, shoes, and gifts fell over as I searched. The large bag sat way in the back. Years had passed since I used the equipment it contained.

"I didn't hear you come in," Dad said, scaring me into hitting my head on the closet shelf. I felt his hands on my sides, in case I fell back.

"That was the point."

I finished swearing and rubbed the back of my head, irritated by his knack for sneaking up on me.

"Going on vacation?" He looked at the bag with puzzlement.

"No. I'm going after the man who was kidnapped today. Hopefully, I'll get a lead to Denise at the same time."

He bent down and picked something I couldn't see off the floor.

"This where you going?" Dad handed me the slip of paper with the address on it. I had shoved it in my jacket pocket earlier. It must have fallen when I smacked my head.

"It's one of the places we have to check out." I took the paper back, folded it carefully, and put it in my pants pocket.

As I shoved the junk back into the closet, I winced and promised myself I'd straighten things out later.

Dad followed me into the bedroom, his bleary eyes becoming worried as I strapped a holster on, checked the Glock for bullets, and put additional ammo in my jacket pocket.

"You think it'll be a bad one?"

"Just making sure I'm prepared." It could be a nightmare given the gifted people involved, but didn't tell him that.

"Will Denise be there?" He eyed the extra bullets I put in my pockets.

"I don't know." I hoped she would, but away from any action or danger. However, if she was anything like the sister I grew up with, she'd be in the thick of things. "Why don't you stay here for the rest of the night and go home in the morning?"

"I'm not sure what I'm going to do yet." He joined me by the door. We stood at Denise's picture.

"I'm coming for you, Denise," I said and touched the frame. Dad watched silently then grabbed me into a tight hug. *I've met my quota for the decade.*

"Be careful," he told me. I hugged him back, then picked up my bag and left.

13

I hit the "end" button on my cell phone and terminated the call with Beam. He'd purchased the equipment I'd asked for and would meet me near the address in Central Islip with his team.

The drive to the island seemed torturous this time. Being keyed up with a combination of anxiety and excitement at the prospect of seeing Denise again didn't help. Nor did the underlying worry for Patronio. We didn't have a lot in common, but I liked him.

Thankfully, there was no traffic at this time of night and I arrived in just over an hour. When close, I called Beam and we decided to meet in one of the parking lots surrounding Central Islip State Mental Hospital; our destination bordered on its property. The hospital was still open for outpatient care. While some of the buildings and property served other purposes, the vast majority appeared unused and abandoned.

I drove into the darkened hospital complex and shivered at the sight of the looming building in the distance. It towered twenty stories high, dark and neglected with the doors and windows on the first few floors bordered over and the higher window broken and empty like eye holes.

Eventually I spotted Beam's silver two-seater sports car – talk about your mid-life crisis: my-penis-still-works-when-I-take-Viagra car. Steve and Doug probably came in another vehicle, but the idea of the three of them squishing into the two-seater made me smile.

They waited for me in two cars parked in an out of the way place under low hanging trees. I pulled up next to Beam's diagonally parked car and got out.

"Are there security guards here?" I assumed they'd call the local police, or, if they had a deal with Yardley Pham, call him.

"I've already taken care of that." Beam's comment made me nervous. It must have shown on my face for he chuckled. "Don't look so alarmed, Detective. I bribed them with a few hundred dollars and a promise of more if they call the cops if the cars aren't gone after five hours."

Steve and Doug approached. "Did you have a chance to look around the place?"

"Yes. It's a Victorian monstrosity with four entrances and an outside door to the cellar. No guards or anyone watching from the windows. There are eight cars parked in the driveway," Steve answered.

"We haven't seen Mr. Patronio through any of the windows but there are at least eight people in there – otherwise why have so many cars? Mr. Patronio is either in one of the upstairs bedrooms with no lights on or in the basement. We didn't see any fire power, but the curtains are closed. It shouldn't be a problem to get in and out with Mr. Patronio," Dean said.

"Don't count on it," I cautioned. "Have you explained anything more about Patronio's kidnappers?" I hoped Beam had better luck than I did.

"No. My information is limited with educated guesses. I thought you'd have more answers, Detective." He was lying. From the darting glances between Dean and Steve, they thought so as well.

"It isn't much but it will help explain my approach," I told them and avoided an outright lie. I wanted to punch the smirk off Beam's face.

"You've got an idea of what we'll be facing." I looked at their faces and hoped they were as observant as I thought. Steve looked puzzled but Doug nodded.

"They've got some new designer drug, is that it? Makes you forget or puts you into some kind of trance for a while? They've used it to get over on people and Patronio's figured it out?" Doug sounded outraged. I thought about it and decided to go with his explanation. It made more sense than mine. Beam waited for my answer without expression but I saw the amused glint in his eyes. I pacified myself by imaging putting sugar in his gas tank.

"That's close," I lied, unhappy about it, but they wouldn't follow me into the house if I told the truth. "The cars in the yard are pretty nice, right?" I hoped I was right.

Steve nodded.

"That money came from somewhere. They've got a variety of drugs with different uses. They've caught the attention of the rich and famous, like the Chung family, who will pay a lot of money for them for personal use or investment."

Steve and Doug nodded this time; they understood powerful drugs drew powerful people for a variety of reasons, few of them pleasant.

"They've figured out a way to administer them in different ways; some by touch, some by smell, others by ways I haven't guessed yet, including getting it into eyes and ears." I waited for them to nod they understood. Beam turned away and walked to his car. He opened his car trunk and took out three bags. After leaving one on the ground, he brought two others back to our group.

"Which brings us to the first part of the plan." Beam handed a bag to each of them. I waited while Steve and Dean opened and shone their flashlights into the bags.

"Wetsuits? What are we gonna do with these?" Doug gave me an incredulous look and shook his head.

"Wear them," I answered. "They're the best thing we came up with on short notice that protects us."

"There are also extra-fine polyprene gloves, goggles to protect your eyes, and face masks with filters to cover your nose and mouth," Beam added. He set his own bag down and emptied its contents on the ground. Then he handed me gloves, goggles, and a face mask; I had my own wetsuit. I scuba certified years ago after investigating a case involving multiple murder victims dumped into the East River.

They watched Beam as he undressed, as if to be sure they weren't being punked. Then Steve shrugged and emptied his bag. Doug followed his lead. We were silent for the next ten minutes while stripping and struggling into the wetsuits, then put Kevlar vests over them.

It took a few minutes for us to work out ways to carry our weapons. I loosened my shoulder holster and pulled it on over the wetsuit and vest. My alternate gun, badge, and handcuffs clipped onto my belt. I doubted it would help me with the people in the house, but if more cops showed up, I wanted it.

"What's the plan, now we look like idiots?" Steve asked. We left off the goggles and breathing masks.

"Two of us go through the front door. Two around the back. Tell anyone you meet you're looking for Mr. Patronio. If they give you a legit answer, tell them leave. If they run, let them. If they try to touch you, get in your way, or doing anything you don't like, use this." I pulled four Tasers from my bag and handed them out.

"You want us to taser them?" Doug frowned. "Seems a little extreme coming from a cop."

"If necessary, yes," I answered, and then held up another four items.

202

"But before it comes to that, try spraying them with mace." I showed them the trigger at the top.

"Cool, cop toys," Steve said.

"Beam and I will take the front door. You two take the back. If they're locked, break in any way you can.

"And if Mr. Patronio isn't on the first floor?" Steve, it appeared, liked to think ahead.

"Stay together," I emphasized. "Check-in every two minutes. If we can't get an idea of where, you two go upstairs. We'll go down. Don't lose communication or sight of one another. Here's the last toy." I handed them each a walkie-talkie. "They're tuned to the same frequency. Check in every minute or so."

"Whoever finds Patronio first, get out and bring him here. If the other team is bogged down, get Patronio to safety." If Beam and I found Patronio, I'd send Beam and Patronio out then find Denise. I didn't care if I had to spray the house with mace or bullets; I wouldn't leave without her. "Any other questions before we start?"

No one answered.

"Lead the way." I gestured to Steve.

We walked single file through the small brush and trees that marked the edge of the hospital property. Coming to the edge of the lawn that marked the end of the perimeter, we stopped. The house had two stories, high sloping roofs, and a turret. A lot of the shingles were missing and paint peeled from the window and door frames. The wrap-around porch missed many of its posts. Three large windows on the first floor would provide easy egress from the porch. I wondered what the house looked like in its glory days before it had become a faded, painted lady.

A light gleamed to the right of the front door. It revealed an empty room. Given the eight cars parked along the edge of the driveway, I expected to see more lights and people around or blue flickering lights from television screens or computers.

"Change in plans. Beam and I take the front. You two take the back. I don't like that we can't see any activity. Until we know where they are, we meet in the hallway or a middle room. Then make a plan from there." Steve and Doug nodded. Beam made no comment. "Masks and goggles on. Let's go."

We donned our head gear and Doug and Steve walked away from us. The goggles worked well – they were wide and didn't limit vision in any direction. The mask strapped over both the nose and mouth allowed us to speak without taking it off. Beam and I waited a few seconds to let them get closer to the back door before we headed toward the front.

I took the lead as we walked up the creaky stairs and peered through the window in the door into the interior of the house. The entry hall had stairs leading upward, a darkened room on the left and a dimly lit room on the right. I caught a flicker of movement from the lit room and motioned to Beam to wait. A few seconds later, there was another flicker of a shadow. We both took out Tasers and unsnapped the flaps over our handguns. I put my hand out to the doorknob and waited for Beam to indicate he was ready.

No surprise – locked. The butt of the gun helped break the glass in the door. When there was no reaction, I pushed the shards out of the way and reached through to twist the knob. Nothing happened except we could hear muttering coming from the lit room. Beam and I took our guns out. I was surprised by the bright white walls and lack of dirt and dust; I had expected the place to be a dump.

"This is the police. Identify yourself," I called out. No response; the muttering continued. Sounds came from the back of the house – *that should be Dean and Steve*. "I'm coming into the room. Put your hands on your head and stand still."

The muttering sped up.

The dim light coming from around the other side of the wall let me see the bay window that curved outward on the other side of the doorway. Plain white curtains draped it. In front of the window sat a large, shabby but clean, couch. The wooden floor continued into the room, but I could see the edge of a throw rug. Again, I was struck by the cleanliness of the room – there wasn't a single dust bunny in the corners or under the couch.

I entered the room with Beam close behind me. Our guns drawn, ready to fire. I froze upon seeing the back of the bald head of a small, thin child; from his size, he looked to be about eight years old. He wore jeans and a blue t-shirt with black sneakers. Facing the opposite wall, he rocked back and forth from one foot to another and touched first the wall then a knee with his right hand. Next to him a faded, black leather wing-backed chair squatted beside an open door. With his left hand, he made a swirling motion above his head then tapped it. I holstered my gun, but kept my mace out. Using mace on a kid who could possess a gift as weird as the siblings' didn't faze me. Closer, I realized the muttering came from him.

"One, two, three, four. Pham will be mad about breaking the door." He punctuated each number by touching the wall or his pocket and swirling his other hand while he spoke. "Four, three, two, one. Run, run, run, run." His voice reminded me of a munchkin.

The closer we got, the faster his rocking and hand motions became. I glanced at Beam, but with the mask and goggles on, I couldn't get a read of what he thought. Hopefully he understood my intent as I holstered my mace and gun.

He nodded and kept his weaponry out.

"We're not going to hurt you," I said and crouched next to the boy, but stayed out of touching range. His motions became more pronounced and his scratchy voice louder. I leaned forward to catch his eye and froze. His face was too small for his head with a tiny chin, and a slight, pinched nose. I could see veins and blood vessels through his skin.

There were wrinkles on his forehead and around his mouth and eyes. The skin on his rail-thin arms sagged. I guessed he had the premature aging disease, progeria.

"One, two, three. Don't touch me. One, two, three. Don't touch me," he repeated over and over, changed his hand motions and shuffled away from me. Other than that, he showed no other reaction to my odd appearance. Given the rocking and the repetitive gesture, he may suffer from obsessive-compulsive disorder. Life dealt him a bad hand.

Steve and Doug came around the corner and entered the room with guns and Tasers drawn. In this homey setting, their appearance was out of place and frightening. The boy made no comment, but his arm movements changed and rocked even faster. Steve approached, glanced first at Beam then me and lastly the boy. He holstered his gun, knelt, and put his nightstick down on the floor, not fazed by the boy's condition.

"Hey, Kiddo. How's it going? We're not gonna hurt you. We're looking for a friend of ours. Maybe you can help us out," he said in a soothing voice.

The boy's eyes bulged as Steve spoke to him.

"Four, three, two, one. Run. Run. Run. Run. Four, three, two, one. Run. Run. Run. Run." He switched his rhyme again.

I felt like a bully. Steve must have felt the same way.

"It's okay, dude. We look scary but won't hurt you, I promise," he said, voice garbled because of the mask. Steve took off his goggles.

I shook my head but he ignored me. "See, we're just wearing these to protect ourselves. We know you won't hurt us either."

Steve leaned down further. The boy reached out and pulled the breathing mask away from Steve's face.

"Jesus Christ!" he said and leapt to his feet. "Get the fuck out of here!" He said to me, eyes wide, face pale and his breathing fast. Then he ran out of the room and through the front door, his goggles spun on the floor.

I repeated my instructions to Beam and Dean. "In case you haven't guessed, don't take your mask or goggles off." They nodded. I leaned forward to get a look at the boy's face. He still rocked and chanted but there was a smirk on his face that hadn't been there before.

"You know what you did, don't you?" I tried to sound like my mother had when she caught me getting into mischief.

He ignored me, but the smile didn't fade.

"Where is everyone else? Do you know? Can you tell or show me?" I was starting to sound desperate even to myself.

Again, he ignored me.

"This doesn't seem to be getting us anywhere," Dean said. "I'll go get Steve and bring him back." He grabbed Steve's gear off the ground.

"Make sure he puts everything back on before he comes inside," Beam told him.

Dean nodded and left.

"We need to keep moving. What do you want to do about our friend here?"

"We'll have to leave him behind us as we look," I answered, not happy about it. I wouldn't force the boy into a room or chair. His arms and neck were severely under-muscled and thin; we could break something.

"What if we put him in a closet?"

I wished I could see his face to tell if he was serious. Different people thought differently about what to do in these situations. Some would never leave an enemy behind them, no matter how frail they appeared. I could now appreciate their position.

"One-two-three-don't-touch-me. One-two-three-don't-touch-me. One-two-three-don't-touch-me!" The boy's motion and words became frantic. This might be the first time his gift hadn't worked. The ludicrous outfits and equipment worked so far.

"Do you know where Anthony Patronio is?" I tried again.

He continued his mantra.

"I don't think we're going to get anything useful from him." Beam left the room. A light from the next room came on. "I'll look around for a place to put him," Beam called out to me.

"What about Yardley Pham? Do you know where he is?" That hit a nerve. The boy rocked even faster and his chant became unintelligible.

"How about Denise? Do you know where she is? Or Kim?" I whispered. No change. "What about Captain? Do you know where Captain is?"

He stopped and looked at me for the first time.

"Captain will be mad if you hurt me," he replied and resumed his chanting. His odd motions never stopped.

"We're not going to hurt you. I want to find Captain because she is my sister. I want to help her." I wasn't sure how much he understood or how he would respond.

"Captain doesn't like a mess. You broke the window, she'll be mad at me," he said. Not exactly what I hoped to hear but he stopped chanting and looked at me out of the corner of his eye.

"If I clean it up will you tell me where she is?"

He continued to look at me sideways. I took that as a 'yes' and moved back to the front door. Carefully, I picked up the glass shards on the floor as well as the ones still in the door frame. It took me less than a minute, but when I turned around, the boy was gone.

Beam came back into the room carrying kitchen towels. He stopped when he realized the boy was gone.

"Where did our friend go?"

I shrugged, angry and unsure how to handle this situation. The boy may not be important. Was he the guard they posted or had he been left behind by the others? Were the people here criminals or victims? I preferred to deal with drug dealers, kidnappers, or murderers, arrest them, and feel no guilt.

The boy was likely the tip of the weird iceberg.

"We could call it a night and come back with backup," Beam suggested with a neutral tone.

I rejected the idea. The longer they had Patronio, the more likely something bad would happen. They could either kill him or disappear like Denise had. I refused to let the opportunity to find Denise slip away.

"No," I said. "If it's not tonight, it might be never."

Beam nodded.

The front door opened and Steve and Dean came in, both wearing their masks.

"Sorry. I shouldn't have taken anything off. Or let him get that close." Steve checked his mask as if to show us it wouldn't happen again.

"Did you smell or hear anything?" I wondered if there was any telltale sign.

"Not that I can remember. As soon as the mask was off, I became terrified. I had to get as far away from him as I could. It wasn't rational. I couldn't control it."

"When did it stop?" Beam looked at his watch.

"In the driveway. It just went away," Steve answered.

"Were you afraid to come back?" Beam clearly knew it only helped to figure out these powers.

"No."

"Are there chemicals in that room, Steckler?" Beam turned to me. It was hard to tell but I was certain Beam mocked my earlier claim about designer drugs.

"No," I answered, annoyed. "Back to business. Change of plans. There's nothing on the first floor, except perhaps, the boy. Let's go upstairs. I doubt anyone is up there. They would have heard us by now. Either they are downstairs or they gave us the slip and aren't in the house anymore."

"There's a stairway next to the kitchen. We passed it on the way in,"

Dean said.

"Good. You and Steve use that one and Beam and I will go up the front staircase." Each nodded in agreement. Steve and Dean left the room and Beam took the lead up the front staircase.

"Might as well do this with the lights on," he commented and flipped the wall switch as he passed it. As we climbed the stairs I wondered where the boy had disappeared to and if he had used a gift to disappear, or simply had a cubbyhole or secret passage. What was a kid in his condition doing alone? Who was in charge here?

Five bedrooms and two bathrooms made up the second floor. Each room neat and clean. Most held two beds, one had three, and the master bedroom had one king-sized bed. A few items of clothing hung in each the closets or sat neatly folded in bureau draws. All male or all female— no mixes to suggest heterosexual couples. Immaculate and empty, the place creeped me out.

"It's got to be in the basement," Dean said as he and Steve joined me and Beam. I ignored Steve's grimace, he ran screaming out of the place once. He couldn't be thrilled to stomp around in the basement.

"Was there a way down from the kitchen?" If not, we'd have to use the entrance outside.

"There were stairs going down but they may lead to one basement and the outside one to a dry cellar. We didn't try the outside door before we came in," Dean answered.

"First, we'll try the one in the house," Beam said.

"That'll be four of us going single file down a staircase. I'm not sure that's the best strategy," I commented.

Beam surprised me. He didn't bristle. "You have a suggestion? I prefer not to split the team up."

"If the two doors lead to the same basement area, we should be able to see one another or the beam from our flashlights. If that's the case, we meet in the middle and proceed from there. If not, we choose the better entrance based on what we see," I answered.

"Works for me," he said. Steve and Dean nodded in agreement.

We walked down the back stairway to the first floor. I reminded them to keep an eye out for the boy. We hadn't searched for hidden passages yet and hoped it wouldn't be necessary. Another scare-fest might send us all screaming into the night.

After making it back to the kitchen, we found the switch for the lights in the backyard. The kitchen, spotless, reminded me of a realtor's open-house. I checked out a hunch and opened a few of the doors and cabinets. The place, so clean and clutter-free; it had to be a safe house, not actually lived in. The utensils in the drawers, plates in cabinets, and cold-cuts and open food containers in the refrigerator contradicted my initial instinct.

"Someone in the house is definitely a neat freak," I explained to the others.

"Freak being the key word," Steve added.

"Probably." I betrayed Denise by agreeing with him. She kept things super clean. "Let's check the basement now. You and Dean"–I pointed to Steve–"take the back stairs. We'll take these. One of each team go to the first landing or bottom while the other waits at the top. The two at the top can signal to one another if the two at the bottom can't see one another."

"What about the walkie-talkies?" Beam checked his.

"Use them if we can't see one another while we explore," I answered. "And don't take your equipment off no matter what," I reminded them.

"I believe we know that now, Detective." Beam chuckled. "Isn't that right, Steve?"

"Totally on board," Steve answered with an emphatic nod.

"Great. Let's go." I pointed Steve and Dean toward the door.

"You want to go down or wait at the top?" Beam questioned my bravery, but I didn't take the bait. Now wasn't the time for a pissing contest.

"I'll go. You know Steve and Dean well enough to know if anything is wrong if they don't say anything."

Beam positioned himself so he could see me on the stairway and Steve and Dean in the kitchen window.

On the right of the stairs where the first floor ended, the plaster wall changed to poured cement. Handles and a banister stuck out from the wall. On the left, opposite the plaster, free-standing shelves lined up against the stairway. The shelves sagged with canned foods and household supplies, all neatly arranged. The stairs and shelving ended at the same place, which made it impossible to see around them and into the basement itself. Probably deliberate.

As I reached the bottom step, I looked up to let Beam know I was there.

"Steckler, there's something going on–" Beam called down but was cut off and all the lights went out.

"Beam! Beam! You up there? What's going on?" I called up the stairs and turned on my flashlight. Silence. No sounds of a struggle either. I pointed the light up the stairwell. No sign of Beam. I considered going forward to explore the basement but knew I should check on him first. Before I went three steps back up, the door slammed shut. Then someone threw the bolt.

"Great, just great," I said and almost giggled. *Don't get hysterical, you've still got your guns.* I went up to the door and tested it. Locked. I called out and hoped Steve or Dean stood on the other side but got no response. I could use my gun to shoot the lock off, but didn't know Beam's location. I didn't want to shoot him, Steve, Dean, or the boy.

The walkie-talkies failed to reach Beam, Steve, or Doug. I was on my own for now and hoped they were okay. Searching the bottom of the steps failed to reveal them or another way out; perhaps the outside door hadn't been locked.

An extra step waited at the bottom. It was a tool used as a delaying tactic by gangsters and pirates chased by police or other thugs. They'd go down the stairs, jump over the step and the people chasing them would trip on it giving them time to escape. Usually, there was a secret passageway out. Maybe the back stairway had been it.

I flashed the light around the room. Small and crowded, the air felt much cooler than upstairs. The walls, covered with shelves, held anything from canned peas to toilet paper. All neatly arranged and in alphabetical order. In the corner opposite the stairway stood a closed door. I opened it and hoped to find Steve and Dean.

It revealed a small alcove on the other side. On the left, storm cellar stairs led up to the backyard. Plywood covered the wall on the right. Before me another wall loomed, but after pushing on it, I found it to be a hinged door, ajar. I pushed it further open and found a wooden staircase leading down. Wood slats and two-by-fours lined the walls around this staircase. It reminded me of pictures I'd seen of mining tunnels from the last century. I knew I'd have to go down those steps but checked the storm cellar door. Locked.

Dean and Steve might be outside, but I doubted it. Everything pointed toward the hidden stairway and where it led. I returned to the alcove and pushed the disguised door all the way open. The stairs surprised me by being sturdy and made of pressure treated lumber. Built recently and well maintained, I wondered about their purpose.

I remembered the extra step from the inside stairway, but there was no trap this time. At the bottom was a long tunnel leading off into the distance. The flashlight revealed a naked bulb hanging from an extension cord, which, like the bulb, looked new. I spent a few moments trying to figure out which direction the tunnel went and where it led. It could only be another escape route or connected to one of the state mental hospital buildings. *Why would someone have secret passages to them?*

As I looked down the length of the tunnel, I saw a flicker of light in the distance. The walls turned to the left. I covered my flashlight with a hand to see better. Yes, it flickered again. Whoever they were, they already knew I was here, so I uncovered the light and checked the floor for anything that would trip me. Finding it made of smooth cement and clear of obstacles, I shut off the light. Maybe approaching in the dark would give me an edge.

I walked forward and trailed my hand along the wall to provide a sense of direction and avoid the studs that lined the walls. It seemed like it took hours. As I approached the turn in the tunnel, I saw a dim light around the corner. Carefully, I edged my way around the corner, Taser in hand, when my foot scrapped on a raised portion of the floor. I blinked at a sudden flash and waited for my eyes to adjust and the after image to fade. Something creaked in front of me. I froze.

"Don't try to hide. I can see you despite the darkness and your scuba suit," a raspy and deep female voice said. I remained silent and tried to get a fix on where he, or she, hid, and if they bluffed.

"You're too short and thin to be either of the bodyguards, and too tall to be Beam. That makes you Steckler," the voice said.

"That's right, Detective Steckler. Where's Anthony Patronio? Where is Denise?" I stepped forward and pointed the flashlight where the voice came from. I hoped to momentarily blind them and take control of the situation. Again I froze, this time in surprise.

Before me stood a man wearing surfer shorts. His skin shone white – not pink, tan, or olive white that we associate with the term "Caucasien" but white like an albino person. His pallor reminded me of fish or sea creatures. Long, white hair surrounded his face. Before he put on a pair

214

of sunglasses I caught a glimpse of solid gray orbs with no whites showing.

"So it's true, you're Captain's brother?"

"Yes. Where is she? Will you bring me to her?" I stepped closer to him and reached for my Taser. He took a corresponding step backward.

"She kept us going for a long time with promises you'd rescue her and us from Pham. And here you are in a scuba suit with a flashlight and toy buzzer." He laughed.

"It was a last-minute trip and I didn't have anything else to wear." I caught a glimpse of a smile and saw his lips had no tint; they were the same white as his skin.

"You have Captain's sense of humor. I wish what she said was true, but doubt you can help us." As he spoke, lights appeared under his skin like sparks struck from within, and swam around his torso. He stepped toward me and raised his hands above his head.

I pointed my Taser at him.

"One more step and I'll shoot." I stared at him, mesmerized by the flickering. What kind of gift did he have and what it would do to me.

"That will just tickle. Besides, I don't need to be any closer," he answered and the flickering turned into a flash. An arc of lightning or electricity spiked out from him. I flew backward and hit the wall of the cave behind me. I fell to the floor twitching.

"So much for Captain's brother, the hero," a new, deep voice said behind me. I couldn't open my eyes to see him.

"It was a nice dream while it lasted," I heard the white man say with regret in his voice.

"What do we do with him now?" the new voice asked.

"Take off the wetsuit and put him with the others until Pham is lucid again," the white man answered. I felt hands underneath my legs and back and I forced my body to struggle against them.

"I'll hurt him if he fights me," the deep voice said.

"Pham is only going to kill him anyway," white man answered. "Kitten said he has no gift."

"He's Captain's brother. If I hurt him without a good reason, she'll get even. Pham will have to force me to do anything to him."

"Me too," the white man said.

"Would you please just knock him out before he wakes up?" the deep voice grew sharp.

"Okay." Then I felt a hand on the back of my neck, a searing burn and that was it.

14

I woke up on a cold, hard surface. Thankful for that small miracle, I kept my eyes shut and took inventory: a slight headache and burning on my chest where the electricity hit me. Several people breathed near me. I cracked one eye open and saw a grayish-green wall and ceiling above me. The other eye, once open, didn't show me anything different. I'd have to turn my head to discover something new, but didn't want to let anyone know I was awake.

"You opened your eyes. How are you feeling?" Beam leaned over me. Despite being unhurt, I felt embarrassed to find myself naked except for a sock on my left foot. A quick look at Beam revealed him in the same state except his sock was on the right foot.

"Not too bad, all things considered," I answered.

Dean, wearing only a t-shirt, leaned against a wall. Steve sat naked on the floor. On the right of me, a thick door with steel bars for a window, a keyhole and a small slot at the bottom locked us in. Face pressed against the wall, another person lay on the floor. The odd proportions and long, thick, midnight-black hair meant it could only be Va^n, either in or post-transition. To the left of me, a built-in-the-wall toilet and sink – like the ones in prisons – protruded from the wall.

"Is Va^n awake?" I averted my eyes and sniffed, but didn't smell any jasmine.

"Some grunts, groans, and occasional mumblings but that's it," Beam said. "That's one of the siblings, isn't it?"

I nodded.

"The skin doesn't look all that sensitive," he observed. Oddly enough, I was able to follow his line of thought.

"It's not. They wear the robes as protection against other gifted. That's what made me think of the scuba suits. Their robes are light weight polyethylene and their head coverings serve as face masks."

"I wish we had one of the robes right now," Dean said, his hand sliding down to cover his groin. I took my sock off and put it next to the toilet. One of us might need it later.

"Get past it. We could be here for a while. One of the first steps to break prisoners of war is to strip them of all but one item of clothing. It's a constant reminder that you're naked and vulnerable. If you're completely naked, you adjust to it and forget about it that much sooner," I said.

Dean shrugged and took off his shirt. Beam removed his sock.

"What happened to you?" I wanted to know how they'd been caught. Something about Va^n bugged me and I knew it was important.

"I was at the top of the stairs. Somebody hit me on the head and I woke up here. I don't have a headache or anything, though." Dean rubbed the back of his head.

"Same with me," Beam said and we turned to Steve.

"They hid under the stairs and tripped me. Then gave me a shot to the head. I'm not banged up or anything, though." He examined his legs and hands as if to double-check. I stayed silent about it, but suspected we had healing help at my sister's request.

"I got a little further into the basement and followed the tunnel. A white guy; I mean really white, waited for me. He electrocuted me." I looked down at my chest, but there weren't any blisters or redness. *Thanks, Denise.* "Then some big guy came up behind me and held my arms while Electro-boy got me again," I added.

"That wasn't a guy, it was a giantess," Beam corrected me.

"Well, then that does it," I said with a strained smile, "The circus is officially in town." That got a chuckle. I glanced at Va^n and something clicked. "Shit." My smile faded.

Beam followed my gaze. "What is it?"

Va^n hadn't moved.

"Va^n isn't finished transitioning." It bothered me when I first saw Va^n's prone body. The skin tone wasn't as white as I remember Cha^a's being. The legs looked similar to one another and still had hair.

"So?" Beam shrugged, indifferent.

"I assumed Va^n was the one who got to the two of you"–I looked at Dean and Steve–"and taken Patronio to Pham. But look at him. He's completely out of it."

"These people aren't getting to us with drugs, are they? They've got some kind of powers or something. Like freaky supermen or something, right?" There was accusation in Dean's voice.

"You must have suspected something like that after working with the siblings," Beam said, turning the accusation back on him.

"We talked about it. But the siblings were so weird, we assumed we imagined things," Steve put in. "We were paid to protect them, not spy on them."

"If Va^n didn't kidnap Patronio, who did?" Beam asked.

Without answering, I struggled to a standing position. I walked over

219

to Va^n, squatted down, and inhaled deeply through my nose. He already smelled of jasmine. I motioned Dean over.

"You said the last thing you remembered before Patronio disappeared was the smell of flowers. Did it smell like Va^n?" Dean gave me a puzzled look and sniffed Va^n's hair. I stopped him from touching it in case something happened.

"Yes, that's the smell. Why?" Steve came over to smell Va^n.

"The siblings use that smell to draw you to them. If you look at them, they can mesmerize you. You'll do whatever they say if they touch you," I said. We all took a step away from Va^n when he unexpectedly took a deep breath. We watched anxiously, but Va^n made no other moves.

"That means it was one of the other siblings," Beam answered his earlier question.

"Are they working with Pham?" Steve looked angry now.

"I don't think so," I answered. "They have history with him. He terrifies them."

"Then why kidnap Patronio and lead us here with that note?" Beam turned away, not really expecting an answer.

Someone spoke outside the door. A key turned, a bolt drew back and the door slid open sideways.

With the exception of Va^n, we all stood, ready to take advantage of the situation if we could. Outside the door, Kim posed with two women on each side of her. One loomed too tall for me to see her shoulders or head — I assume *she* stood behind me in the tunnel. The other over-weight woman had skin so brown it was almost black. Her mouth caught my attention; light gray lips covered with glistening saliva. Each of the strange women held pistols.

Kim stayed outside the door, and sized each of us up, her gaze lingering at our groins. If she meant for us to feel uncomfortable, she failed. I suspected Steve and Dean were Special Ops and had been dropped into forests, maybe even cities, buck-naked. Beam didn't appear to give a rat's ass that anyone saw anything. With my recent facelift, *thanks, Sis*, I wasn't embarrassed either.

"That didn't go as well as you hoped, did it?" Kim smirked as she walked into the room. The two other women followed her.

Dean made a move toward Kim.

"Don't touch her, Dean," I cautioned him. "You won't like what happens." He froze in place.

"Liar." Kim grinned at me.

"What's going on, Kim? Where's Patronio? Where's Denise? Give us our clothes and get us out of here." It was worth a try, but she had a crazy look in her eyes again and her movements were quick and jerky.

"Pham's back among the living. They're with him. He's unhappy with Denise and trying to addict Patronio," Kim answered. "I want to bring you to him so he has somebody other than Denise to make miserable."

"Who's Denise?" Beam gave me a suspicious scowl.

"His sister and my wife," Kim said. "Let's go." She pointed out the door. Beam flashed me an irritated look.

"I'll break you like a toy." Steve made a grab for Kim's gun. She shot him in the leg and he went down with a groan.

"That was stupid," Kim commented, then nodded at the short, stocky woman beside her who made a hacking sound then spit on the ground. When it hit, it smoked and ate a hole in the cement. "Do anything else and Pica will kiss you."

Pica smiled at Dean; her teeth were thick and gray. They looked like stone.

"What do you want with us, Kim? Let us get Patronio and go," I pleaded with her, hoping she wouldn't shoot anyone else.

"We're bored," Kim answered. "I promised Denise I'd leave you alone, but I didn't say anything about the other three." The look she gave Steve didn't bode well for them.

"What did they do to you?" I hoped to distract her.

"They're men. What they didn't do to me they did to some other girl. We're just here to even the score."

I flinched from the hatred in her eyes. An argument could make things worse.

"Freya, you take the injured one. Pica and I will handle the other two," Kim told the tall giantess who bent down and picked up Steve as though he were a child. Steve struggled and Kim stroked his arm. He immediately relaxed. Before either of them could react, Kim grabbed Beam and Dean. Her touch on them caused the same effect; each lost their threatening stance and became aroused.

"I like the little one." Pica leered at Beam and let out a deep, throaty laugh.

I tried to grab the gun from Kim.

Freya swung her hand at me and I hit the wall opposite the door, almost on top of Va^n.

"I didn't make any promises," Freya said with a deep laugh, and left the cell with Steve in her arms.

"Don't press your luck, Carl. Captain's used you as a symbol of hope for twenty years. You finally show up and totally fail Denise and the rest of us," Kim told me, bitterness in her eyes. "Come on, lovers," she said to Dean and Beam who stood waiting for her. They followed the two women out the door without a backward glance.

Va^n was right below me, and I moved away from him the moment the cell door slammed shut. His skin had paled even further and the hair from his legs lay scattered on the floor around him. I sat on the floor and tried to figure out what to do to turn the situation around. If I could get to Denise, it would help.

"Detective Steckler, are we alone?" Va^n spoke.

"Yes," I answered, unhappy to be locked away with a killer.

"Help me sit up. I'm very weak."

"No. I know what that will do. Tú explained a lot after you shot

Cha^a."

"My transformation is not yet complete. My gifts haven't come to their fruition. You are in no danger."

I stayed still.

"Please. We do not have much time before they come for one, or both of us." Va^n sounded exhausted.

I relented, but kept my eyes averted. I'd seen too much today as it was.

Va^n spent a few moments recovering.

I said nothing; I didn't want to create any sort of camaraderie.

"I did not willingly kill Lisa Taylor or Cha^a," Va^n said.

"Whatever."

"Detective, I know it's hard for you to believe me. Tú made me do it."

I pursed my lips. Either I had to beat Va^n senseless or listen. At the very least, it would take my mind off the other guys, Denise, and Patronio.

"I'm listening. Why would Tú want you to kill Lisa Taylor? There was no need. Patronio would have gone with you that night. Lisa didn't see your faces." I let Va^n hear the anger in my voice.

"Tú wanted to ensure you would investigate the case."

I wanted to argue it wasn't possible to know what detective would get assigned to a case, but remembered Captain Perez said she saw a sibling talking to the dispatchers that day.

"Why?"

"I told him about your sister's belief that you have a gift that would allow you to kill Pham. I tried to warn you at the bar, but Tú stopped me. Cha^a knew what Tú was doing, but wasn't strong enough to stop Tú. Then Tú made me kill Cha^a and go in search of Pham so I could lead you to him."

"Where's Patronio now?" I demanded.

"I have no idea. I've not been out of this cell since I got here." I suspected as much, but hoped Va^n heard what I said earlier.

"Why'd you take Cha^a's robe?"

"You've seen only a few of the gifted Pham controls. If they scared Tú, with all of the gifts of a sibling, I needed something to protect myself," Va^n answered. That confirmed my suspicions their robes and head coverings protected them from others as much as they protected people from their gifts.

"Did you know you would become a sibling when you killed Cha^a?

"No, I knew I took a risk working at the bar, but I'm gay and my parents owe much to the siblings. By working there, I was able to repay a portion of their debt. They would rather risk me than my brothers who would give them grandchildren."

"Did Tú make you run my car off the road?"

"No, that was my idea. I hoped to scare you away," Va^n answered.

"You could have killed us!"

"What do you think will happen to you now?" Va^n answered with ire.

"You have a point," I conceded. "How did you get involved with Pham in the first place?"

"Kim and Denise came to the bar. They heard rumors about the siblings and came to check them out. They asked me some questions and I told Tú who suspected they were connected to Pham and had me talk longer with them. Afterward, Tú forced me to pretend I would deliver the siblings to Pham while I was actually spying on Pham and trying to find a way to kill him."

Va^n leaned back against the wall, pale and sweaty, heat radiating outward like a furnace.

"What's happening?"

"The transformation continues. It comes in waves," Va^n grunted at me.

224

I smelled jasmine and leapt to the other side of the room.

"You are in no danger from me, Detective. My transformation is far from complete."

When I glanced at his crotch, the usual stuff was still in place.

"Thanks, but I'll be the judge of that." I turned away.

We were silent for so long I started to get sleepy.

"Detective." Va^n broke the long, almost tranquil, quiet. He stared at me, waiting for me to answer. "Detective. Please. Help me."

Va^n's pain made me turn back despite my better judgment.

"What do you want me to do?"

"Kill me."

"What? Why? Is the pain that bad?" I remembered Tú's answer about how painful it was. "It should be over soon."

"It isn't the pain. But you are right, the transformation is nearly complete," Va^n said.

"I'm a police officer. I'll bring you to justice, but not kill you. Besides, you told me Tú forced you to kill Lisa." My sympathy faded.

"Tú did," Va^n answered, eyes closed. The skin on Va^n's torso twitched and heat radiated at me. Not sure what to do or how to help, I squatted down, ready to jump away, but Va^n passed out.

Then a hand shot out and grabbed my arm.

I shouted in surprise and tried to pull it out the grasp, but Va^n was stronger than I guessed.

"Detective. Listen to me." Va^n took a breath, ignoring my continued attempts to pull my hand free. "The transformation is nearly complete. Pham touched me with his gift. Your sister and other gifted are addicted to him and under his control. But their gifts are nothing compared to the siblings. Please, kill me before Pham makes me do more evil than Tú ever considered." Va^n suddenly released my arm and I fell over.

When I checked again, Va^n was unconsciousness.

225

I stood over Va^n and wondered if there was anything I could or should do to help. Banging on the door might get attention, but I was sure it would result in laughter or make things worse. I paced, but couldn't think of any way out. The NYPD had no idea where I was, and it would be some time before the Patronio brothers notified them. That would be too late.

Tired, I squatted back down on the floor. Va^n groaned and I looked again. In the short time since I woke up, Va^n's hair had gotten thicker, blacker, and his lips had turned a brighter red. I forced my eyes away and turned my back to him, knowing the pronoun no longer applied.

My mind kept coming back to Denise – where was she? What was Pham doing to her? What did Va^n mean that Pham addicted people to him? Had he addicted Denise to him? Is that why she hadn't broken away from him? Part of me was afraid of what may happen when I got out of the cell; another part didn't care as long as I could see Denise.

I distracted myself from that train of thought and pondered Denise's nickname: Captain. She had been Captain of the junior and varsity Girls' softball teams with an outstanding ability to get them to focus and play their best. Under her captaincy, the teams made it to the state championships. I wondered if that was her gift, getting people focused on a goal.

Despite the seriousness of my situation and worry for the others, I became drowsy and dropped off to sleep.

The sound of the door sliding open woke me. I blinked up at the giantess, not sure how long I slept, but didn't think much time had passed. Va^n was still out.

"What now?"

"Pham wants to see you." She handed me a pair of long pants. "They're from Captain." The thought of overpowering her occurred to me but one look at the muscles in her forearms and the smirk she gave convinced me not to try. I took the pants and turned around to put them

226

on – my sense of modesty overwhelmed the fact she'd already gotten an eyeful.

Her grin when I turned back told me she understood the irony of my actions.

"Where are the others?" I made no move to follow her.

She turned back to me. "They're fine. We distracted Kitten and put them into another cell." She waved me through the door. I complied to keep her talking. Earlier, she mentioned being disappointed I hadn't rescued them from Pham.

"Distracted her?" I guessed, referred to Kim. "Is there something wrong with her? She was wild when Denise and I first met her, but now she seems …"

"It happens to all of us after we've gotten a treatment. It fades soon enough," she answered and closed the cell behind me.

She didn't lock the door.

"What kind of treatment?"

"Same kind you got, making her younger and stronger."

We walked down a long corridor with other closed and locked doors.

"That could make me crazy?"

"Probably not. The first few times only makes you jumpy. Crazy doesn't happen until you've had a lot more of them."

"How many have you had?" We came to the end of the corridor.

She took a key out of her pocket and unlocked the door. The key struck me as improbably small in her hand. She waited as I walked through. The door swung shut with a thud. We were in another corridor; this one seemed less like a prison and more like a hospital hallway. There weren't very many doors or lights along it. It was empty. I noticed she hadn't locked the door behind us again.

"A few. Pham's only had me a few years." Her biceps were the size of my thighs.

"How many has Denise had?" I worried about her sanity.

227

"More than me, but a lot less than Kim," she answered as we walked down the corridor. There wasn't anyone in the corridor or the rooms we passed.

I noticed again how clean everything was. Who did all the work?

"Kim's the same age as Denise and me, why would she need more?"

The tall woman snorted. "Kim was one of Pham's first. She's a lot older than she looks," she said.

"How old is she?"

"No clue."

"How old are you?" I scrutinized her face.

"Didn't your mother teach you any manners? You never ask a lady her age." I managed to stop myself from telling her she was no lady. She looked at me and chuckled, knowing what I hadn't said.

"We're in the state mental hospital, right?" I hoped our exchange had softened her up.

"Yes," she answered, her tone now short. I shuddered. The place and the stories about it creeped me out as a kid. The way our steps echoed didn't help.

"In the basement?" This time, she just nodded and frowned. I made a wild guess and asked, "Pham fixed it so you can't talk about where we are?" She shot me a quick look and nodded. We came to the end of another corridor and she opened a door. Behind it was a cement stairway leading upward. Faded paint on the wall said we were in sub-level three.

"What happens if you don't do what Pham wants?" I could guess the answer but wanted to keep her talking.

"Pain. A lot of pain," she answered, and motioned for me to go up the stairs.

"Ugh," was all I could think of to say as I walked upward.

"No shit."

"You can't fight him?"

"We do what we can."

I noticed she said "we" and remembered the unlocked doors behind us. There was a small glass panel in the door at the top of the stairs. A security guard walked by us. I thought about getting his attention, but then felt her hand on my neck. It was so large her thumb and fingers nearly met under my Adam's Apple.

"Don't try anything." She tightened her grip on my neck. "I don't want to hurt you; you seem like a decent guy and you're Captain's brother." She waited a moment and then opened the door. We entered another long corridor. The guard must have walked around a corner.

"I could force you to hurt me to get their attention." I tested her.

"Pham has control of most of them, including all the guards."

I groaned. Beam checked in with the guards at the gate. Pham knew we were coming all along.

She took her hand from around my neck and pushed me in the opposite direction from the guard.

"What's Pham going to do to me?" I thought I had a good guess.

She shrugged.

"He's angry with Captain. She set this up but won't do anything to her; her gift is too strong. He may make an example of you or make you one of us."

"I have no idea what you're talking about." I admitted. She hadn't said what I expected.

"He may kill you or just addict you to him. If he addicts you, you'll do whatever he says whenever he tells you to do it."

"You're addicted to him?"

She nodded and slowed as we came to a double door in the hallway. Swallowing nervously, she reached out to push the door when it swung open. We both jumped.

The red-headed man who licked my face stood in the doorway. He wore carpenter's overalls and a shirt declaring him a cookie monster. I couldn't see his face with him looking down at the floor.

"Puppy! Jeez, you scared me half to death," she chided him and moved toward the doorway. He kept his head down and didn't move out of the way.

"Puppy, let us in." He shook his head back and forth like a terrified child. This confirmed my belief he was definitely developmentally disabled.

"Why not? Did Pham send you?" He nodded his head up and down, eyes fixed on the floor. His breath caught. It sounded like he would burst into tears at any moment.

I touched his arm. "It's okay, Puppy. Don't cry," I said.

He glared at me from under his hair, teeth bared in a silent snarl.

I dropped my hand and looked up at the giantess, but she hadn't seen the exchange. She was too tall.

"Puppy, Pham wants Captain's brother brought to him?"

Again he just nodded.

"You can take him." The tension dropped from her face and shoulders. I moved forward, then felt a light touch on my neck.

"Good luck," she said quietly.

"Thanks."

Puppy stepped backward to let me in

Behind him, a reception area led to a long hallway lined with offices. Scattered randomly about, dusty and damaged furniture gave testament to my belief this particular place no longer served an official purpose.

Puppy shut the door behind me. "Here, take this." Puppy held out a .38 magnum. His voice sounded different.

I took the gun and checked for bullets. "What's going on, Puppy?"

"I'm not Puppy, I'm Wolf." He looked straight at me for the first time and bared his teeth. Now he stood straight, shoulders back, eyes clear and intelligent. I faced a very different man than the one who straddled me in my bed.

"What am I supposed to do with this?" I ignored his statement, held up the gun.

"Kill Pham," he said.

"Do it yourself!"

"I can't, Pham controls Puppy. If I go against his understanding of Pham's directions, Puppy takes over again," Wolf growled at me, frustrated. I took what he told me at face value. Given everything else going on around me, a person with dissociative identity personality disorder didn't faze me at all.

"You're not addicted to Pham?" I wasn't sure how that would work.

"Pham doesn't know about me."

"Will a bullet work on him?"

"Probably. It's worth a shot." His quirked lips told me the pun was intentional.

"What happens to the people addicted to him if he dies?"

"We'll go into withdrawal. Some of us may die. Pham controls our withdrawal pain and makes it worse so that we do as he says. If he's dead, most can get through it."

"Most?" I probed, hoping he would tell me Denise was strong enough to survive.

Wolf shrugged. "I'd rather try and die than be on his leash."

"Great. Good to know. Where is Denise? You call her Captain," I said, to get us back on point.

"I know who Denise is," Wolf answered me.

I didn't like the way her name lingered on his lips.

"Where is she?"

"In the main office on this floor with Pham and the others." He pointed down the hallway past the foyer. The hallway lights were off. I couldn't see anything past the first few office doorways that lined both sides.

"Who else is there?"

"Trainer, Kitten, and Frankie," he answered.

"Kitten is Kim, right?"

He nodded.

"I know what her gift is." I shuddered. "What about the other two, what can they do?"

"Trainer is strong and fast. He was at your condo that night. He can make your body stronger by touching you," Wolf said.

"What about Frankie?"

"He sings and puts you to sleep. Frankie does anything Pham says, he stopped fighting a long time ago. Trainer just likes that Pham lets him hurt people."

"Great," I said. A muffled scream come from the back of the hallway.

"Are they hurting Denise?" I stepped past him toward the back office.

"Wait." Wolf stopped me with a touch of his hand.

"I don't have much choice. You said Puppy wouldn't let you go against Pham."

"He won't. But I can find the others and send them to you." I heard another agonized moan.

"I can't wait," I said. "Send them when you can. Or let them go." I checked to make sure the safety was off.

"You don't have a gift, do you?"

I shook my head.

"Shit. I hope Captain knows what she's got us into."

"Me too," I said and walked past him.

My heart pounded as I walked down the darkened hallway. Office doors randomly punctuated my path. In each, a small, dirty, window reflected my image as I passed. The hair on the back of my neck bristled as I waited for more of Pham's weird menagerie to burst out. I checked up once to make sure a spider or spit-ball-boy wasn't glued to the ceiling waiting to pounce on me. Halfway down the hall, I heard a whispered, "good luck," and Wolf, or Puppy, left.

I was aware of the silence behind me after his exit. No sounds came from the hall for a few minutes. Maybe they were on a torture break and nothing more serious happened. With that thought, I ran the last yards to the end of the hallway.

This door was different from the others; larger, made of wood, no window. The doors behind me were white, thin, and narrow, and looked like I could kick them open even before my anti-aging treatment. The one in front of me, the boss's office, seemed heavy and solid. No super-cop move would bust this one open.

I listened and tried to determine if anyone was in the room, how many, and where they might be. After hearing nothing, I knew I had to wing it and hope for the best.

Many of Pham's people resisted him in little ways, left doors unlocked and misdirected attention hoping someone would come along and knock him off his throne. I had no idea if I was the one to do it, but didn't care about that. If Denise and Patronio got away from him, I'd be content. Pham's turn would come once they were safe.

As quietly as possible, I turned the knob and pushed the door open wide enough to look through with one eye. No response from the other side. I couldn't see anything. Time to make my entrance.

15

I stood in the hall outside the room. My heart pounded with anticipation. The time had come at last.

A male voice called out to me, "We've all waited years for Captain's heroic brother to rescue her."

A flush of anger and guilt filled my mind and pain built up behind my eyes.

"Better late than never, asshole." I spat at him and slammed the door open, gun up and ready. A strange tableau confronted me, but my eyes were drawn to the woman sprawled on the floor in front of an Asian man I assumed to be Pham.

"Denise." My eyes teared up. Sweat matted her hair to her head. She breathed quickly and shallowly: a junkie in withdrawal.

"Hey," she said weakly and clutched her stomach.

I tore my eyes away from her and pointed my gaze, and gun, at the man in the center of the room behind Denise. It couldn't be anyone else but Pham. I thought he'd be large and frightening – instead, he was small, diminutive, and well dressed. He looked forty, but I knew he was a lot older than that.

An overweight man with empty eye sockets, and greasy blond hair sat on a folding chair to Pham's left. He sat still as though he waited for his picture to be taken, a smirk on his face.

I didn't like the situation. It was time to take control. I was tired of being lead around by this asshole.

"Whatever you're doing to Denise, if you don't stop right now, I'll blow your head off," I told Pham, my finger twitched on the trigger. Adrenaline coursed through my body.

"Frankie, sing something for Detective Steckler to soothe his nerves." Pham smiled and Frankie's grin grew wider. I pointed the gun near Frankie's head and blew a hole in the wall.

Frankie scrambled off the chair; one hand covered his right ear. Cuts appeared on his neck from splinters. Frankie whimpered.

Thanks for the warning, Freya.

"Frankie, whatever gift you've got, keep it to yourself. I don't care if you're blind or not. I'll kill you if you make another sound." Pham quickly masked his look of surprise. I grinned in satisfaction.

Denise looked surprised, which hurt.

"Detective–" Pham began, but I cut him off.

"Don't talk or move, Pham. Frankie, get out of here. Use the door I came in." Frankie lumbered to his feet. I stepped out of the way as he moved closer. He fumbled for the door knob. Once he found it, I noticed his smirk returned. I moved closer to him and hit him on the back of his head with the butt of my gun. He went down without a sound.

Pham lunged for me but I dodged and he missed. I kicked his hip as he went by. He fell on top of Frankie and I backed away from him.

I waited to catch my breath. Denise may have given me a few years back and some extra muscle, but my mind told me I was too old for this kind of stuff.

"Detective, others will come to check on me. They will overwhelm you regardless of the gun. Give up now and make it easier on yourself." He stood up slowly, but didn't check on Frankie's condition. Cold bastard, he didn't even wince as he stepped on Frankie's hand and it made a cracking sound.

"Back away and put your hands in the air." I brought my gun up and pointed it at his face.

"If you kill me, Denise will die an agonizing death."

"Based on your tender care for Frankie, I'm sure the same is true if I let you live. I might as well make it quick for her. Now get your hands over your head or you'll lose an eye." I pointed the barrel of the gun at his face.

His eyes narrowed, hands went in the air.

An intense anger swept through me. He ruined my life, and devastated our family. The pain in my head spiked with my anger. It was time for payback.

"Not high or fast enough. Too bad," I said and raised the gun. The world stopped. Sweat flew from my arm and hit Pham in the face. I pulled the trigger and the bullet hit his hand.

He fell on Frankie and sagged against the wall.

Killing him wasn't an option but being shot in the hand, with all of its nerve endings, would be distracting. I ignored the splatter of blood and flesh on the wall behind him as well as Denise's gasp. She hadn't moved. I leaned over Pham, careful to stay out of his reach, and waited for him to look at me over the wreck of his hand.

His face had drops of blood on it and a thin stream came from his nose, covering his lip.

"I told you to stop what you were doing to Denise. You didn't listen.

236

Do it now or my next shot goes to your nuts."

He nodded.

I backed away and stepped carefully to Denise's side, but kept my eyes on him.

"Don't kill him," Denise said weakly. "I can die right now just because he does."

"Is he letting up?" I glanced at her. She sat up.

"Yes, I'll be fine in a minute," she answered, stronger.

"What if I knock him out? Will that work?" I nodded at Pham, and let him see how much I wanted to do it.

"Denise, they feel it already. Soon they'll be screaming and throwing up blood. With no idea why." Pham smirked at her. Pham thought he had Denise.

"Liar. You've never touched them. Even Frankie wouldn't stoop that low," Denise snarled and stood.

"Are you sure, Denise? Are you willing to risk it?" Pham seemed too sure of himself for a man who'd just been shot.

"Who's he talking about, Denise? Kim?" I hoped Kim was feeling pain now.

"Her children, Detective. Your–" Pham answered, but didn't get a chance to finish before I shot his left foot. He screamed in pain.

"Strike two. Stop fucking around with my sister or I'll blow you apart piece by piece." I ignored the part of me that knew I acted like a madman.

"Carl. Calm down and stop shooting him. It's the treatment. It changes you, washes you in hormones, makes you think differently. Try to keep that in mind. We need him alive," Denise said.

I froze, shocked – not at the fear in her voice – I was as surprised by my actions as she was – but the sympathy I heard for Pham.

She squinted at me like when we were kids and tried to get me to understand something without saying it in front of others. I shook my head in anger and frustration.

"Do you still remember Mom, Denise? She drank until she died from a broken heart because of him. Dad had another stroke two years after you left. Pham ruined your life, their lives, and mine."

The pain and despair I felt for all those years, the long lonely nights of useless searching built up until I shook with anger. My head pounded.

I faced Pham again, the gun pointed at his face, my finger on the trigger.

"Carl, the rage isn't you. It's from being young again. I've seen it before. Think past the hormones. I've followed your career; you've solved dozens of crimes and caught criminal masterminds without a single bullet. You've shot that gun three times in two minutes. Calm down and get some control."

She was right, but I didn't trust myself to speak. The smell of gunpowder, blood, and splintered bone registered. I felt sickened, though still justified, by what I'd done.

"She's using her gift on you, Detective. She's no different than I am," Pham said. I kicked his injured foot. His grunt of pain made me smile and I yanked my hand away.

I'd never let perps goad me into action before.

"I can't let him touch me, flesh to flesh, right?" I ignored the hurt look on her face.

She nodded.

"Can you touch him without anything bad happening?"

I knew she meant if I had myself under control and nodded to reassure her.

"He's already addicted me to him. Touching him won't do anything more."

"Good. Then help him up and we'll use him as a shield from the rest of his goons and get out of here."

A sad smile played on her lips for a moment, and then she sighed deeply.

"Carl, it's not that simple. I can't walk out without the rest of them. They're all – even Pham and Frankie – my family."

I shook my head at her in anger, then gestured again at Pham.

"I'm your family. Dad's your family. Those kids he mentioned are your family. Maybe, God-help-us, even Kim is your family."

I pointed the gun at Pham again. "That genocidal pedophile is NOT your family. Now get him to his feet. We're running out of time." The rage was back and I trembled again.

Denise realized it, and rather than argue, moved to Pham's side. The gentle way she helped him to his feet made me want to shoot him again.

"Stockholm syndrome," I said, trying to understand why she cared about him at all.

Denise answered with a shrug, "Maybe, but I think it's more than that. He's changed since I first met him. He's gentler, kinder. He's not killed in years."

She looked at Pham and I hated the tenderness in her eyes.

"I've grown soft because of you," Pham spoke as though I was no longer there. I took a small measure of pleasure as he grimaced in pain.

"You found your humanity again," Denise contradicted him.

"Where is Patronio?" I decided it was time to take control again. Denise's comments could be considered later. It would take years to deprogram her.

"He's locked in an office on the first floor," Denise answered.

"Let's go." I indicated the door I came in.

"Puppy is coming," Pham said and looked at Denise.

"Doesn't matter, we're leaving." I tried to hide any sign I suspected back-up, however psychotic, would arrive.

"Detective, Denise made her point. Her gift, while more subtle than mine, is my equal. Find your friends and leave. Denise knows as well as I do, she isn't going anywhere," Pham said. Denise looked up at me and I saw the truth of his words in her eyes.

Before I said anything, the opposite door to the room banged open. Puppy stood panting in the doorway with the giantess next to him. He looked terrified; there was no sign of Wolf now.

"The siblings are here with heavily armed men with them. They've entered the house and have people at each of the doors to the building" the tall woman told Denise and Pham with a quick glance at me.

"Send Va^n out to them," I suggested.

"That's not what they are here for," Pham contradicted me and held out his injured hand. Puppy dropped to his knees and licked it. It reminded me of people kissing the Pope's ring.

Disgusted, I turned to Denise.

"We have to get out of here. Let Pham deal with them."

"I can't," Denise answered over Puppy's slobbering and Pham's groans of discomfort.

Pham's hand was healing, the flesh and bones knit together even as I watched.

"We'll send Va^n and Pham out to them at the same time. Let them sort it out," I told her.

The hallway behind the giant woman filled with others. I caught a glimpse of the white-skinned man from the tunnel, the small boy from the front room, and the large muscled black man who could only be Trainer. Frankie woke up and groped his way to them. The woman called Pica stepped from behind Trainer and helped him to his feet. Others I hadn't seen before were there as well. There were twelve of them.

"Detective, there will be no sorting out. They only want one thing: revenge." Pham groaned as Puppy slipped off the shoe from his injured foot.

"Then go out and take it like a man and let the rest of them go," I snarled. Some of them came into the room and surrounded him to

240

protect him with their lives despite the terror and fear in their eyes. Even Denise moved closer to him at my suggestion.

"I do not know what you've learned about the siblings but they aren't a forgiving group. Nor do they do things by halves. They will make no distinction between me, my people, or probably even you, Patronio, or your friends. No loose ends will be left."

"Then you better start running," I told him. "Or call the cops; at least they'll give you a trial before killing you."

"The police will be of no help to us or the siblings. The siblings have controlled the police for centuries. The Viet Cong sent me to neutralize them with a team like those you see around me," Pham told me.

"It's not the siblings with the Suffolk County cops under their thumbs," I countered. Pham shrugged and I noticed blood still dripped from his nose. I hoped we wouldn't be treated to Puppy slobbering all over Pham's face.

"This is getting us nowhere. We've got the siblings and their Vietnamese gang members making their way through the house and cellar. They've got this building covered as well. When they see us, they'll open fire. Does anyone have any ideas?" Denise interrupted any additional comment Pham may have made and looked around the room, at me and the others clustered around them.

I understood then if I wanted to save her, I would have to save her friends as well, even Pham.

The others looked at her, their faces creased in concentration.

"Where are the men I came here with?" I looked at Denise.

"Down the hall," the giantess answered me.

"Would you bring them here? They've been in situations like this before. They may be able to think of a way out. You should also get their guns." The giantess took the white-skinned man with her.

"Is there anything any of these people can do to counter the siblings?" I kept my eyes on Denise.

"No. Generator and Frankie have the best offensive gifts that don't require physical contact. None of us have enough juice to counter what the siblings can do," Denise answered me.

Pham nodded and pulled his foot away from Puppy's mouth.

"Can Puppy do anything for Steve – that's the wounded one back in the cell area you had me in." Even if he couldn't, maybe Wolf could think of something if he was far enough from Pham and the fear he inspired in Puppy.

"I don't wanna go!" Puppy wailed, grabbed Denise's leg, and worked her with his big round eyes.

"Puppy, I know you're scared, but I need you to check on Carl's friend. If you can't help him, come right back. You'll do that for me, won't you?" Denise caressed Puppy's head like a mother trying to calm a crying toddler.

I was about to tell him he could stay, but Pham spoke before me.

"Stop pawing Denise, Puppy. Go drool on the Detective's friend. You are only in the way now." Pham wiped his foot on the side of Puppy's coveralls.

Puppy bowed his head, but I saw the flash of teeth from Wolf's silent snarl. Then Puppy returned and lumbered to his feet. His lower lip trembled.

"Thank you, Puppy." I touched his shoulder. He darted his gaze at me, but I wasn't sure which person peered out. We'd have to see if he helped me, Denise, and the others escape.

At that moment, the giantess returned with Beam and Dean. They looked around the room and found me at its center, in front of Denise and Pham.

"What's going on?" Beam stormed over. If he had been abused or hurt while Kim had him in her claws, he hid it well.

"Tú and the siblings used us as their stalking horse. They're here with armed gang members. I don't know if they're afraid of Pham or just want revenge. In either case, they want him dead," I explained.

He looked at Pham, back at me, and shrugged.

"Works for me."

"Agreed. But according to Pham, the siblings will kill not only him, but everyone else, including us."

"You believe him?" Beam gave Pham a cold stare.

"No, but Denise, my sister, says it's true."

He raised his eyebrows. Beam and Dean turned to look at her.

"The one who disappeared twenty years ago? She doesn't look old enough," Dean commented, then eyed me again. "Neither do you," he said with a frown.

"We age well," Denise said, dryly. Pham and the giantess snorted.

I stayed quiet as she shook their hands and used her gift on them.

"Where's Patronio?" Beam returned to business.

"Locked in one of the offices above us," Denise answered.

"Why did you kidnap him?" Beam tilted his head, curious.

"We did no such thing," Pham answered.

"It's true," Denise added when Beam appeared skeptical. "He showed up at the house in a daze. We put him in a cell until we could figure out what to do about it."

"Did he get his hands on Patronio?" I glared at Pham. My gun came up again.

He returned my hostility ten-fold.

"No, I did not," he said and turned his basilisk gaze to Denise.

I quirked an eyebrow at her.

"It's one of the things we argued about," she answered my unspoken question with a small shrug. She touched my hand with a soothing gesture.

I moved beyond her reach.

"Where are our guns and gear? And where is Steve?" The door behind us opened just as Beam spoke.

"Right behind you," Steve said and entered the room. He staggered and grabbed the door frame. A faded scar marked his leg. It hadn't been there before. He wore boxers with cartoon characters on them. I blinked, but didn't say anything, happy to be alive.

"Where's Puppy?" Denise looked at the underwear and answered my unvoiced question about Steve's choice of clothing. She stepped away from Pham, anxious about her friend.

Steve held up his hand to reassure her. "If you mean the redhead, he's fine. I woke up with him licking my leg. I got a little freaked out and yelled at him, but then I realized he was healing me. When I asked him about pants, he gave me these." His face turned red but continued. "Then he pointed me in this direction and went down another hallway." His eyes stopped on the white-skinned man. He stepped forward, ready to fight, but I jumped in front of him.

"We've got bigger fish to fry right now," I told him. "Besides, we were tricked into attacking them tonight. They defended themselves." I stared him down. He wouldn't get by me.

Dean shoved his way between me and Steve. He gripped Steve's bicep briefly.

"Welcome back," he said and turned to face me. "How many and who, besides the siblings, are we up against?"

I waved the question to Denise and the giantess.

"Like I said, the siblings and twenty–" a series of gunshots interrupted her.

"They've gotten through the tunnel; I can hear at least three of them now they've started running," a blonde woman said, and pushed hair away from her face. It revealed her ear, which was stretched and deformed; its opening long and dark. It appeared infected.

She saw me staring and glared, but said nothing.

"More of them are coming in the front, side, and back entrances. They're using cell phones to coordinate the attack," she told Pham and

Denise.

"Fight back," Pham said, definitively. He faced each until they met his eyes. It was clear he gave them no choice.

"No! We run! We know this place and the back ways out. None of them will. Use them! Go before they get here!" Denise shouted at us. She ran to the door behind me, pushed past us and opened it. "Run! Get out now! Use Spook's gift to hide and keep them away while you run!" She glared at Pham and dared him to contradict her.

They locked gazes but it was Pham who looked away first.

"Go. Run if you can. You would only be cannon fodder." Pham returned her stare. "A conscience is a useless gift, Denise." He shook his head as most of the strange men and women rushed past us.

Each touched Denise as they went by. In seconds, only me, Denise, Beam, Steve, Dean, the giantess, Frankie, Pham and the white-skinned man, Generator, were left in the room.

"We have to get Patronio. Then we're out of here," Beam said. "And where are our guns?"

"They're in the next office," the giantess said, waiting for Pham's permission. He nodded, and she left the room again.

"Bring Puppy back. He's probably terrified," Denise said to Pham. He nodded and closed his eyes.

"What now?" I wondered why anyone but Denise and Pham had stayed.

"We've got to get Pham out of here. There are places we can go to ground," Denise answered.

"Dean will get you out of here. Leave with him and I'll catch up with you after we get Patronio," I told her. Dean nodded at my unspoken question.

"We have to get Pham out of here," Denise repeated and frowned at me. I frowned right back. "I already told you, if he dies, we all do."

I turned my glare to Pham.

"That better be true."

Pham smiled, knowing exactly what went through my head.

"Do you want to risk it so soon after your tender reunion?" his smile widened and my gun pressed against his nose. Then the giantess came back with an armload of handguns. She also had a pair of nunchucks.

"The security guards delayed them, but a sibling got them. The other guards are going into withdrawal," she told Denise. Her voice sounded grim. She handed Beam the handguns and put the nunchucks in her back pocket.

"What does that mean for the guards?" Pham didn't say anything. Denise, turned away.

"Pham has to conserve resources. If he doesn't get to them soon, they'll die," the giantess, Freya, answered for them. I decided she was on our side.

"Shit!" I hated I would have to save his sorry ass, if only for the guards' sake.

"Let's get Patronio. We'll take care of the guards as soon as we can," Beam said. "Which way?"

"He's up on the first floor," Freya answered and opened the door. We heard a series of gunshots, but no shout or scream.

I hoped the others made it safely away. Freya shut the door and locked it. "We should take the back way." She pushed past me and the others, but took Denise by the shoulder. She didn't look back to see if Pham followed her.

"What about Puppy?" Denise pulled away from her.

"He'll have to find his way to us," Freya said.

"He knows I want to see him." Pham added.

"I suspect he's fine," I pushed past Denise to check the next room before she entered it.

"Put something in front of the door and shut off the light." Beam gestured at the door behind us now. "We don't want them to know where we are or have been."

"Whatever, let's just get out of here," the white-skinned man said and put a folding chair under the door knob. I raised my gun when he got close to me.

"Relax, we're playing for the same team now," he said with a smile and a long look at my chest. Sparks flew between his lips.

"You won't be charging my battery anytime soon." I frowned at him. He chuckled, as did Denise.

"Some things never change. Come on. There's nobody back this way," Denise said.

"How do you know?" I followed her through the doorway and pushed past her again.

"It's part of my gift to know where people are within a few hundred yards. Get out of my way, will you?" she said irritably. I smiled; it was just like old times with her taking charge.

"Can we get to Patronio from this direction?" Beam scanned the area.

"Yes, there's another stairway at the end of this hall," I answered. "Freya brought me this way earlier." I nodded at the giantess.

"We should split up, there's no need for all of us to go. I'll take Dean, you stick with your sister and Steve since he was just hurt," Beam suggested.

I felt torn, I wanted to find Patronio; we had become friends despite the strangeness of this case. My feelings must have shown.

"You just found Denise. Don't lose her now," Dean told me.

We heard another round of gunfire and screaming. Then another gunshot and the wailing stopped.

"Who will show us where Patronio is?" Beam queried the group.

"I will," the white-skinned guy said. "He's on my team." He laughed then checked with Pham for permission.

Having received it, he said, "Come this way." He ran ahead.

Beam, Dean, and I followed. Sparks flowed under the extremely pale man's skin.

"Which way for us?" I turned to Denise. Pham was behind her surrounded by Freya, Trainer, and Frankie.

"We should go back the way you came in, there are more exits that way," Denise answered.

"Block this door and let's go. Will we pass the rest of our clothes on the way?" I asked. "We wore Kevlar vests when we came in. They'd come in handy right now."

"They're by the room you were in. We'll pick 'em up on the way by," Freya said and wedged a file cabinet against the door. She moved it like a paperweight.

We walked quickly down the office space where I met Wolf. I stopped them when I came to it.

"Is there anyone out there?" I waited for Denise to answer. She shook her head. "Where is everyone?"

"Probably hiding wherever they can," Freya said.

I scanned the hall, despite Denise's assurances. After seeing no one, I motioned to the others to follow me. I glanced at Freya, trying to determine which way led out. She shrugged and answered my unvoiced question.

"Left goes toward the back of this building, right leads to the front."

"Which way are the sibling's forces coming from?" I tried to guess but couldn't.

"Both," Denise answered.

"Is there a way out from a direction they don't have covered?" I watched Denise and Freya, hoping they knew. Hell would freeze before I willingly sought advice from Pham.

"There are only three ways out from here. The front stairs, the back stairs, and the tunnel to the house." Pham smirked. He knew how much it cost me to listen to what he had to say.

"We should split up. You get Va^n and go out to the house," Denise

248

told me.

"No. We don't have enough guns or any protection against their gifts. The only advantage we have is our numbers," I told her and ignored Pham's continued smirk.

"Are there any other ways out that you haven't told them about?" Steve watched Pham, his tone neutral.

"No, we've all been here long enough to know entrances and exits," Denise defended Pham and that irritated me. I was about to tell her to stop when gunshots sounded in the distance.

"That's coming from the front of the building," Freya said.

"That settles it then. We'll head to the back after we get Va^n." I started across the hall past the offices I saw before. We'd have to leave our vests and other gear behind.

"Anything we can use as weapons in the offices?" Steve didn't sound hopeful.

"No, they've been empty for years. We searched them when we first set up house for Gerbil Mom," Freya answered, then gasped and grabbed her chest.

"Enough chatter, Freya," Pham told her and walked around her stooped figure, unconcerned with her pain. My gun came up again, but before I could point it at him, Steve tapped my arm.

"We don't have time for another showdown. Let's get out of here before you settle old scores." I let my arm drop as Freya took a deep breath and straightened. We continued walking and his words reminded me of Pham and Denise's earlier exchange.

"Where are your children, Denise?" It disturbed me that she hadn't said anything about them yet.

"Safe," she answered, and slid her eyes at Pham and back, telling me not to ask anything else.

"Yes, Carl, your children are safe, thanks to my recently acquired conscience," Pham added, with a mocking laugh and a scornful look at

Denise. His grasp of English wasn't as good as I thought if he still messed up possessives.

"Quit looking to borrow trouble, Yardley. None of that will matter if we don't get out of here. And we're still in the basement. Focus your gift to help us escape so you can live to stir shit tomorrow," Kim told him.

We stopped and looked as Kim joined the group. By the look on Denise's face, I wasn't the only one surprised at her being the voice of reason. She shrugged and put her arms around Denise protectively.

I kept my face neutral when Denise returned the gesture.

Freya, fully recovered from Pham's attack, blocked light from behind us with her body and opened the door into the stairwell leading down to the cells.

"I don't see or hear anyone," she said and gave Denise a quizzical look.

"With so many people around me, I can't get a good read," Denise told her with frustration in her voice.

Freya opened the door wider and as a group, we crept toward it.

I stopped. "We all don't have to go, but I need to get Va^n." I felt bad, but wanted to get Denise out more than I wanted to save Va^n. "Do the stairs lead up to the first floor?"

"Yes, these lead up to the opposite side of the building at the loading dock. We have cars parked in the lot there. We can meet there," Denise answered.

"There's enough room in my car for you, Kim, and your kids." Denise's eyes welled with a sadness I couldn't understand.

"Great"–she used the same tone we had as teenagers–"but let's cross that bridge when we get there."

Glances passed among Denise and the rest of Pham's clown clan that made me uncomfortable.

"Dean, Steve, and I can go down after Va^n and meet you at the loading dock. Will you be able to get Patronio on your way out?" Beam checked with me, then Denise and Pham.

"The office he's in isn't far from the stairway," Denise answered, Pham didn't gainsay her.

"I'll go with these three," Freya said, nodding her head at Beam, Dean, and Steve. "They don't know where their stuff is and I've got the keys." She looked at Pham who gave her a blank stare and I remembered the comment about Pham's gift being over-stretched and him needing to cull the heard.

"Fine. Just be careful. If we get separated ..." Denise hesitated and I knew she changed her words, because she didn't trust me. It felt like a knife in my heart. "Get to one of the safe houses and send word to us."

"Okay, enough talk, let's get this over with," Steve interrupted any further exchange, pushed past Freya, and started down the stairs.

"Agreed," Dean said, and followed Steve. Beam shrugged but said nothing. Freya grinned as she held the door and waited for Kim to take it from her before going down the stairs.

"Our turn." I walked past Kim and went up the stairs, not caring if the others followed me or not, especially Denise.

At the top of the stairwell, I stopped in front of the door with large, faded "1" painted on it and waited for Pham. "Why don't you lead the way, Pham, since the guards are under your control? Who knows, there may be a welcoming party on the other side of the door," I said with a cold smile.

Denise shot me an exasperated looked. "I don't sense anyone near the door on the other side."

"None of my guards or gifted are close," Pham said.

"Good. Move." I motioned with my gun for Pham to go first.

"To the left." Kim pushed past me and Pham and took the lead.

Denise followed Pham, safeguarding him. I couldn't tell if it was her choice or his.

We shuffled into the dark hallway. None of the regular lights were lit but every twenty yards were dim, flickering emergency lights. This part of the building had been used in the not-too-distant past, but the lights still didn't look like they'd been serviced or updated for twenty years.

I kept my gun out, safety off, and watched as Kim pulled a handgun from the waist of her pants. Given our meeting at the morgue, I knew she could use it.

Kim led us to the left from the door and checked the dark rooms we passed where the doors were open. I tried to insert myself between Denise and Pham so she was last but she pushed me back, shook her head, and huffed in annoyance.

We heard gunshots, stopped, and tried to determine which direction they came from, but the sounds reverberating down the halls made it too difficult. Once the echoes died, all else was still. Denise nodded that we should keep moving without even a glance at me. The years of separation severed her reliance on me.

The smirk on Pham's face almost made me shoot him again, despite the consequences. I managed to get my anger under control and shoved forward so Denise and Pham were behind me.

We passed several more rooms, the dim lighting making long, blurry shadows behind the standard Government Issue desks, chairs, and cabinets. At closed doors, we paused and waited for Denise and Pham to give the sign the room behind was empty.

A door banged open on the opposite end of the hall. Then a man, small and thin, ran across the hall followed by Puppy. Seconds later, there was a thud and a scream abruptly cut off.

We froze and waited for an indication of what happened. Puppy's lumbering form appeared around the corner and he made his way toward us. He wiped his mouth and hands on his overalls. An emergency light revealed sharp intelligence in his eyes; Wolf was ascendant, but by the next light, it had dulled, his bloody lips and jaw loosened. Puppy was in control again, or Wolf pretended he was.

252

Denise gave Puppy a quick hug. "What happened?"

"He said he was going to kill Pham," Puppy said, his eyes tearing up. "I stopped him."

"Good job." Denise gave him another hug.

"Who's on the other side of the door? And how many of them are there?" Pham ignored Puppy's efforts or tears. As Denise released her grip on the grubby man, a flash of hatred showed on Puppy's face but quickly faded.

"There were a bunch of guys that looked like him." Puppy gestured in the direction of the man he killed. "They had guns and the creepy one in black that smells like flowers told them to separate and shoot us. Not to let us gang up on them."

Pham smiled.

"That was how I routed them out of their home in Vietnam." Pham smiled, as if he relived a cherished memory.

"How many of the siblings are out there? And what is on the other side of the door? Is it another room?" I peppered Puppy with questions.

"The maintenance room and loading dock," Kim answered the second question.

"I only saw one of the creepy, smelly ones," Puppy answered.

"Where is the rest of your wonder team?" I shot at Pham and Denise sarcastically.

"Some of them got out the side door and are beyond the parking lot, waiting for us. A few are on the second floor waiting to join us. And Freya, along with your friends, will be with us in just a moment," Pham answered, then turned and looked down the hall. The door to the stairwell opened and Beam and Dean came through and waved when they saw us in the distance.

Denise indicated we should continue down the hall and wait for them there. As we approached the door, both Pham and Denise drew their breath in sharply.

"Get down!" Denise yelled and dragged Kim and Pham down with her. The maintenance room door banged opened. Two men rolled into the hallway, guns firing.

Puppy and I dropped to the floor at the sound of the bullets hitting the walls. I returned fire.

"Stay low!" I heard Beam call out and automatic weapons fired. Two distinct grunts split the air. Two men in front of us fell to the ground. We waited a moment before continuing down the hall again. Beam and Dean ran to catch up with us.

"Do we know what we're up against?" Beam approached me, impressively cool under fire.

"At least one of the siblings and a gang under their control," I answered. "We don't know how many of them. Denise?"

"Too far away for me to get numbers," she told me and glanced at Pham.

"Besides Tú, there are three of my security guards and ten of the gang members. Va^n and Patronio, are out beyond the loading dock." He rolled his eyes at my relieved sigh.

"Tú is interfering with my control of the security guards," Pham continued. Pale and sweating, his nose once again bled.

"What's his problem?" I frowned at Denise.

"It's the fight with Tú over dominance of the guards," Denise answered and I saw blood drip from his nose. She squinted at my forehead and then away. It made me want to look in a mirror.

Kim said Pham was over-stretched because of the number of people he addicted to him. Maybe with all of them in one place and the sibling in there, he was about to break.

Another adrenaline rush crashed through me at the thought I could help smash him into little bitty pieces.

"What's the plan? If all the bad guys are out on the loading dock and Patronio escaped, why don't we head out the front or side doors? We can connect with him once we get out of here."

"Tú has people out there as well. I don't know how many, but I can sense them," Denise answered.

"Besides, I said he was out there, I didn't say he was free. I have no idea if that is the case or not," Pham added.

"It might be better to go out of the side doors as opposed to the route where Tú is." I wasn't sure what approach Beam would think best to go after Patronio. If possible, I would help, but my primary concern was to keep Denise safe and away from Pham. Beam probably reached that conclusion about me.

"We could split up. Tú is after Pham, no one else. He can go out that way and we could take the other exits," Steve suggested and brought up his weapon.

"As attractive as that idea is to me, it won't work. If he dies, so do all the people addicted to him, including Denise," I told him.

Pham glared and reached his hand out, threatening me with his gift.

"Are you sure you can handle another addict at this point? You've already got pit stains from the strain," I sneered.

"We don't have time for this," Denise hissed at me. "We all have to get out alive." She touched each of us with a hand. "Now start thinking of some way for that to happen."

An overwhelming desire to do as she said and please her rushed over me.

She remained longest with Pham who returned her gaze with irritation.

"Is there another way to the maintenance room? Can we come at them from two different locations? There's only one sibling. The rest of them are normal. They just have guns, right?" Beam looked at Denise and Pham.

"No, there are two siblings," Pham corrected him. That meant Va^n had transitioned. Hopefully, they would be locked in a battle resulting in both their deaths. "And Anthony Patronio is out there too."

"Does that work in our favor or not?" Beam frowned and sounded confused.

"That depends on if he is in control of what he does or if it is one of the siblings," I answered.

The door to the maintenance room banged open. Two more gang members came through, guns blazing. At the same time, a loud crunch sounded above us. Two more came down behind us. Dean and Steve's training took over. They opened fire on the two from the floor above before they stood from their crouch. The gangbangers fell dead in seconds.

Kim, Denise, Puppy, and Freya leapt into position around Pham, shielding him from the bullets. Beam and I opened fire on the men from the maintenance room but not before they got off several shots. Freya, closest to them, staggered from the impact but didn't go down. My shot hit one of them in the head; Beam's hit the other guy in the shoulder, throwing him backward.

Freya roared and took two long strides and crouched over the downed man. She grabbed him by the shoulder and throat and literally tore the head from his body. Blood fountained from his neck and sprayed the wall behind.

Freya dropped the pieces and turned back toward us. Beam and I kept our pistols raised, frightened by her strength and the crazed look in her eyes. When she was close enough, Pham reached out and touched her arm. Whatever he did brought the sanity back.

"Are you hurt?" Denise touched the giantess' arm. Freya shook her head and absently brushed off her surprisingly bloody and gory free shirt.

"Just a couple of scratches and bruises. The bullets didn't penetrate," she answered. My eyes widened in surprise; there were holes in her shirt and pants. She smiled grimly at me.

"Being such a big girl growing up, I learned to be thick-skinned," she told me. Kim guffawed.

"Enough," Pham said. "They've figured out how to block or confuse our ability to sense people."

Denise nodded her agreement.

"They also don't care how many people they kill to get at you," I said.

"Such a waste," Denise commented sadly.

"True, but before they send anyone else in, let's block the door with their bodies and take their weapons and ammo," I said and went forward to the body of the man I killed. I took the gun from his hand and found three clips in his pocket. Freya and Puppy did the same to their assailants.

Dean and Steve helped move the bodies to block the door.

"Do you have any way to contact the others?" I checked Denise and Pham.

"Digame, that's the one with the infected ears," Denise said, and pointed to her ears. "Can hear us from anywhere in the building. If the others are with her, we can tell them our plan."

"What is our plan?" Kim took an extra gun from Freya.

"Do any of you have offensive gifts that work from a distance? Like the electric guy, um, Generator?" I ignored Kim.

"Not with the same impact, no," Pham answered. "I sent those with offensive gifts out ahead of us."

"I can toss these bodies twenty or thirty feet if that would help," Freya said.

"Is anyone immune to the sibling's gifts?" I scanned their faces.

"Spooky maybe. Kim's gift doesn't work on him," Denise answered.

"Which one is he?" I couldn't keep all their nicknames. straight.

"The young boy you met when you first came into the house," Pham answered. "He has courage."

We stared at him, outraged. There was speculation in his tone.

"He is a boy!" I yelled.

"A boy with a devastating disease. Even with all the gifts at our disposal, he won't make it for more than a few more pain-filled months. Why not let him die fighting and give meaning to his death?" Pham locked gazes with Denise.

"You can rationalize killing a child to save your sorry ass?" Steve leaned over the small man. Pham glared back while his addicts averted their gaze or stared at the floor. This wasn't the first time they faced this kind of situation.

"I don't want Spooky to die," Puppy said, tears ran from his eyes. "I don't want to die!" He sobbed. Denise hugged him.

Pounding sounded on the door but it wouldn't open with the bodies piled in front. We all pointed our guns at the ceiling, waiting, but apparently they decided not to try that particular trick again.

"We can't stand here all day. They're going to surround us if we stay here much longer." Dean warned Beam and me.

"Spooky agrees with my assessment, he's making his way to the loading dock," Pham told us. Denise and the other addicts sighed in resignation and sadness.

"You're a bastard," Beam told Pham, surprising me. I had Beam pegged as the same kind of guy.

"The others are following more slowly. They will do what they can to cover him. Hopefully, Spooky can scare them off before they shoot him," Pham said.

"Can you tell where he is?" It still irritated me to ask him anything.

"Yes, he should be close enough for them to start feeling it."

"Then let's distract them as best we can," I said, then looked at Freya. "Let's open the door and you chuck the head at one of them, at Tú, if possible," I told her. "It might break Tú's concentration, or at a minimum, freak the others out enough to run." She nodded. "We have to do it quickly. While she throws the head, try to pinpoint Spooky's location. Or Patronio's. And all the gang members. Three seconds later we open the door and fire." Dean, Beam, and Steve nodded in confirmation.

"Let me in the front. I'm smaller than everyone else, and probably a better shot," Kim said. I agreed based on her performance at the morgue.

"Stand behind me," Freya told her. "Shoot from between my legs," she said, unable to say it without a smile, even under these grim conditions. Kim nodded and returned her grin.

I looked around at the others.

"Ready?"

Denise, Pham, and Puppy held back. I was particularly glad Denise and Puppy did. Puppy could be available for the injured and I wanted Denise safe. If only I could convince Freya to throw Pham rather than the head, but knew she wouldn't go for it.

16

Freya stepped forward, grabbed two of the bodies, and dragged them away from the door. She moved the headless body just far enough away to allow her to open it, and then casually grabbed the head by the hair.

"One," she started, "two." We got into place. "Three!" She roared and slammed the door open, scanned the area and threw the head straight into the face of a gang member standing guard at the door. Freya crouched to allow the rest of us to get a look past her. The lights were off, making it difficult to see in the gloom. I got a glance of one of the siblings surrounded by five or six of the gang members. I didn't see Patronio.

Freya shut the door as the guns in the room came up and the sibling's hand approached its hood. I turned to Denise and Pham.

"I counted seven, including the sibling in the corner opposite the door. Did either of you get anything different?"

"There are three more behind the wall behind Tú. One of them was Patronio," Pham told me.

"Crap, a hostage," I said. Pham shrugged, indifferent. "Any sign of Va^n?"

"He's out there somewhere, but not close. There are also eight guards out in the parking lot. Most of them are mine," Pham said.

"Are they armed?" Beam sounded hopeful.

"No. They are not paid to carry weapons," Denise answered.

"Can we count on them for help?" Dean tried to find an upside.

"Only the five addicted to me," Pham told him.

"What good will they do without guns?" Steve frowned at Pham.

"Fodder for their bullets and a distraction," Pham answered. This guy was definitely a psychopath. "Spooky is moving forward," he prompted.

"Let's do this before Spooky dies. Where will they be coming from?" I wanted to do everything we could to prevent that.

"There's a door one floor above us. The stairwell leads to the right of the door on this floor," Kim answered.

"Kim, Steve, and Dean, try to take out the sibling. Beam, you fire right of it, I'll take left." Each nodded at me.

"Digame, let them know what we're doing. We'll open the door on one," I said quietly, looking at Denise for confirmation that Digame could hear me. Denise nodded.

"Five … four …" Freya walked up to the door, unfazed by the guns pointed at her back. "Three … two …" Her hand twisted the knob.

"One."

Tú stood in the center of the room, hood down, the scent of jasmine strong. Four of the gang members huddled shoulder-to-shoulder, arms intertwined and locked, blocking a direct shot, and a direct view. Within seconds, they were riddled with bullets but remained standing, despite being dead.

The door to the metal stairwell above us clattered open. A second later, an object came hurtling down, striking Tú in the head. Tú's form crumpled to the ground.

"Ha! Got you bitch!" A voice boomed above us, and the stairs creaked as someone ran down them. Others followed.

"No!" Denise yelled as Trainer and Spooky reached the bottom landing. Two men leaped from behind the standing dead men and fired at Trainer and Spooky. One shot caught Trainer in the head. He went down, landing on top of the boy.

"Get back in!" I yelled and backed up. Freya stood in front to shield me and the others. Before she slammed the door, Freya reached around the door frame and hit the light switch turning the lights on in the room.

"What happened?" I screamed at Pham, positive he had misled us.

"It's the siblings, they've figured out how to mess with our gifts." Denise stepped between us. "My gift tells me there are a bunch of them in there with Tú."

"Trainer and Spooky are in there!" Freya turned to Denise and Pham. "We should go in after them."

Steve nodded his head. Apparently he'd taken a liking to Spooky despite what happened.

"Trainer is dead," Pham told us.

"Shot to the head," I added.

"What about Spooky?" Several of them spoke up.

"He is alive," Pham said without emotion.

"We can't do anything until we figure a way out of here," Beam said.

"Did Trainer kill one of the siblings?" I queried Pham, calmer now.

"No. One of my security guards was killed. Several gang members were killed as well," Pham said.

Doors banged open in the distance followed by the sound of running.

"They've sent men through other doors. They're surrounding us," Beam said. Sounds came from the floor above us.

"We're screwed," Dean concluded.

"Any ideas? We need something brilliant. If anyone has a gift we don't know about, now's the time to use it. No repercussions for hiding it." Denise looked at each of us. She put her hand on my arm, and this time, I moved closer to her, no longer caring if she manipulated me or not.

"Hanging out with you again could get on my nerves," I told her.

She smiled and Kim laughed.

"Think!" Denise commanded again.

"What does Tú want?" I wiped sweat from my brow. Denise's eyes followed my gesture.

"My death," Pham answered.

"Definitely. But Tú wants control and security even more. Let Tú have it," I said.

"What are you talking about?" Denise sounded intrigued.

"Go out there; give yourself up," I told Pham. "Let Tú touch you. You can't lie to them while they're touching you. Tell Tú if you die, all your addicts die. If Tú controls you, then the siblings control all of your gifted. Tú won't be able to resist that."

"Tú will kill me out of fear." Then he gave Denise an accusing look. "You burdened me with a conscience; you can easily give one to the siblings."

I hated the fond look the two exchanged.

"Do it now or we go out in a blaze of guns and glory," Kim said. We could hear people running toward us.

"Let's go. Pham and me first. Hopefully, they'll be more likely to listen to me," I said, making for the door.

"No, I'll go and block the bullets until you get their attention." Freya gently pushed me aside and opened the door. She crossed her arms over her face and crept forward. I almost grabbed Pham to put him in front of me but stopped in time. Pham glanced at my forehead, making note of the sweat we both knew glistened there. Then he stepped behind Freya.

"Get on the floor with your hands up when they get here. I doubt they'll shoot you. At least not until they get additional input from Tú," I told Denise and ignored the exchange. My head pounded again. "It's the best I can come up with."

"Don't get yourself killed," Denise commanded me with a quick hug.

"Or us either," Kim said. I frowned as I crossed the threshold.

Four shots rang out. Freya grunted and paused with each one.

"Tú!" I called out. "It's Detective Steckler. Pham wants to surrender." Another two shots fired as I spoke.

"Then step aside, we shall kill him, and this will be over. We have no quarrel with you," Tú responded.

"I can't let you do that. As much as I would like to. His gift addicts people to him. That's how he controls them. They'll go into withdrawal and die without him."

"Then they will die," Tú said.

"No, there's another way." I took several steps forward and pushed Freya to the side. Behind me, I heard people approach Denise and the others. In front of us stood ten of the gang members, guns drawn, their faces deadpan; Tú had them under control. I couldn't see beyond them but caught a glimpse of the hooded sibling.

"We are not interested in another way. We want Pham dead," Tú said. Another person spoke the same words at the same time. It could only be Va^n. It was clear who won the contest of wills. "Bring them in and keep your weapons pointed at them," Tú called out to group behind

264

and above me. Perhaps he was interested in what I had to say, or perhaps he wanted us all in one place to make it easier to get this over with and clean up.

"Think about it," I called out and tried to keep the desperation out of my voice. My head throbbed and I felt a deep welling anger surface. I spent years looking for Denise and now, having found her, she would be taken away again. "You could control Pham and exact revenge." I heard Denise and the others catch their breath. "Through him, you could control them. You could learn more about the gifted and about yourselves. You could make use of their gifts," I tempted Tú.

"You seek to delay your death through trickery," Tú said.

"You're right, I don't want to die. I just found my sister Pham kidnapped twenty-five years ago. Death is too good for Pham. Keep him alive and let Bi`nh experiment on him." I let Tú hear the truth in my words.

"Spooky," Denise whisper behind me.

"Tú, there's a gifted boy hurt under our dead. Can we help him, please, while you decide? His gift repels people as much as yours draws them in."

There was a long pause.

"Very well," Tú answered and I knew I piqued the sibling's curiosity.

"Puppy and I will get him," Freya said. She and Puppy went to Trainer's still body. Freya lifted Trainer and Puppy gently took Spooky into his arms and began licking him.

"Your colleagues are not upset about the death of their friend?" Tú smiled, baiting us. I was about to reply when Kim spoke up behind me.

"No, he was a sadist and a rapist, we're glad he's dead." Her voice was defiant and somehow discordant. I suspected she had her crazy on again.

"And the boy?" Tú tried again.

"He is just a boy who is very sick and has been almost his entire life.

He deserves to live the rest of his life laughing and playing," Denise said, defiantly.

"How do I know this isn't a trick?" Tú frowned, suspicious.

"You can touch Pham, he won't be able to lie to you then," I said.

Tú laughed.

"Detective, I am not so easily tricked. Pham could addict me to him with a touch," Tú said.

"Your gifts are greater than his," I said.

"That may be true, but I am not willing to risk that," Tú said. I stepped forward and the gang members centered their guns on me.

"Then touch me," Denise said and stepped to my side.

"No!" Kim and I said. More than twenty years and we finally agreed on something. Denise' eyes focused on my forehead, which still ran with sweat, and then at Pham who also looked at me. I felt another wave of anger sweep over me as I realized they had another plan in place and hadn't bothered to share.

"I've been with Pham a long time and know all his secrets. I'm Denise Steckler, Carl wouldn't risk me for a trick," Denise said. "We found each other today; please don't take that away from us so soon." The pleading tone in her voice tore at me, diminished the anger and made me want to please her.

"That sounds almost believable," Tú said. "I will take you up on your offer and add to it. Approach me with the young boy being healed. Pham, separate yourself from your human shields. Go to the right. If anything is amiss, both of your lives will immediately be forfeit.

Additional people came into the room behind Tú. The hooded figure had to be Va^n. One hand wrapped around Patronio's throat, the other held a knife. Patronio's neck appeared bloody, bruised, and misshapen. Va^n's other hand kept Patronio enthralled. Next to Va^n stood three security guards.

Denise took Spooky's hand and the two of them walked to Tú. As they approached, three more security guards came up behind Tú. With each step my anger and desperation to protect Denise increased, the pressure built behind my eyes, blinding me.

"What is your gift?" Tú demanded of Denise.

"People want to please me, to do their best," Denise answered.

"Doesn't sound very scary," Tú said.

"It's not. It's effective," Denise answered coldly. As they spoke, Va^n and Patronio closed in on Tú and the security guards circled Pham.

"You sound very much like your brother. It will be good to have one such as you under my control," Tú said to her.

"There is a joy in controlling others," Pham encouraged Tú.

"I'd rather she die than lose her again to one of you!" Dad appeared out of nowhere, yelling.

A guard screamed and several things happened; the air filled with an overwhelming smell of oranges and burnt popcorn; Patronio broke free of Va^n, took the knife and slit Tú's throat from behind. A security guard, who I hadn't noticed until then, yelled, stepped forward, and swung a cudgel at Pham.

Pham moved faster than I thought possible, caught my father's hand and twisted it with sharp crack.

"Dad, no!" I yelled when he screamed and fell to the ground, clutching his heart with his unbroken hand. He gurgled something and laid still, his eyes sought out mine.

"Bastard! Rot in hell!" Patronio stood over the bleeding and gasping Tú. One of the gang members stepped forward and shot Tú in the head.

I spun back to see a smug, satisfied smile on Pham's face directed at Denise. Her gaze darted between Pham and Va^n, bottom lip caught between her teeth, a sure sign she worried. Pham's smile widened as he raised his arm and held out a hand to Va^n. Denise's eyes widened. Pham addicted Va^n to him without her knowing. She lost whatever game the two of them played.

Pham turned his eyes to me and then flicked them at Dad lying at my feet. He smiled again and I realized he'd touched Dad, addicted him as well.

"No," I said, got up from my knees to stand over and in front of my father. The sudden pain in my head became a welcome distraction from the thought of losing Denise again. I sweated heavily, droplets running down my face, chest, and arms. Denise and Pham noticed it at the same time and froze. Pham's smile faded as he stepped back. Denise's eyes snapped to mine and I felt the weight of it, willing me to understand what she needed me to know.

I thought about Denise's gift, and nickname, "Captain," a woman able to bring people together and focus on a goal. Dad always said Denise was as gifted at bringing people together as his father had been.

Mother's hospital newspaper nicknamed her the "human defibrillator."

The siblings discovered "gifts" had a genetic basis and could be catalyzed with exposure to others with a fully expressed gift. I spent a great deal of time with Patronio, the siblings, and now, others through the "treatment."

Denise believed I had a gift that would help, that had been stunted by Kim, but was now corrected.

They kept looking at the sweat, the way it poured off me each time I got angry, the first time with Luddy, then twice more today with Pham. Each time, moments later, blood dripped from their nose.

The pieces came together. Pham knew I figured something out. My anger swelled again as I thought about all the pain he caused my family. Making a fist, I pulled my arm back, ready to drive it through what was first a fearful, then smug, expression.

It changed back to fear as I pulled my punch and my clenched hand stopped short of his face, opened, and my sweat spattered across his cheeks, eyes, and mouth. He gave me one last look of hatred, then his

268

eyes rolled and he fell to the ground, unconscious. Everyone else froze.

"What did you do?" Denise glanced up at me, while she ensured Pham still breathed.

"You tell me." I watched her face, angered by the remorse in her eyes. We divided back into our original groups: Pham's gifted, the gang, and the security guards. I was gratified when Patronio stood beside me alongside Beam, Steve, and Dean. Everyone was tense and breathed hard.

"Great. We finally find Denise and there are bodies splattered all over the place and guns pointed everywhere," I muttered to my father. Dad breathed, unconscious or badly hurt. I had to get things under control and get him help.

"Okay, everyone, let's all take a deep breath and figure this out," I called out, put my gun in the waist of my pants, and kept my hands in plain sight.

"Which one of you speaks for the gang?" One of them had to speak English. Hopefully they were in control of themselves with Tú dead. The one who shot Tú in the head stepped forward.

"I do." They kept their hands on their guns, but pointed them downward. He was one of the guards who had been at the meeting with Commissioner Cast.

"Denise? Who speaks for your group?" I called out.

"Me." She stepped forward, but her eyes were on our father.

Freya, Kim, and Puppy, or Wolf, surrounded her, their guns, and I suspect their gifts, cocked and ready to fire.

The three security guards still standing backed away, terrified and confused.

"Va^n? What's happening with the siblings?" I guessed at who it could be. Va^n's hood was up again and gloves now covered white hands.

"Tú is dead. The other siblings are in Manhattan. They fought with

269

Tú about these plans. Tú was still dominant but couldn't force them to come out here without fear of a constant struggle, which would have gotten more difficult once my transition was complete."

"Who is dominant?" The gang leader obviously understood how the siblings were organized.

"I am," Va^n answered.

"There are blood and other debts to be paid tonight," the leader said, the warning clear.

"Agreed," Va^n said. The leader's shoulders relaxed and let out a long breath.

"Wonderful. That's one out of any number of details worked out. What happens now, Detective Steckler?" Patronio pushed into the circle to ask. He looked exhausted, but satisfied with himself.

"That's what I'm trying to work out, Mr. Patronio." Calling the local police would be tricky since Pham had them under his thumb. It would also result in all of us being arrested.

"Who needs medical attention?" Denise looked at her group and then the gang. Generator and the woman called Pica stepped forward. There was blood on her shirt and his pant leg, but I couldn't guess the nature of their injuries.

"If they aren't already dead, I have several men who need help," the gang leader said.

"Puppy can try to help them," Denise told him. "Watch." She held out her hands to Puppy and Generator. They ignored the weapons the gang members trained on them.

Generator whispered something to Puppy and turned to reveal an ugly bullet graze across his ribs. Puppy leaned forward and licked the wound. Generator's face was creased with pain, but after several seconds, it relaxed. A few breaths later, Puppy stood up and backed away from him. Under the saliva and remaining blood, the wound had healed. Murmurs of surprise came from the gang and security guards.

270

"Puppy will try to heal your men if you let him," Denise told the leader.

The leader nodded.

"Do not seek to heal Tú or Pham or this truce ends," Va^n said.

"I'm good with that," I muttered. The others agreed, though the addicted gave Pham's still form worried looks.

"There have been enough deaths today." The gang leader waved his men forward. Freya helped carry two men to a corner while three others made their way to where they could be tended to in private. She carried my father to Puppy with care.

Denise followed close behind.

We found four dead men tied standing to a table. Behind the table was another dead man wearing white face paint. That answered my question about the sibling I thought we killed. I shook my head in disgust over the wasted lives. No one deserved to die that way.

"When the siblings call in their debts, there is no refusal despite the cost," the leader said to me.

"You weren't, um, enchanted by Tú?" I wasn't sure what word to use.

"We would have been if we refused to do as bidden. Future requests from our families would have been refused. The families of those who run are ostracized from our community. Many of our families owe the siblings a great deal of money. After tonight, the siblings will forgive those debts and pay blood money. Many of us would die for far less."

He surprised me. I hadn't expected more than a yes or no answer.

"Pham kidnapped my sister a long time ago. Tú figured that out and set things in motion for me to kill him. That didn't work out as Tú expected." I chuckled, but stifled it before it turned into a scream. As a cop I've seen murders and grisly deaths before, but they paled in comparison to this.

"We have to clean this up," Patronio said as Va^n joined us, completely covered, but I still smelled jasmine.

I willed Denise to pay attention to me, like we did growing up. When it worked, despite the situation, I smiled and called her over with a gesture.

"What are we going to do?" I called out to the group when Denise was within earshot.

"You're not calling more cops?" The gang leader's eyebrows rose in surprise.

"No, not right now. There's too much that can't be explained," I sighed. My career just went down the toilet along with my pension. There might even be jail time. Even seeing Denise again didn't completely take away the sadness. Then I caught sight of the four dead men tied to a table; at least I was still alive.

"Any ideas?" I looked to the others in our small circle.

"How many dead?" Denise spoke to the gang leader, seemingly unruffled by the nature of the question.

He spoke to several of his people in what I now recognized as Vietnamese. After several exchanges, he turned back. "Ten, and three wounded, but they are almost healed."

"I'm sorry," I said, uncomfortable. I shot at least three of them.

The gang leader shrugged. "I am sorry they are dead as well," he responded. "But those are the fortunes of war. Your actions against us were no more personal than ours were toward you."

"The two people most responsible for this are either dead or nearly so. I don't have any interest in pursuing this further," I answered.

"Nor I." We shook on it and I looked at Denise.

"This was between the siblings and Pham. He had no plans to go after them and, even if he did, he won't be in any condition to do anything for some time. You gave him a stroke."

"What about using Puppy?" I changed the topic, not ready to address Denise's accusation.

"There's no way for him to get at it. There is not an open wound."

272

He hasn't had any luck with brain injuries before – Spooky has them and Puppy hasn't been able to fix them," she explained with a look at Va^n.

"The siblings hold no grudge against you or the others Pham addicted to him. Tú led us against you and overrode our objections. Until the next sibling transition, I lead the siblings. Unless, Mr. Patronio wishes to pursue legal action against me." Va^n turned to him.

"Having been under Tú's influence, I can't hold you responsible for what you did to me. Lisa's wife Angie may feel different, but I'm not sure there's anything to be done about it," Patronio answered. He checked with Beam.

"No issues here. Everything extra just gets put on your bill."

Patronio pursed his lips in irritation, shrugged indifferently and turned to Puppy. "I know you were there, somehow."

Puppy looked at Patronio confused.

"No, I wasn't," Puppy told him. He returned to licking the arm of one of the gang members.

Patronio glared at him, inhaled through his nose, and shook his head, frustrated.

I looked away, unwilling to reveal Wolf's existence. He had done what he could to help me.

"Fine, I'll leave it be. For now," Patronio said.

The gang leader broke the silence. "We will take our dead. As well as Tú." Va^n nodded in approval. The leader issued orders to his uninjured men and some cut the dead men from the table while others went to gather bodies.

"What about Trainer? What will you do with him?" I wasn't happy having to question my sister.

"Freya will bring his body back to the house. We'll take care of it from there," Denise answered. "It's not the first time." Her tone suggested I not pursue it further.

"What about the blood? Bleach won't get rid of it." I pointed at the floor where the table had been.

"If no one calls the cops, why would they look for it?" The gang leader shrugged.

"It still needs to be cleaned," I said, looking around the room for a bucket and mop. This was a maintenance room after all.

"We can take care of it," Denise told me. She turned back to where the gifted clustered around Pham's fallen form. "Pica, would you help me, please?"

The short, stocky woman made her way to us. Despite the blood on her shirt, she was healed. I tried not to look at her lips, but couldn't help myself. They were thicker and covered with more mucus than I remembered.

"What's up, Captain?" Pica answered, her voice low and guttural.

"Would you take care of the blood in here, the hallway, and ..." Denise looked at the gang leader.

"Two of my men died in the front entrance," he told Pica.

"Sure thing. She gave the two of us a wide smile, and showed us her square, gray teeth.

I forced myself not to take a step away from her.

She knew the impact her smile had and laughed. While walking away, she started making a loud chewing sound.

We all watched as she approached the blood and gore. Pica squatted down, smeared an index finger in the blood, and put it in her mouth. She grunted, stood, leaned forward and wretched. A large volume of fluid gushed from her mouth and splattered onto the floor. She stuck her finger in her mouth several more times and wiped it in various places in the room, wherever she saw blood spots.

"If you have blood, flesh, or bone on your clothes, don't go near the blood pools in this room or anywhere else I'm going for cleanup. Or take it off and throw it in the puddles. It'll dissolve with the rest of it, just do it in the next five minutes and don't touch any of the gore with

274

naked flesh." With that, Pica turned, gave me another creepy smile, winked, and left.

Curious, I moved to one of the spots where Pica spewed. On the ground, dark blotches spread into the blood, making a quiet fizzing sound, and dried, which took only seconds, the floor underneath looked clean and dry.

Several gang members and gifted threw clothing into the middle of the gore and watched as they dissolved. Patronio took his bloody t-shirt off and threw it, as well as what looked like a bloody strip of leather, into the puddle. Both dissolved as soon as they hit. Patronio gave me an expressionless look and walked away.

"I bet you're glad she wasn't your first kiss, right Steckler?" Kim said, coming up beside me. She looked up at me and then away quickly.

"How long have you been with Pham?" I ignored her jibe, looking at his prone form.

"Since the seventies," she answered quietly. "I was one of the first he addicted when he got to the U.S."

"Is he going to live?" I speculated, curious about her opinion.

"Probably. He was old when he addicted me; he's had years to figure out ways to use gifts to survive. He just needs time."

"You don't sound unhappy about that," I commented.

"If he dies, I'm sure the rest of us will too. I've seen men and women die of withdrawal from him. It was horrible. I don't want that to happen to me, Denise, or even Frankie," Kim replied.

Denise walked over and the two wrapped one another in a casual embrace.

"How's Dad?" Denise had sent Puppy over to him after the others had been seen to.

"He's still out cold, but Puppy thinks he'll be okay," Denise answered. She smiled at my skeptical look. "He's not been wrong since I've known him."

"And he's been with Pham a lot longer than I have," Kim added. "He's been through and seen a lot."

"You know Dad's gifted, right?" Denise changed the subject.

"I pieced that together after he appeared out of nowhere like he did to us when we were kids. Keep him away from Pham." It was my turn to direct the conversation.

"That shouldn't be a problem," Denise answered. "We've got to be going." She gave me a wan smile.

My heart sank. She didn't just mean leaving the building.

All signs of violence and dead were gone from the room. Va^n and the gang members had disappeared as well. That left me, Patronio, Beam, Va^n, Denise's gifted crew, and three security guards who wondered around aimlessly, scared and confused. I watched two of them touch Pham's hand. Several of the gifted addicts did the same.

"We have to touch him to get our 'fix'," Denise explained. "When he is unconscious or asleep, we need to touch him more often. When he is awake, he can do it with his mind." Her cheeks flushed red while she answered.

"What about the guards? What will happen to them?" Denise looked away and didn't answer.

"They'll have to come with us," Kim answered. Two of them looked to be in their thirties and both wore wedding rings; the other appeared barely twenty.

"Can't you stay?" My voice cracked. Tears streaked down both Denise and Kim's face. Denise shook her head and wiped tears from her cheeks.

Generator handed Denise a set of keys then turned to the others. "Let's get back to the house and pack. Denise and Kim, we'll get your stuff and meet you in the parking lot by the loading dock door in ten minutes." He called the last part over his shoulder.

Freya, carrying my father as if he weighed no more than a child, came up to us next. Dad's unconscious form limp in her arms.

"Give me your car keys and I'll get your father into it," she said to me. Denise nodded and I handed them over.

"He's not addicted?" I had assumed he was.

"No. Pham has to know the person and be ready for them for that to happen. He was ready for you, not Dad," Denise answered.

"Where's your car parked?" Freya tapped my shoulder to get my attention.

"We'll show you," Beam told her with a look at Steve and Dean. "We'll do a quick scan again to make sure we didn't leave anything behind, like your shirt," Beam said with a tap of his finger on my naked chest.

"I'll bring your car and father around in a few minutes," Freya said. I reached out and touched her arm.

"Thank you." Her arm felt like steel covered in leather. "For carrying Dad, and for opening doors."

"You're welcome, Carl," Freya said and surprised me with a quick kiss on the cheek. "Maybe you're a hero after all." She walked back to the door we entered.

"Detective Steckler, I'm going back to the city with Mr. Beam." While I spoke to the others Patronio had cleaned up at the maintenance sink.

"That's for the best, Mr. Patronio," I looked at him and then Beam. "Be careful, though. You heard Va^n – another dominant sibling could emerge and want revenge."

"It was Va^n's idea to wrap my neck with the flesh from one of the dead men to fool Tú. It protected me from Va^n' gifts. In order to truly enthrall they require direct flesh to flesh contact. Va^n and the other siblings kept fighting Tú and providing distractions. Tú never noticed I wasn't under Va^n's control," Patronio told me. "I don't think I have anything to worry about from them."

He walked away, then turned back to look at Denise. "Your brother is a good man. He never gave up on you," he said and left.

"We'll talk again soon, Steckler," Beam told me and followed Patronio. Dean and Steve nodded at me and left as well.

Denise, Kim, Puppy, and I stood in a group. Tears ran down Denise and Kim's face. Puppy's lip began trembling, seeing them. He wasn't the only one.

"Denise, what's going on?" I feared I knew the answer.

"Carl, we have to go. We can't stay in New York," Denise answered and fought back tears. Kim sobbed, tears streaming down her cheeks.

Denise hugged Kim to her chest. "We can't protect them." Kim didn't say anything but nodded.

"Can't protect who from whom, Denise?" I knew part of the answer as she handed me a key.

"Protect our children. Lee and Lilly," Denise answered. Then she gave Kim another hug. "Lee is so much like you, Carl," she added, and started to sob. Despite the horrors of the day, the long years of separation, and my anger at her, it still felt natural to reach out and comfort her.

"Denise, don't run. I can help you. We can go to the police," I said, even though I knew we wouldn't.

"Carl, you've met only the sanest and most normal ones," Denise whispered to me, I think in order to avoid scaring Puppy. She succeeded in frightening me. "There are a lot of them who were so evil and twisted, Pham was afraid of them. Pham kept control. With him out of commission, they will come for total freedom or revenge."

"Maybe it makes sense for us all to disappear for a while," I told her.

"Take care of them, Carl," Denise whispered and grabbed my hand. I gave her a puzzled look which became one of betrayal as Kim reached out to take the hand Denise captured. Then everything became an erotic haze.

278

Epilogue

When I came back to myself I was alone in the maintenance room. No one would know six people met their death there. Even the smell of blood, urine, and feces had faded. I found my fist clenched around something hard and sharp. The key Denise handed me. The number read "312".

"I hate you, Denise," I muttered and felt the weight of responsibility for her children as it fell on my shoulders. My mind was numb as I went back into the hall, made my way to the stairwell, and climbed to the third floor. Designed for resident living, the wide hall had old carpeting and doors with curtained windows. Unlike the lower floors, fresh air blew through the rooms and looked as though people lived here.

It took a moment to find room 312. Curtains on the door blocked my view. I searched for the courage to enter.

"Hello?"

A young boy and girl glanced up. They sat on one of the perfectly made beds in the brightly lit and painted room. At the back wall, under the window, a long table and two chairs made up the rest of the furniture. School books and spiral binders covered the table.

"You're Uncle Carl, right?" the girl, Lilly, smiled at me. I nodded.

"Not only do you look just like your mother, you're the one who takes charge, just like she did with me, right?" I asked her with a smile and gave Lee a rueful look. I hoped the tears in my eyes wouldn't upset them.

"We should pack," Lee said to Lilly.

"Mom told us if you showed up without her, we should go with you," Lilly answered the implied question in my raised eyebrows.

"Yes, you should start packing," I told them, my tone solemn.

"Is everyone dead?" Lee drew in a deep breath, as if to prepare for my answer.

"No, they'll be back soon, though," I assured them. They stopped. The way they eyed me said they recognized the lie.

"Where are we going?" Lee let out a sigh of relief.

"First, to my car where you'll meet your grandfather who saved your mother's life today," I said, and they gave one another an excited smile. "And then we're going home."

Meet T.S. Kay

T.S. Kay is the author of Familiar Scents, his first novel in the Gifted World. He grew up an avid reader, all but living in bookstores and libraries. Dogs have always been a part of his life and he and his wife currently share their home in upstate New York with three. Their personal space is encroached upon by more than a thousand frog figurines they've collected from around the world.

Follow T.S. Kay on Facebook:

https://m.facebook.com/tskaywriter/